EBU

BOYS D

Meghna Pant is an award-winning author, journalist, feminist and speaker.

Her books—*The Terrible, Horrible, Very Bad Good News, How to Get Published in India, Feminist Rani, The Trouble with Women, Happy Birthday* and *One and a Half Wife*—have been published to commercial and critical acclaim.

Pant has been felicitated with various honours and her works have been shortlisted for distinguished contribution to literature, gender issues and journalism. She has won the Bharat Nirman Award, Laadli Media Award, FICCI Young Achiever's Award, The Lifestyle Journalist Women Achievers' Award, FON South Asia Short Story Award, Muse India Young Writer Award, Amazon Breakthrough Novel Award, Frank O'Connor International Award and the Commonwealth Short Story Prize.

Pant has been invited as a speaker for the nation's biggest literary festivals and conferences, and has appeared as a panellist on prime-time news and international channels to discuss gender issues. She has written articles for and been quoted in leading national and international media.

She has worked as a business news anchor for Times Now, NDTV and Bloomberg-UTV in New York and Mumbai.

Pant currently lives in Mumbai with her husband and two daughters.

BOYS DON'T CRY

A TRUE STORY, ALMOST

MEGHNA PANT

EBURY
PRESS

An imprint of Penguin Random House

EBURY PRESS

USA | Canada | UK | Ireland | Australia
New Zealand | India | South Africa | China | Singapore

Ebury Press is part of the Penguin Random House group of companies
whose addresses can be found at global.penguinrandomhouse.com

Published by Penguin Random House India Pvt. Ltd
4th Floor, Capital Tower 1, MG Road,
Gurugram 122 002, Haryana, India

First published in Ebury Press by Penguin Random House India 2022

ISBN 9780143455097

Typeset in Adobe Caslon Pro by Manipal Technologies Limited, Manipal

Printed at Repro India Limited

www.penguin.co.in

*'Stay away
from men who peel the skin
of other women, forcing you to
wear them.'*

—*Ijeoma Umebinyuo*

P.S. Thanks for the scars. They helped me bloom.

S.K. Everyone else is the journey, you are the destination.

TODAY IS the day. The day that he will finally kill me. I hear the doorknob turning. I push my hand under the pillow. I feel the edge of the kitchen knife I've begun keeping under my pillow in case he attacks me. I tell myself to use it. To not be afraid. To kill him before he kills me. He enters the room.

CHAPTER ONE

THEN THERE'S the business of flowers. I've been told that all the darkness in our lives can be extinguished by the bloom of a single petal. And isn't this what today is about? So, I walk to the florist near my building and tell an attendant: 'Bhaiya, I need flowers for a party. What do you recommend?'

A man with a single fingernail, long and curved like the stem of a rose, asks, 'What's the occasion, Madam? Engagement, birthday, havan?'

He doesn't meet my eyes.

'It's for a divorce party,' I say.

I hear a short, clean sound, like the stem of a flower being snapped. The attendant looks up from the hibiscus he's trimming and sniggers, 'You mean you want flowers for a *daphanana*?'

Daphanana? I stare at him. Burial?

Well, I guess, a man in a flower shop will always think of a corpse first.

'No, I mean divorce . . . talaq,' I say. 'The opposite of a daphanana.'

He blinks in confusion.

'I am throwing a divorce party this evening, and I want flowers for it,' I say. It has to be said bluntly. After all, the worst mistake a woman can make is to wait for a man to grow up.

'Divorce party?' the attendant chuckles. He looks at another attendant, whose attention is drawn by our conversation. They exchange a smile.

'So, Madam, you are divorced?' he asks me with a smile, his teeth showing.

'Yes,' I say, not showing mine.

'Madam, we do not have special flowers for all this . . . you know, *things*?'

I take a deep breath. So much for India's modernity.

Everything else for the party—the food, the cake, the alcohol—has been ordered on the phone. These are things that require no human interaction. That's how I make my way around the world now. But flowers demand to be touched and felt, like clothes, before showing their worth. I will have to see this through.

'Well, if you want to make money, you must keep such flowers,' I say flatly, with the tone of a woman who is divorced but not broken. 'It's 2013. Divorces are rising by thirty per cent each year. Imagine how many new clients you'll get!'

I speak business. It's the language that Mumbai most understands.

'Maybe you should try another shop,' he says. God, he's a fool!

I place my hands firmly on the display rack. It's scratchy as though made of a thousand thorns. I don't pull away. Because even the moon doesn't have to be whole in order to shine.

It's then that—finally—I see the blinkers from his eyes disappear. His eyes meet mine. He nods. A man tending to flowers knows that rain is better than thunder.

'Okay, Madam,' he says, his eyes now squinting effortfully. 'You might like the yellow carnations.'

'Why carnations?'

'What?'

'Why carnations? Why not something else?'

'Well,' the attendant leans over and says. 'They symbolize rejection, I think. They will be good for a divorce party, no?'

The difference between a florist and a gardener is that the florist cuts the flowers while the gardener brings them to life. This florist will never understand what it is I truly seek—a feeling that lasts a lifetime.

'Divorce is not about rejection, Bhaiya,' I say. 'It's about celebration. Freedom! Happiness! You understand?'

'Errr . . .' he says. He has no idea what I'm saying. 'Perhaps you'd like roses?' he adds.

Too blasé, I want to say. Our desires, our breath, our clothes are all a necessity. Flowers are not. They are more than life. They are hope. I want that. Something extra.

'No.'

'Lilies? They are popular.'

They are. But their ovaries are superior to the male parts and this is not about female superiority. No. I shake my head.

The man looks around the shop, inspecting it like he's interrogating it for answers.

'Petunia?'

I look at the dainty blend of crimson and white. They speak nothing of a new life, a tough past. No.

'Gladiolus?'

Too clustered. I need a flower that is brave enough to stand up to its own truth. No.

'Hydrangea?' He presses the flowers against my nose. I feel the tickle of God's blue belly hair on my nostrils. No.

He's looking for flowers. I'm looking for a story. I tell myself to be patient.

He continues searching. The flower shop can barely mask the metallic halitosis of the city. It must be tough to smell sweet inside the lungs of an alligator.

Finally, he says, 'Kaner is for new beginnings. I think you will like them.'

The attendant looks at me expectantly. I see a bee buzzing behind his head, its feet dusted with the fragrance of a thousand flowers. Does the bee ever find something to rest upon, even for a moment, and just be?

'I do like it. Thank you,' I say. Kaner. Oleanders, I remember, represent leaving the past in the past and enjoying what's in front of you. 'Please pack thirty.'

'Madam, they only come in dozens. For good luck.'

Greed bleeds into his eyes. He knows I haven't asked their price. It's a mistake. I don't care. My loss has always been someone else's gain.

'Okay, three dozen then,' I say nonchalantly.

His long fingernail quivers as he packs the oleanders. He adds some rajnigandha, though I haven't asked for them. I pay him and turn to leave.

'Enjoy, Madam,' he says. 'I hope we get more business from you.'

I turn around and say, 'With all due respect, Bhaiya, I hope I never have to see you again.'

My words are softer than their meaning. We exchange a smile.

I come out of the flower shop, with three dozen white oleanders in my hands, and squint into the sun. No matter how hot it gets in this city, I never complain. Having survived three cold winters in New York, where night bleeds into day, I love sunrays on my skin. I step on to the kerb and pause. For a moment I debate whether to look down, as if into a microscope, so I can avoid falling into Mumbai's notorious manholes or its crater-sized potholes, or to look up, as if into a telescope, to avoid being crushed by its crumbling flyovers or its faulty air-conditioners diving off crusty buildings. This is the bane of every pedestrian in this mofussil metropolis, where neither footpaths nor roads are built for the people.

It is that or suicide.

I do neither. I look straight at the oncoming traffic, cross the road and walk home.

It'll take more than a city to kill me.

*

Unlike other city parties, mine begins on time. I assume this is because people are enchanted by the idea. They want to know what happens at a divorce party. For who doesn't love the bite of scandal? I don't tell them that I don't know; that this is also my first time attending one.

The party will be at a quarter past love, I'd written in the original invite. But people in Mumbai lack imagination. It's understandable. Living in this city is like drawing blood with thorns. Who has time for culture when a heavy mortgage has to be paid for a house one can cover in six long strides? Whose fingers have time to turn a book's pages when they're busy honking furiously at traffic? Creativity is reserved for bulls and bears. Thoughts are preoccupied with salacious gossip about the latest Bollywood diet.

So, I'd sent another invite saying: Be there at 8 p.m.!

And, here they are.

My house has been divorce-proofed. There are quiches on the dining table that Jeet, my gay neighbour, has laid out to spell 'Good Riddance'. My best friend Sherna, who is down from the US, has put up a banner that says: 'Happily Divorced'. My two-tiered cake, priced at a princely Rs 8000, reads 'Free at Last'.

The oleanders are in two vases, the fridge is filled with beer and white wine, and my bar is stocked with bottles of other alcohol and paper glasses. There's no sangria or red wine, for these are the colour of brides, of new love. Jeet has made a customized playlist—the snarkiest in music history he calls it—and one that includes everything from Rafi's *Kya Hua Tera Wada* to Green's *F**k You*. The music is loud. No worries. I have invited my neighbours, as any smart host does.

'You look beautiful,' someone says as they enter, touching the silk of my dress, the one oleander flower clipped to my hair, my purse shaped like a broken handcuff. Many had asked what the dress code for a divorce party was. Green, I'd told them confidently, like I'd done this before. Green is growth. Green is renewal and abundance. Green is—'Pakistani,' a guest had complained.

'We didn't know what to get you,' is another grouse I hear as people enter. They've got something neutral: wine and perfume.

Sherna has come up with an ingenious idea. As soon as the guests have settled in, she turns down the music and puts a steel bin in the centre of the room. We all gather around it. From a packet she pulls out my *mangalsutra*, a *sindoor* box and the red bangles I had worn during my wedding *pheras*.

'How did you get all this?' I ask her.

'I know where you keep your things, remember?' she says and gives me a peck on the cheek. 'You don't mind do you, Manu? I wanted it to be a surprise.'

'What surprise?'

'Watch,' she says.

I watch as she throws these things into the bin, along with the photos of my wedding and ex-husband. Photos of exes are like fresh paint masking the smell of piss. She seems to have found all the ones that I'd printed. I look at my ex-husband for the last time before he's consumed by the fire: those brown eyes like sand running through fingers, that aquiline nose that bends like whiplash, that smile that curls outwards like a sail too loose, and skin like a dove bathed in honey. My heart that has been a bird flying from branch to branch becomes still. A small cicatrice is made on my memory. I am healed.

'So, *this* is what you do at a divorce party,' someone remarks. We laugh.

As the smoke clears, a guest points out an intriguing gift: a condom bouquet. An acquaintance, Richa, takes one out and makes a balloon. The others do the same. My ceiling is filled with condom balloons. Jeet plays *It's Raining Men*. Everyone begins to dance.

Just as well.

My childhood friend Sanaya comes up to me, 'I think this is awesome, Manu. Best. Party. Ever. And I'm seriously happy that you're out of that nightmare.'

I blink in surprise.

'She's been so strong. I can't even imagine going through what she did,' I hear Jeet say.

To brush the bloom, you have to tear the flower from its stem.

I hug them.

'Sorry, I don't agree,' Richa interrupts us. She's drunk. 'This party is making me sad.'

'You're clearly not woke enough, babe,' Jeet says defensively. I touch his arm. His India is not everyone's India. We have to be tolerant of those who are intolerant.

'Why would you even have a d-i-v-o-r-c-e party?' Richa continues. 'It's inappropriate.'

Where do I begin explaining? I haven't seen her in years. She can't even say the word 'divorce' out loud.

'Well, I did try to find a pandit to conduct a divorce havan, you know,' I say, 'but Hinduism doesn't have a cleansing ritual for *apavitra, ashudh aurats* like me—'

Richa looks at me wide-eyed and turns to blend into the crowd. I chuckle. My sarcasm has rarely got me anywhere, but I go nowhere without it.

I take a deep breath. Of course, I had wondered for a few days—who wouldn't, after all?—whether having such a party was at all appropriate. In India, failure is rarely acknowledged, public failure never so. And here I am owning to the most public of my failures. Embracing and celebrating it. What if I break down during my own party? What if I begin crying in front of my guests? What if everyone looks at me with pity? It's certainly not wise to ignore one's emotions for the sake of one's principles. Because *there is* the bigger issue of my own confused feelings, isn't there? In my marriage of five years, I had meandered from disorder to chaos, in the general direction of decimation. I had imploded and scattered. My pieces were everywhere. I resented this time and how I had squandered my love on a man of all things. If I couldn't make my marriage work, what was the point of my existence? It was the one thing I *had* to get right. I'd been told this since I was a little girl. Such feelings flap around me, frayed and random, completely out of my control, no matter how hard I try to rein them in. But I also know that a divorce party, a celebration, is that helpful height from where I can see clearly into my past, present and future. It shows me that I have gathered my pieces back together. I am whole again. I don't have to pretend to be strong about my divorce because I am strong. As I stand at my party, a published novelist with awards to boot, eight years after I first met my ex-husband, I decide to not cry because I've travelled too far to allow my tears to fall. I will not break down because I'm grateful for the horror and pain. My failed marriage has not diminished me. It's not been futile. Its collapse has not been a coincidence, but a tightly structured design to lead me, like a magic carpet, into a future that is bright and hopeful. This provides me with great consolation.

My doorbell rings. Sherna opens the door. I can't see who the guests are. She runs up to me, her eyes filled with laughter.

'There are some gigolos at the door. They're dressed as cops. They're asking for you. I didn't know it was *that* kind of a party!'

She winks at me.

I look at her quizzically.

It isn't *that* kind of a party.

I walk to the door. Clashing thoughts run through my head. Is this someone's surprise gift? Or perhaps someone's idea of a joke? Did the smoke from the bin tip someone off? Is our music too loud? Too raucous? Are my guests too many? Did I forget to get a liquor licence? Or are there actual policemen at my door? Have they come because it's a divorce party? Fuck.

'Put out that joint,' I tell a friend's friend.

'Burst the condom balloons,' I tell a few others.

'Hide the booze,' I tell Sherna.

Of course, the man at the door is no gigolo. He's a real cop. Tall, strong and fair, with the face of a man who's never let himself eat a vada pav. There are two constables with him. They're all in khaki—short-sleeved shirts and long pants.

Nothing in my life has been a coincidence. This man is here for a reason.

He says something when he sees me. I can't hear him over the music.

'Turn it off,' I tell Jeet. He turns off the music. There's a groan from the guests till they realize there are cops at the door. Everyone stands to attention. There is complete silence.

'Are you Maneka Sodi?' the cop asks me.

'I am Maneka Pataudi,' I reply confidently, as though I've faced many cops before.

The cop looks at me in confusion.

'I used to be Maneka Sodi. But I've gone back to using my maiden name,' I say.

The cop doesn't blink. His eyes are black like a raven's.

'Miss Pataudi, your husband Suneet Sodi was found dead in Dubai a few hours ago.'

There's a collective gasp from the crowd.

'Ex-husband, not husband,' someone says loudly.

I don't react. The cop looks at me like a hawk looks at a sparrow.

'You don't look surprised. Your husband is dead!'

'Ex-husband,' I say.

The cop squints in displeasure. 'Aren't you even going to ask me how he died?'

'How did he die?' I ask, my voice level, though I've never been good at disguising my feelings.

'Would you like to tell us?' he asks.

Frankly, I'd prayed for him to be hit by a truck. A 100-tonne truck.

'Must've been his snake,' I mumble instead.

'What did you say?' the cop asks. He's clearly startled by my insouciance.

I cross my arms and stare at him, then I add, 'Sorry, Sir. I didn't catch your name.'

This riles him up, as I know it will. I have learnt what riles men up: women they cannot control. I watch as the cop stands up to his full height and says, 'Maneka Sodi . . .'

'Pataudi.'

'Maneka Pataudi, I have come to arrest you for the murder of your ex-husband.'

The crowd behind me gasps again.

The cop handcuffs me and shunts me away from my shocked friends.

'You can't do that!' a few of my friends protest. Even Richa.

Two of them block the cop's path. My friends love me. I smile.

'You need a warrant!' someone shouts. I have friends who are lawyers.

The cop produces a warrant. 'Now move.'

'You need a lady constable to arrest Manu,' someone shouts.

'You cannot arrest a woman after sunset,' someone else shouts.

The cop doesn't answer. The constables push my friends away.

'*Challa, challa!*' they shout. They look like burnt bread under the corridor's white light.

Sherna and Jeet run to the elevator. 'We will come with her.'

'You cannot,' the cop says sternly. 'Stay back or—'

He places his hand on his holster.

'We insist,' Sherna says. She looks like a twig facing a storm.

'You can come to the station once she calls you,' the cop says.

'Which one?'

He names the station.

'Don't worry, guys. I'll be fine!' I shout.

Sherna hugs me. I step into the lift.

'PFO. Party's fucking over, guys!' someone shouts.

'But you have to keep celebrating!' I shout to my guests. I jangle my handcuffs the way I had once jangled my wedding *chooras*. 'For *this* is what happens at a divorce party!'

I hold up a victory sign. My guests cheer.

My divorce party is a success.

The lift doors close.

I squeeze my eyes shut. My optimism is a guise. Because I know by the time I return to my house, the oleanders would have wilted. That's the problem with owning something so beautiful. You have to watch it die.

CHAPTER TWO

OUR LOVE story began the way most big love stories begin, after great sex. It didn't matter that it was in the bathroom of a low-cost airline called Air Deccan, that we'd nicknamed Air Dhakkan because its engine rattled throughout the journey, like a lid on a boiling pan. It didn't matter that the air hostess had to force open the bathroom door after banging on it for ten minutes. The only thing that mattered was that when we got back to our seats, he'd said, 'Close your eyes and look into the darkness, *jaanu.*'

This was how Suneet spoke. I wanted him to know that I understood him. I shut my eyes.

'What do you see?' he asked.

I took a deep breath. 'I see you,' I said.

'Smiling?'

'No, frowning.'

He punched my arm. We laughed.

'Be serious. I want you to see me. Do you see me?' he asked.

'I see something,' I said. 'I see the clouds above you . . . the aisle behind you. I see you lifting your hand to your mouth and chewing your fingernails.'

13

Silence. Even in the darkness I could sense his disapproval.

It was 2006, two days before Valentine's Day. Suneet and I were returning to Mumbai after a weekend trip to Goa. It was the type of trip that only new lovers can take. The type we took after meeting each other randomly in the US and spending eight months chatting on Skype and MSN. The type where people watched us with their hearts in their eyes, wishing they could experience a love like ours. The type where he whispered into my ears, 'You're an oasis for a desert full of thirsty men, everyone wants a sip!'

But Suneet was flying back to his job in Boston the next day. We didn't know when we would meet again.

'Sorry . . . I see you. Of course, I see you, *jaan*,' I said. He was actually all I saw.

'Good. Now, tell me, my angel. Do you know what love is?' he asked me.

Love? I smirked. Of course I knew what love was. Everyone knew what love was. We'd all said it to someone. We'd all had someone say it to us. But when I opened my mouth, nothing came out. What the fuck? I was drawing a blank. Why had no one taught me what *love* was?

My orderly mind crumbled. Loosened fragments arranged and rearranged themselves at random. Bits of life made themselves prominent, the small and insignificant injustices of love, the silence of victories from deep within the noise of love. My heart that had been broken at twenty-one by my straying first love. The hearts I had broken in the following years to draw blood back into my own. The men who'd said they loved me, some of whom I'd said I loved back, only because crushing someone's hopes seemed like the worst kind of sin.

'I can't . . . you know . . . define love. I need a dictionary,' I mumbled and smiled.

'Answer me.'

'Fine,' I said quickly. '*You* are love.'

'No.'

'No?'

'No.'

How can a correct answer be incorrect?

'I am not love, jaanu, because I cannot be everybody's love. Only yours, forever yours,' he said.

Ah! I was his and he didn't even know it.

'Okay,' I said.

'Love is yielding.'

'Love is caring.'

'Love is acceptance.'

'No! No! No! No clichés,' he said. 'You call yourself a writer, don't you?'

The previous night I had given Suneet a half-written love letter, in which I had told him that he was the song for those who didn't sing . . . his love an anthem that rose like hope. I wanted him to fill in the rest, because I knew his heart. Now he wanted to know mine. *Could I tell him?*

'I guess I . . . I don't know what love is,' I admitted.

'Love is something we can't control,' he said quickly, as if he'd been anticipating my failure. 'If I tell my hand to hold your hand, it will hold your hand. If I tell my foot to kick you, it will kick you. I can control my physical body. But what I have inside . . . the stuff I cannot see, and you cannot see . . . is what I cannot control. I cannot tell my cells, "Okay, today you will not grow." I cannot tell my liver, "Okay, today you cannot make bile." I cannot tell my heart not to beat. But when my heart thinks of you, it beats faster, on its own. That is love.'

Something inside me stirred, as if a long slumbering giant had awakened.

'*You* are love,' he added. 'You're an amazing person with an energy that is pure and innocent.'

'That's so sweet, Suneet,' I said. He always found ways to define what I couldn't. I kissed him.

'Now . . . slowly . . . ' he added, 'put your left hand into your right hand.'

I put my left hand into my right hand.

'Is it warm?' he asked.

'Yes,' I said slowly. 'It's warm.'

'That warmth belongs to me. Don't you ever forget that.'

I opened my eyes. They were fluttering with delight. Isn't the eye where the heart comes to rest? I looked into his eyes. They were brown. I liked everything brown, I decided: chocolate, mud after rain, rusted doorknobs, the first fallen leaf in a desert.

'If you ever miss me just hold your hands together, feel that warmth, and you'll feel me,' he added. 'That's love.'

I understood what he was doing. You can't explain love to a plant or philosophy to a dog. We feel only what we understand. And he felt love for me. He wanted me to understand that.

I went numb with joy.

'Do you love me?' he asked.

If you put a frog in cold water and heat it slowly, it will not notice. And, before you know it, you'll have a boiled frog. Love's like that. You're bumbling through life not knowing what you're doing, and suddenly, it's there and you're in love. I knew I was in love. I loved the curl in his arms, strong, even though he didn't exercise. The way his butt looked after he came out of the shower. Taut like the crust of a freshly baked baguette I wanted to bite into.

I nodded. I really did. I really loved this man.

'And I love you,' he said. 'I feel so lucky to have met you. You're fabulous.'

I smiled. He said this to me all the time.

He smiled back at me and said, 'That's why I wanted to ask you, Manu, will you smoke my snake for life?'

I didn't understand what he meant. He took out a joint from his sock.

'What . . . are you crazy?' I whispered fiercely. I looked around. The cabin was dark. 'You'll get caught.'

'Shhhh . . . ' he said calmly. 'You know I call my weed my snake, right? So, I want to know if you would like to spend the rest of your life smoking my snake with me?'

I was still too alarmed for his words to sink in. 'What?'

'Will you marry me?' he asked.

I fell back in my seat and felt the breath go out of me. I looked out of the window. The moon was shining like a button in the black blanket of the night, lit with our love.

'Should I?' I asked.

I hadn't known Suneet for long. It had only been a few months. In that time, with me in Mumbai and him in Boston, we'd only spend nine days together in total. Could I marry a stranger?

'Give me one reason why we shouldn't get married,' he asked. He didn't look upset.

'Because we don't know each other very well, Suneet. We've only met during trips like this,' I said. He was one of the few people with whom I didn't censor my thoughts. 'Shouldn't we give ourselves more time?'

'It's not the time spent but the love given,' he said. He paused as I let his words sink in. 'Don't overthink this, Manu.

You're one in six billion. I never thought I'd meet someone like you. I really never did! It's renewed my hope in mankind and in myself. Of course, it's also ruined me for anyone else!'

I laughed. Suneet always knew exactly what to say and when.

I also knew that I was twenty-five years old which, by Indian standards then, made me a leftover bride: the one who attended only other people's weddings. I didn't know what I was waiting for. Back in Mumbai, there were men who were interested in marrying me, but I didn't want their money or stability or goodness. I couldn't bear their predictability. I wanted a man who was made only for me. I wanted striving. I wanted elevation. I wanted passion. Suneet offered me all that. A middle-class NRI boy working in the US, paving his own righteous path in the world, he was different from the rich spoilt deathly-dull south Mumbai boys I'd grown up around. In the musical chairs of potential matches, Suneet was the only one I wanted sitting down.

He held my hand tightly. 'Manu, do you know that before I met you last July, I'd never felt alive. My life was a burden. Then you came and everything changed. I never thought I would meet someone so perfect, so amazing! It was like God had made an angel in the sky just for me, and dropped her into my lap. Since the day we met, I've woken up every morning feeling so grateful that you're in my life. I can't take a single breath without remembering you. You have no idea what you mean to me and how much, my darling.'

I sighed. I'd never met a boy who spoke this way.

We seek the extraordinary because it rarely occurs in our life. We don't even know how to recognize it. Here was my chance. I could make the ordinary come alive and make it extraordinary.

'That's why I want to marry you,' he continued. 'I know how lucky I am to have you in my life. I don't want to spend another moment without you, my angel, my princess. You are the only thing I need in my life.'

I smiled. His words sounded poetic and deep, hence true.

'I like to think that my hobby is to change people. I was trying to do that for you, but you ended up changing me,' he continued. 'For the first time in my life I trust someone. I feel so safe and secure with you. I cannot live without you.'

'But will we make each other happy, Suneet?'

'I don't care about my happiness as long as you're happy,' he said quickly. 'Promise to stay happy forever, my *sonu*. If not for yourself, please keep doing that for me. I don't ever want to see a frown on that beautiful face.'

I smiled. Sometimes you need to be loved a certain way to find what you're seeking.

'Remember one thing, Manu, if you're not smiling then I'm not doing something right,' he added. 'You're such an amazing person with so much potential. You're going to do great things with your life. And all I want is a ringside seat to cheer you on!'

Life had taught me that it was important to be with someone who wanted you urgently, so I said, 'Yes. Yes! Suneet, let's smoke the snake together, forever. Let's get married.'

I knew then only passion and none of its consequences.

'Pukka, my little *bhondu*?' he asked.

'Ermmm, actually, let me think about it for forty more years,' I said and laughed.

'*Chal hat*!' Suneet said with joy and hugged me.

He looked so happy. It made me so happy. After all, we are all beggars of love.

'Good.' He held my hand and whispered, 'I don't want you to belong to anyone else but me.'

I looked into his eyes. My *nani* had told me to never trust someone with light eyes. 'Light eyes mean a dark soul,' she'd always say. But I'd always loved men with light eyes. It was the way of my heart.

'We are going to be happy, aren't we?' I said.

'Better than all the rest,' he said.

My happiness was flying so high that it went and sat on the moon. I now understood. Love is when you lose yourself so completely that you forget where you've kept yourself.

'Now put your snake back in its hole or . . . '

*

'Stop! Stop!' the cop says. 'Madam, this is a murder case. I don't need to know all this love-shove poetic nonsense about snakes and moons. Kindly stick to the facts.'

I smile. Is there a single truthful fact in this world?

'I can't talk about him without thinking like this,' I say.

The cop leans back.

'You really hated him, didn't you?' he asks me.

I smile. A constable with the name tag 'Wanave' walks in with two cups of tea and places them in front of us. The cop and he discuss something in Marathi. I take this time to look around the cop's office. It's the way I had imagined a police station—dusty files, tied with red threads, line creaky cupboards. The wooden furniture is as old as the legal cases. His desk has rust that settles on my fingernails. The cups are chipped at the rim but—what a surprise—are filled with green tea. This cop is different!

'You obviously don't speak Marathi.' I hear him tell me. 'You thought you'd marry an NRI and leave Bombay forever, huh?'

Or, maybe, he's not.

'It's Mumbai, not Bombay, Sir,' I reply back.

He glares at me.

'I moved to Mumbai from Delhi when I was nine years old,' I add. 'My parents worked with the IRS and thought they'd be posted somewhere else soon. So, no, I didn't get a chance to learn Marathi but that is my biggest regret.'

The cop looks at me, unimpressed.

'I moved back to Mumbai this year because this is the only place in the world I call home,' I add.

'We have a saying that a person living in Maharashtra who doesn't speak Marathi is like a snake who bites without having venom.'

'Well, you have no reason to fear my bite then,' I say.

The cop laughs. He seems placated by my honesty.

'I told Wanave not to disturb us while we speak. I know ladies feel safe this way. So, now feel free to say anything you want,' he says.

'Great! Did you know that eagles live for eighty to ninety years?'

'What?'

He's easy to manoeuvre. Or maybe my marriage has taught me to get the better of anyone. I continue: 'Any idea why eagles live that long?' I don't wait for a reply. 'Because when they get oldish, around forty, they rejuvenate by breaking their own beak, talons and feathers. Divorce is my rejuvenation. It's broken everything inside me, so I can get better and stronger.'

'Ah! I know what you're doing, Madam,' the cop says. 'You're trying to buy time because you know we have to produce you before the court in less than twenty-four hours.'

I smile.

'These mind games are not going to work with me, Madam,' he says. He leans forward. 'All you have to do is answer my question: Did you kill your husband?'

'Shouldn't I be interrogated by a lady cop?'

'Why?'

'Empathy?'

'Don't men have empathy?'

I shrug.

'Is that why I get the privilege of sitting here with you, with my phone and my purse, sipping green tea, while other criminals are beaten in the interrogation room?' I ask.

'You're a well-known author and journalist. Not as famous as Bhagat, obviously, but people know you. That comes with its perks.'

I smile.

'So, did you do it?' he continues.

'No.'

'No? Your mother-in-law says you did.'

'What else will a mother-in-law say?'

'Why would she accuse you of something as serious as murder unless she had a reason?'

'Sir, do you know that the snake plant is also known as the mother-in-law's tongue? Coincidence? I think not.'

'Madam, please!'

'Sir, she does not need a reason. She needs proof. Which you clearly don't have. Why are you wasting my time?'

'Who killed your husband?'

'I don't know who killed my *ex*-husband.'

'Do you know how he died?'

'Of boredom at a police interrogation room?'

He ignores my sarcasm and says, 'He died of a drug overdose.'

'Oh.'

'Oh? Aren't you surprised?'

'No.'

'So, who killed your *ex*-husband?'

'No one killed my ex-husband.'

'No one killed your ex-husband?'

'No one has killed a lot of Indians. No one killed Jessica. No one killed Sunanda. No one killed Gauri. In India, no one kills anyone. There's no case here, Sir.'

'Madam, please don't act smart. His post-mortem report states they found traces of poison.'

'I must say I didn't expect the force to be quite so efficient. Post-mortems! Arrests! Interrogations! And it's not even been twenty-four hours since his death.'

The cop blinks, slowly. He's seen worse than a quick tongue.

'Is it because my ex-father-in-law works for the Dubai police?' I ask.

The cop ignores my taunt. 'Weren't you having problems in your marriage?'

'Well, the fact that we're divorced would be an indication of that, no?'

'Your in-laws said that you've been on the run since you tried to kill him.'

'Well, if they call building a new life for yourself a crime, then maybe they need a refresher course to the twenty-first century.'

'Your in-laws have given a statement that you purposely left poisoned drugs in Suneet's room.'

'Sir, I never did drugs. Suneet did. Remember the airplane story I just told you? He must've poisoned the drugs himself. Maybe it was suicide.'

'Why would a man suddenly kill himself?'

'Why not? Does every man need a woman to blame for his suicide?'

The cop glares at me.

'Instead of interrogating me, why don't you question his parents?' I say. 'He lives . . . lived . . . with them. Maybe his mother got fed up of him. She must have made his last meal. She might have cooked that gucchi mushroom sabzi that he loved so much. Mushrooms can be poisonous.'

'How do you know that?'

'I used to cook for him.'

'You don't look like the cooking type.'

I look at the cop's pinched face: 'You don't look like the chauvinist type.'

He allows himself a smile.

'None of us are who we look like, Sir. You should know that. You need to establish a motive for me to kill my ex-husband and there is none. I'm not even in the same country as him! How could I have killed him?'

'Your in-laws said that you planned his murder in advance. You went to his house, even though you both were separated, and planted poisoned drugs.'

'Sir, you're mistaking their broken hearts for the truth. Isn't that the worst way to investigate a death?'

'So, they're lying?'

'Well, they've always had a troubled relationship with the truth, I can tell you that. You should question my father-in-law. He's a doctor. The last time I saw him he'd had a big fight with his son. They weren't even on speaking terms. Maybe he killed him out of frustration.'

'Why would his parents kill him? Come on. Just tell me the truth, Ms Pataudi.'

'What's the truth, Constable Sahib?' I say on purpose.

'DCP Sahib,' he says evenly.

He hasn't lost his temper. It's a good sign. I smile.

He points to his nameplate. I've seen it before. It says: DCP Anmol Munde.

'Sorry, Anmol.'

'Let's stick to DCP Sahib, shall we?' he says.

'Sorry, DCP Sahib,' I say. Murder is rude. I am not. 'What is it that you want to know? What is it that you want me to say?'

The cop gets up from his seat in frustration. 'Why are you being so difficult?'

I look at the photograph on the cop's desk. A family photo. A wife, not much older than I am. A girl, his daughter, around six years old, her smile bright against a missing front tooth. They seem to be strengthened by his presence, not diminished by it, as most women are around their men. I see Anmol going home after a long day of dealing with thieves and murderers and rapists, to read a bedtime story to his daughter, to help his wife with the dishes. This is a man who understands women. *Will he understand me?*

I watch him circle the room. I see him glance at his phone as it pings. It must be a message from his wife telling him to come home. I'm the one keeping him from love.

'Fine,' I say.

'Fine what?'

'I'll tell you my story.'

He heaves a sigh of relief. 'Thank you.'

A cop who says 'thank you'. That is unexpected! My instinct about him is correct.

I know he wants this done with. I do too. He has only about twenty hours left before he has to present me in front of a judge. He needs the story. I need it too, if I want to avoid going to court.

I pause and look at him.

'Think about your reputation, Ms Pataudi,' he adds. 'You've just started your career as a writer. You want it to end before you become famous?'

'Assuming that fame is the end-goal for a writer is a plebeian way to think, DCP Sahib,' I reply. 'Because, honestly, all we want to do is tell our stories and be left the fuck alone.'

'Fine, tell me your story,' he says. Smooth. 'All I want is to hear your version. The truth. I'll record it. The court can use it how they want, if they want. Then we can both get out of here, okay?'

I take a deep breath. I didn't know then. I didn't know that night on Air Deccan when I said yes to marrying Suneet that a day would come, not too far along, when I would want to kill him. Because that day we'd smiled at each other till our faces crinkled. He had turned to me and said, 'We are going to live happily ever after.' Because these are the only words the world has given us for marriage.

'You are to tell me the truth, okay?' I hear the cop say. 'Please remember, I have access to emails and witnesses. I'll be able to verify everything you say.'

I look at the state emblem on his rank badge. There is a star below it. He can be trusted. A little bit. I can do this.

'As I said, I'll tell you everything from the beginning, exactly as it happened.'

'Good. But this was years ago. How will you remember?'

'Sir, people don't always remember what exactly someone said or when exactly they said it, but they never forget the feeling that someone left them with. I'll say things as I remember them. But I'll insert one lie in the story, and you'll have to recognize it.'

'You cannot lie. You're under oath.'

'We're not in court,' I quip.

'Not yet,' he quips back. 'Don't get into all this *lafda*, Madam. Don't lie.'

'I will not. The only lie I'll tell you is the lie you'll want to hear,' I say. 'Trust me. Please.'

'Why should I trust you?'

'Because isn't it better to believe a lie than to doubt the truth?'

Anmol sits back and sighs.

'Fine. It's not like I have a choice.'

I smile at him. He really doesn't have a choice.

'Proceed. But remember I have access to . . .'

'Eek-mails . . .'

'What?'

'Emails . . . yes, I know. I was a part of them, remember?'

'Okay.'

'Shall we begin?' I ask the cop.

He turns on the video camera and nods: 'Let's begin.'

CHAPTER THREE

THE FIRST thing I did was to forget.

I took a step forward to begin our first phera around the mandap. I heard the pandit chant: *Om esha ekapadi bhava iti pratham*, the promise of the groom to look after the happiness of the bride. I stopped. *Could I partake of this lie?*

I was mentally unfortified, like we are at tough points in our lives. Despite the tick of time, it is impossible for us to discard our truths and untruths. That's why our past sits in our present and our memories live inside our experiences. So, I couldn't resist when my memory rose like a wave of pain and washed over me. Everything turned dark for a moment. I gasped and remembered.

By the time our big fat Indian wedding had been fixed, Suneet had moved from Boston to New York City to do his MBA at a famous university. I had quit my job as a TV news reporter in Mumbai to join him in New York. I'd left everything I had—my country, my family, my job, my friends—to surprise him on his birthday, two months before our wedding in December. It had been a foolish and impulsive decision, but I wasn't the first woman to forsake her career for love. I wasn't the only woman who wanted to spend time with her future husband before she married him.

I was in love. He was in love. Our eyes crinkled from smiling all the time. We whispered sweet nothings into each other's ears. We gave each other nicknames. Charsi for him, because he loved getting high, and Chikni for me since he said I was cute. We teased each other about what kind of spouses we would be: him *khadoos*, because he easily got into a foul mood, and me *karamjali*, because I always burnt the food I was cooking. We laughingly named our future children Chintu and Chutki, one boy, one girl. He sewed a fallen button on my sweater. I helped him with his MBA assignments. He taught me how to cook. I learnt how to make his favourite baingan ka bharta, without burning it. One long weekend, we lay in each other's arms for three days straight, not getting up for anything unnecessary, not even a bath. We subsequently broke out in a rash that lasted a week. Such was our joy.

My decision to leave everything I knew had felt right during those heady first few weeks.

We moved into a one-bedroom apartment in Newport, a lovely little residential community across the Hudson River. Newport let us live close to Manhattan without emptying our pockets, even though our rent was still a good $2000 a month. Since Suneet was a student and I was unemployed, our priority was to curb expenses. We decided that my savings would take care of our expenses for half a year. Suneet's older step-brother Samit, who lived ten minutes from us, would cover Suneet's tuition. The rest of our expenses would come from Suneet's savings and my salary, once I found a job.

The problem was that I wasn't able to get a job. With my Indian accent and brown skin, it was becoming obvious that no one would hire me as a television journalist. I'd have to restart my career from scratch. I didn't mind. I was willing to do anything for love. 'Our aim must be to get rich,' Suneet told me one day. 'You should get a job that pays well. All this low-paying journalism and writing nonsense should be a hobby, not a career.' I found myself agreeing with him. After all, we were adults now, on the brink of marriage. Practicality was more important than passion. So, with my double degrees in MBA and finance, I decided to become a banker—much better paying. His eyes gleamed. The first step towards that was for me to clear the national CPA, the Certified Public Accountant, exam. Though the exam was just three weeks before our wedding, and only a month away, I said I'd take it.

And, so, slowly, we settled into a routine. I would get up at 6 a.m. to make breakfast and lunch. I'd serve Suneet his omelette and pack his sandwich lunch for the university. After he left, I'd have a quick toast and chai and then study non-stop. I was competing with Americans who'd been preparing for years for this exam, so I had no choice in the matter. More so, I wanted to impress my soon-to-be husband with my devotion to making us rich, as he wanted. Suneet would be back at 5 p.m. and we'd make a simple pasta or khichdi for dinner. I'd never been much of a cook, but I forced myself to learn basic cooking so I could at least fill our stomachs. We'd eat together while watching our favourite animated show *South Park*, study, snuggle and go to bed. My only indulgence was a gym, which I'd go to thrice a week, so I'd fit into the bridal clothes I had purchased earlier that year.

It didn't matter to me where we lived or what I did. I loved our home. I loved our routine. I loved our sacrifices. I loved how in love we were.

*

'Move,' I heard Suneet say. I startled. The fire crackled. I looked at my hands that were covered with henna. I couldn't find the initials of my husband's name there, as was the custom, no matter how hard I tried. Maybe I wasn't trying hard enough. I moved. It was just a few steps around the fire. I could do it. I could do anything for love.

Kutumburn rakshayishyammi sa aravindharam, the pandit chanted. As a bride I was asking the groom to love me solely. I looked at Suneet. Would he love me the way that I deserved to be loved: solely and completely? No, I would not go there. After all, everyone was watching us. Hundreds of guests, and counting. I had to walk. I had to forget.

I smiled as I walked under the canopy.

But what I forgot was that life has a memory. DNA . . . dogs . . . dreams . . . everything remembers. Even a plant has memory, for how else would a creeper grow facing the sun? The universe had recorded everything that had happened to me. And now it played it back to me.

I remembered how, one day, in the dead cold of a December evening, he entered our home.

I heard him call my name.

'I'm here!' I shouted. Suneet opened the door to the bathroom and saw me sitting inside the bathtub, an accounting book open in front of me.

'What are you doing?' he asked me.

He was not smiling. I smiled.

'This is the only part of the apartment that's warm. I figured it'd save us heating costs.'

I looked at him for validation but his face was pinched.

'I want to talk to you,' he said.

'What's wrong?' I asked. I pushed myself up from the two pillows I'd been sitting on and walked up to him. He went out. I followed him to the alcove outside our bedroom. He put his bag down on the floor, as if counting cards at a blackjack game, slowly and carefully.

'You're hiding something from me, aren't you?' he asked. His back was to me. His voice was thin. I got confused. Sure, he was moody and unpredictable; I had accepted that about him. But this morning he'd left home in a decent mood. What had happened since then?

I looked at his back and thought that perhaps this was one of his pranks. He had a strange sense of humour that I was still trying to understand. I walked towards him and said, 'What could I possibly hide from you, jaanu? Why would I even do that?'

He turned around sharply. His eyes were red. He was crying.

'Baby, what's wrong?' I went to him. 'Why are you crying?'

Without any warning, he pushed me into a corner against the wall and pinned me there. His hand was around my neck.

'What the hell! What are you doing?' I asked, alarmed. My voice reached a thin pitch it never had before. I was terrified. I gripped his wrist with both my hands to ease the pressure.

'Your walls. You have too many walls. I can't take it anymore. I'm going to break your walls today,' he said. His whole body was shaking.

'What are you doing, Suneet?' I asked. He was not making any sense. 'What are you talking about?'

Suneet didn't answer my question. Instead, he started shouting at me. His dark cheeks turned red. His brown eyes, which I loved so much, were in indescribable rage. His index finger was pointing at me. This was the same man who often said that a finger pointed at someone meant four fingers pointed back at you.

'Stop it! What's happened to you?' I pushed him away. 'What are you doing?'

I stepped away from him. He was scaring me. Who was this man? This was not the man I loved.

'Tell me, Maneka. Why are you so interested in this exam, huh? So you can get a corporate finance job? So you can be surrounded by men to fuck all day?' he asked.

I blinked in shock. I'd never heard him talk like this. This could not be real.

'What?'

'Tell me, why?' He walked towards me menacingly. I shrank back against a wall. 'Why do you have so many walls? Why are you in the house all day? What are you hiding?'

'You need to calm down. Do you want some water?' I asked.

I needed to get away from him. I went towards the kitchen. He followed me.

'Why do you have so many walls?' he asked again.

'Suneet, I really don't know what you're talking about,' I said. I turned around and looked at him in confusion. 'Trust me, I have no walls around you. I've told you everything about my life, things that I haven't told anybody else. I love you.'

'Really? Then what do you do at home all day? Who comes over when I'm not home, you dirty whore?'

'Mind your language, Suneet! Do you even know what you're saying?' I asked.

'Excuse me? Are you talking back to me?' He walked towards me, all 6 feet of him. Again, he pinned me into a corner against the wall. He pointed his finger at me accusatorily. 'Who do you think you are?'

This could not be happening to me. I was too modern for this, too educated, too well-travelled, too independent, too . . . unprepared. I started crying.

He didn't stop. He called me names.

'Get out of my house, you slut!' he shouted. 'You're nothing but a whore!'

Then, he spat at me. That's when my anger took over.

'How dare you!' I shouted. 'Have you lost your mind? What do you think you're doing?'

I wiped the spit from my face and pushed him.

'You bitch!' he shouted. 'You have the fucking audacity to talk back to me? To hit me? Who the hell do you think you are?'

And then, from nowhere, he punched me. During the initial second of confusion, I thought that his fist was simply resting on my face. You see, no one had ever hit me before. But then my skull shook. My glasses flew off the bridge of my nose. My cheeks burnt with a hot acid sensation. Everything around me turned blurry and red.

In one moment everything beautiful about us became ugly.

Now here I was, weeks later, walking around the wedding fire, with the man who'd raised his hand to me. I felt like a rope was pulling me from one round to another. I stopped. The gold around my neck began to itch. It was drenched in my sweat. I wanted to remove it and toss it into the fire. But there were so many people, so many, staring at me. There was such hope in their eyes. What could I do? I took a deep breath and continued walking.

I remembered that once at a party, I'd asked a historian about sati. 'What did those women feel, walking into the funeral pyre of their dead husbands? Did they go mad, in those final moments, with the realization of their own insignificance?' 'No, they felt elated,' the historian had replied. 'Sati was not suicide for them but a celebration. Their sacrifice validated society's joy.' I understood: Indian women were raised to self-immolate so their existence could be celebrated. My pheras were my sati.

Suneet shuffled over in front of me. He whispered. 'Babe, it's my turn to lead now.'

'The bride leads the first three walks around the fire and the groom takes over from the fourth,' I heard the pandit say. There was a tug at the knot tied at the end of my sari, the *granthi bandhanam*, symbolizing a sacred bond. I didn't move. Tears welled up in my eyes. I was overcome with a mad impulse to make a dash for it.

I saw my mother look at me. Could she read my mind?

I saw my father smile at me, assuming I was emotional for different reasons.

Could I let them down?

They had spent a good part of 2007 arranging my wedding. Finding a pandit to set the mahurat date, which comically fell on Christmas Day. Complying with my in-laws' demand to have the wedding in New Delhi, even though we lived in Mumbai. Booking the lawns of the majestic Siri Fort for two days. Reserving guesthouses and hotels for the out-of-town relatives I'd never met before. Finding caterers and mehndi-wallihs and decorators and ghazal singers and make-up artists and photographers. Arranging the many ceremonies: from the Ganesh Puja on the first day to the mehndi and sangeet the next day, and the pheras and reception on the third day. Depleting their hard-earned savings for a seventy-two-hour party. Distributing the wedding invitations from house to house, refusing tea after tea and then drinking it, exhausted from the same conversations, but assuaged that their only daughter was finally getting married.

The marriage is for the child. The wedding is for the parents.

After all this, how could I let them down? I moved.

The need to be loved is so strong that we choose it above the need to be right.

Without warning, it began to drizzle.

Some guests ran to the hall where dinner was being laid. Others stayed.

A guest behind me said, 'Rain at a wedding is bad luck.'

I looked at the wedding pyre. Would it bring me good luck or bad? Would it extinguish and set me free? Or would it keep raging?

'Hurry,' I heard Suneet say.

The fire was sputtering. There was only one phera left.

I looked at Suneet. Completing the seven pheras would mean I'd be with him for seven lives. Could I do it?

Sherna hugged me from behind and said, 'Don't look so worried, Manu. Rain brings great luck to newlyweds.'

She didn't know for I had told no one. Not even her. The way Suneet had continued to shout that evening. I don't remember what he said. I don't remember what he did. It was all so unreal. Unimaginable. Surreal. It was like watching myself star in a horror movie where you want to tell the girl to turn around because the murderer is standing behind her. I wanted to pluck myself out of that moment. But I had no idea how to. Because the physical pain was the least of my concerns. I had become numb. I had gone into shock. I felt like someone in a coma: hovering above my own body.

This could not be happening. Not to me. This happened to glamorous women in movies, and to victimised women behind doors far far away. This could *not* be happening to *me*.

But it was. For the man I loved grabbed me around the neck and began to choke me.

Again, I pushed him away and told him to stop: was he trying to kill me?

'Congratulations,' someone said.

The mangal pheras were complete. The drizzle had stopped. I was married. I was married to a man who had hit me three weeks before our wedding. There was nothing I could do now. I brought my mind to the present and tried to smile.

Memory is action. Forgetfulness is rest. I needed rest.

I tried to focus on the many faces surrounding us on the reception stage. But they were one big blur of gold and foundation, criss-crossing whiffs of cheap perfume and whisky.

I smiled thinly as they told Suneet, 'You are one lucky guy.' He was not pleased. Not one of them had told me that *I* was a lucky girl.

He would remember that.

A random aunty I didn't know came up to me and said, 'Don't look so worried, Maneka. I know you're a Brahmin and he's a Kshatriya. But women in your family have had great luck marrying men of lower castes. You'll be fine.'

I couldn't even tell her off for making such a regressive statement. My mask was falling. I couldn't let it. I could do this. After all, I was marrying a man I loved. A man who said he loved me. A man of my choosing. Aunty was right. I would be fine. I smiled a little brighter. My jaw hurt.

The wedding was over. What was I supposed to do now?

No, no, I told myself. The universe has been kind to you your entire life. Why would it stop now? You will be fine.

For the wedding night, my parents had booked us a room at The Oberoi hotel. But, as was tradition, my brother Rahul and my friends got to our room earlier to put papads under our mattress and to not let us, the newlyweds, be alone. I was thrilled to see them there. Most of them had flown in from all over the world—America, Dubai, London, Singapore—to watch me get married. I was relieved that we could finally catch up, even if for an hour or two. I didn't know when I'd see them again. I was finally having a good time.

Seeing my friends in our room upset Suneet. Perhaps it reminded him that he had no friends, not even one to attend his wedding. Back in Boston, there was a handful of people he hung out with, but no one was close to him. In New York he hung out only with his step-brother. I had found this odd, but had justified it by saying that the consuming care of oneself, while living abroad, negated care of others. It didn't even matter to me because I thought of my friends as his friends, and I had enough for both of us. But that night it became obvious that Suneet would never think of my friends as his own. He didn't talk for the hour that they were there—teasing us, chattering about how beautiful the wedding was, trying to unsuccessfully engage him. I could see the people I loved the most in the world fall into a growing sense of disquiet. Little alarm bells began ringing inside me. How had I not seen this about Suneet before? How frigid, cold and distant he was! Perhaps he didn't have people around him because he discarded their feelings, as he had discarded mine that cold December evening. After all, friendships are not an option, they are a choice. I wished then that I'd married someone else, the kind of man who would try to charm and embrace my family and friends, not antagonize them.

When Rahul opened another bottle of champagne, Suneet got up with a jerk, locked himself in the bathroom for fifteen minutes, came out in a bathrobe and tucked himself into bed. Fuck, no! In an instant the hotel room became a tomb of silence.

My friends looked like they'd been shot. They quickly made excuses to leave and hustled out. I apologized, 'Sorry, he's just tired. Too much excitement at the wedding.' They hugged me indulgently, gently, and left. My brother stared at me. He had warned me about Suneet and asked if I was certain about him. His doubt was splashed across his face. I squeezed his arms. I stayed at the door as they all left. I heard one of them say at the turn of the hallway, 'I hope Manu knows what she's gotten herself into.'

I went back into the room trembling with anger and disappointment.

A tree falls the way it leans. I should've been careful where I leaned.

Now, it was too late.

No, no, no. You love this man.

Suneet had turned off the lights. There was a tight silence in the room, like it was being choked. I knew better than to say anything.

Because that December evening pushing him back had been a bad idea. It had further enraged him. He dragged me to our bedroom, threw me on the bed and proceeded to choke me again. When he'd had enough, he punched my arms. He punched my stomach. Then he pulled his hands away, flipped me around and twisted my arm behind my back, lifting me as if trying to break my back. I was then yanked around again and slapped a few times. Every time he hit me, every piece of my broken heart would gather on my skin and beat rapidly, covering me in little heartbeats, till I could hear nothing but a giant heartbeat.

I wanted to fight back. But I could not even lift my arms; his grip was so strong. I was absolutely helpless. I couldn't fight back. I couldn't move. I went limp. There was nothing I could do except to let him do what he wanted with me. This feeling was more horrifying than what he was actually doing to me.

The whole time he continued to shout. I couldn't understand what he was saying. Nothing was making sense. I wanted to say something. To tell him to stop. But his hand around my throat had taken my voice. A strong sense of survival kicked in. I knew I would be safer if I kept quiet.

I removed my heavy lehenga and make-up and the long *paranda* attached to my hair. I slipped into the negligee a friend had gifted me for my wedding night. I didn't want to wear it, but this and a salwar-kameez for the morning were all I had carried with me for my *suhaag raat*. I slipped in beside my husband. I didn't know why but I was suddenly afraid.

'Your friends are idiots,' I heard his voice in the darkness.

A jolt ran through my body, as if I'd been struck by lightning.

'Don't say that,' I replied. 'They're smart, accomplished . . .'

'Why were they trying to ruin our night?'

'I had told you that they'd be here, Suneet. I have done the same at their weddings,' I reached for his arm. 'Stop taking this so seriously. It's a silly ritual. It's meant to be fun.'

'Fun? I don't understand you Bombayites. Each one of you is a bigger idiot than the other.'

I didn't say anything. I loved this man. He was just exhausted, like any other groom.

'Because of them we're not going to have sex on our wedding night,' he added.

I shook my head, trying not to snigger. Over the last year, Suneet had had difficulty getting it up. He blamed it on stress. He blamed it on his MBA. Before our wedding, he had finally gone to a doctor. He said he was fine now. I believed him.

But to project his weakness on my friends was unfair.

'We can have sex now if you want,' I offered.

'No, you don't deserve it after the way you've acted. You were having fun with them instead of me. Now suffer.'

He waited for a minute, probably for me to say sorry. I didn't. With a huff, he pulled up the blanket and went to sleep. I sighed in relief. I felt like I had gotten away with murder. I shouldn't have called his bluff. It could have ended badly. But we were in India. There were friends and family. In this country there was an audience for everything. He wouldn't dare do a thing. He wouldn't do anything to me again. He had sworn to it. We were going to be just fine.

Before closing my eyes, I prayed that, if it was possible, I would do what was right, and if it was impossible, I would do what was necessary. I shut my eyes.

*

'Hold on,' Anmol Singh tells me. 'You married a guy after he hit you?'

'Around three weeks later, ya,' I say.

'That sounds . . .'

'Stupid. I know. I was terribly naïve. Or in love. I don't know.'

'It's just——'

'If you don't believe me, it's in the eek-mails.'

'That's not my point. My point is that you don't marry a guy who hits you.'

'Women do. All the time. And they stay married to such men for their entire lives.'

'And was he possibly impotent?'

'Turns out he wasn't. It was a phase or something. Anyway, I had bigger things to worry about.'

'Why would you even marry such a guy? I could understand if you were helpless or forced into it. You were not, I believe. You have an MBA degree. You are financially independent. You have lived around the world.'

'Don't educated, modern women from good families get hit? Every third woman in India is a victim of domestic abuse. It doesn't matter if she lives in a chawl in Bhatinda or in a fancy penthouse on Malabar Hill. Money, status, independence and education do not save a woman from violence.'

'But, you weren't some *abla nari*—'

'Every *krantikaari* was once an *abla nari*, DCP Sahib.'

He smiles. 'Still, Ms Pataudi, to marry a man knowing that he is abusive . . .'

I adjust my chair. I feel like the weight I carry with me will break it.

'Do you know that jellyfish have survived for 650 million years without a brain?' I say. 'Most people survive a lifetime without using theirs.'

He doesn't laugh at my joke. He stares at me.

'Remember, this was 2007,' I say. 'We lived in a world where girls like me had been raised to think that if a man molested us, it was our fault. If someone teased us, it was our fault. I thought I was asking for it. I thought I deserved to be hit. I thought I was provoking him and he would stop once I changed myself and became a better person.'

'Come on.'

'He said he loved me. That hitting me was a one-time thing. That it would never happen again. I believed him.'

Anmol shakes his head in disbelief.

'DCP Sahib, I had a *masi* whose husband used to hit her. Beat her up badly. She was even in the hospital a few times. But she was the most cheerful woman I'd ever met. She disguised her horror for thirty-three years and it manifested in the cancer that ate up her brain cells when she was fifty-five years old.' I pause. I miss my masi. I wish I'd known her truth earlier. 'She didn't speak about it because who would listen? Who would care? Women who speak out are rarely believed, leave alone applauded. Instead, they are told to keep quiet. They are shamed and demeaned. Even in my so-called modern circle, a cousin—that same masi's daughter—told me "*adjust kar lo*". A friend told me that I must have provoked Suneet to "make him hit me". Some uncle told my parents that I must've left Suneet no other choice. People gossiped that I was "making up stories" to justify my divorce.'

I pause. Anmol looks at his daughter's photo. What will she do if she's ever hit? Will she cower or will she fight? What message is the daughter of a cop receiving when she sees the plight of other women, especially independent and educated ones like me?

'What's the point of telling the truth when people choose not to believe you?' I add. 'If they assume a wide distance between abuse and their lives? Society wants domestic violence to stay behind closed doors. They want it to remain a private matter. How can a woman, who is already broken, talk when no one wants to listen?'

'But you are not like most Indian women.'

'Why? Because I wear Western clothes, and drink and work?'

The cop doesn't say a thing. On his desk is another photo of his wife. She's wearing a *nauvari* sari and talking into a mic on stage. He's accustomed to women with opinions.

'I know it sounds foolish, but I didn't know what abuse was. I thought a woman had to land up in a hospital for it to qualify as physical violence. I didn't know then that even a slap qualifies as abuse,' I said.

'You never ended up in a hospital?'

'No. Suneet was smarter than that; the son of a doctor, right? His hitting would leave red marks and minor bruises, but nothing more. His abuse was meant to scare and intimidate me, not kill me.'

'Most abusers don't mean to kill. Not at the start. But they do. I see it every day.'

'I know that now. I didn't then. Now I know that even if an abuser doesn't mean to, he can kill his victim. That even a slap can kill someone.'

He presses his forehead. 'Then why?'

'Love is the presence of light and darkness. When I was madly in love with him, I justified his behaviour. I thought he would change, I thought he was going through a bad phase, he was depressed, he needed me, he loved me, he didn't know what he was doing. When the love went away, I justified my behaviour. I didn't want to face divorce's scandal, taboo, failure or stigma. But sand needs heat and pressure to become glass. To understand my story, you have to understand the how and not the why. So, be patient, DCP Sahib. I will tell you how supposedly modern and independent women like me stay in abusive relationships.'

Anmol nods and orders more cups of green tea. It's going to be a long night.

CHAPTER FOUR

MY WHOLE life was about to change. I was going to step into a black hole and not find a way out for five years. I didn't know that when I landed at John F. Kennedy Airport in the middle of January, face beaming, to begin my newly married life. I had expected him to be happy when he picked me up at the airport. But Suneet was sullen.

'She cheated on him,' he told me in his brother's borrowed car. My brother-in-law's wife, Kamini, with her bovine expression and body, had been screwing her white, much-married colleague for over a year, taking weekend trips with him using work as an excuse. That's why she hadn't come for our wedding. She didn't get leave, was Suneet's excuse to me. A lie in what would be a series of lies. A man who loved me would've told me the truth. I didn't point that out.

When we got home, he didn't let me unpack or rest.

'We have to be with Bhaiya in his time of need,' he said.

I didn't remind him that I'd flown halfway across the world that day, after an exhausting wedding and packing up my entire life in India. I didn't tell him that after flying thirty-six hours in coach, all I wanted to do was sleep. Some men show consideration only when it's begged for. If I'd known what would happen in the weeks to come, I would have never set such a dangerous precedent.

By the time we reached his brother Samit's building, a brisk ten-minute walk away, white puffs of snow were melting on the pavement and turning into puddles we'd have to avoid on the way back. Suneet's mother was also there, sitting on a sofa, her face pinched with sorrow. The living room was stiff as a funeral. I had not expected to walk into this. But I remembered that my mother-in-law had been incredibly loving with me before the wedding. She would see a dress and buy it for me. She would see a piece of jewellery she liked and gift it to me. She would tell me that I was a wonderful girl and the only one who Suneet would marry. 'My *bachcha* had sworn never to get married. You made a decent man out of my *brahmachari*,' she'd say gratefully. Every time we met, she'd repeat how she always wanted a daughter. 'You are not my bahu but my *beti*,' she'd tell me, her eyes brimming with tears. I should've asked her why Kamini could not be her beti. But I was not that bold.

The moment I saw her I decided to forget being a newly-wed bride and become the beti she so desired. I sat down next to her and held her hand.

'Due to Samit's situation,' Suneet told me, 'Maa has decided it's time for DFM, not WFM.'

'What's WFM? And DFM?' I asked.

'Weekly Family Meeting and Daily Family Meeting,' he said staidly.

I laughed. I thought he was joking. They all turned to glare at me.

Some people see the rain and only think of puddles.

I looked at the *chooras* that were listless on my wrists. My mehndi that had begun to fade. My friends were right, what had I gotten myself into?

Suneet opened Samit's laptop. He started Skype. His father's sombre face streamed into the living room. He was still in Dubai, where my in-laws lived.

'The women of today,' said my father-in-law.

'The women of today,' said my mother-in-law.

'The women of today,' said my husband.

Suneet looked up at me. I looked back at him. I'd been married for ten days. Still, I could read his thoughts. Are women so brazen nowadays? Is Maneka any different? She has a career. She has male friends. She smiles at people she meets, men included. What will stop her from sleeping with another man? Fuck him every Saturday in some New Jersey motel? How will I stop her from making me a cuckold?

I smiled at him reassuringly. I had never cheated on anyone and never would. I knew that about myself as easily as I knew that I hated cockroaches.

That's when a thought struck me like a thunderbolt: Was this why Suneet had hit me a month ago? Because he'd heard about his cheating sister-in-law? Was that why he'd gone on about breaking down my walls?

There was a moment that cold December evening when he'd let go off me. Like a rabbit that had found a hole in the hunting net, I wriggled out of his grip and dashed to the nearest safe spot: the bathroom. This much I could do. I locked the door behind me.

I could hear nothing outside.

There was a moment of relief, like a deer that's escaped the deathly jaws of a lion. But then fear returned. And this time it came with horror. I leaned against the door and held myself in disbelief. *What had just happened?* This could not be something that the man I was marrying would do to me.

I was weeping, my sobs coming out of me like pain undone.

I stayed in there. My body felt weak. I thought I'd collapse. I climbed into the bathtub and put my head down on the pillow, where I'd been studying what seemed like a lifetime ago. A red drop fell on it; my lips were bleeding. They tasted like copper. Like love gone sour.

How could one hour obliviate an unyielding all-consuming two-and-a-half years of love? I had loved Suneet at first sight, with all my heart. I was convinced that he was my soulmate, my true love, my better half, my whatever-trite-society-tells-us-our-partner-should-be. He was perfect for me. Despite the many warning shots during our long-distance relationship, I'd overlooked all his wrongs.

The wrongs began in October 2006, when we were dating. I'd flown down from Mumbai to Boston to celebrate his birthday. This was the first time we were meeting after he'd proposed on the plane that February, and we were inseparable, like butterflies and pollen. He took me to New York to visit Samit. He asked me to attend Kamini's brother's birthday party with him. I invited Sherna as well as Farha, another college friend now living in Manhattan, both of whom were eager to meet my boyfriend. We were having a great time together when, at one point, Suneet grabbed me and tried to make out. I pulled away. Kamini was staring straight at us. Later, on the way back home, he accused me of ignoring him the entire night. Through the rest of my two weeks there—when we went back to his apartment in Boston, when we went to the Blue Man Group show, when we ate lobsters at Atlantic Fish Co., when we called our parents to tell them we were getting married—he kept complaining about how I'd given my friends more attention than him.

'I want you all to myself,' he told me repeatedly.

I mistook his possessiveness for romance, as many foolish women do.

I ignored his entitlement to my love, evident when he didn't once thank me for flying down from India to the US to celebrate his birthday. Because the trouble with women is that we think it's normal to be taken for granted. We don't trust our instincts because we've only been taught to second-guess ourselves.

Now, as I lay in the tub, I realized that there was pin-drop silence outside the bathroom door. I wondered where Suneet had gone. What was he up to? Suddenly, I was scared.

After ten minutes or two hours, for time was trivial in comparison to my agony, there was a soft knock on the door. I sat up stiffly.

'Manu? Jaanu?' His voice reached me, muffled but clear through the door. 'Are you all right? Why are you crying so much?'

I stared at the door in disbelief. Was this guy for real?

'Open the door,' he said.

I didn't. What if he had a kitchen knife in his hand? What if he tried to kill me, this time in finality?

'Why have you locked yourself in the bathroom like this? I'm missing you. Come out,' he said.

I didn't answer. I was petrified. He somehow knew how to open our bedroom door from the outside. What if he could do the same with the bathroom door? I stared at the door. It had a latch, not a knob. He could not enter unless he broke the door down. He was too stingy to do that. I heaved a sigh of relief.

'Jaanu, I love you. You have no idea how much I love you. You're the only person I've ever loved,' he said. I didn't reply.

He went away.

My phone was next to me. I flipped it open and texted Rahul.

'Calling off wedding. Will explain later.'

My mother called just then, almost as if she knew something was amiss. Her voice was warm, nudging me away me from the centre of my unhappiness.

'Are you okay?' she asked the second I said hello. There was no fooling a mother. 'You sound sick.'

'I'm fine,' I lied. 'Got a cold.'

She rattled off a list of cold remedies I could take. I didn't listen, wondering how to tell her that her daughter didn't want to . . . no . . . *shouldn't* marry a monster.

'Mom, I . . .'

'I was calling to tell you that Papa and I are in Delhi. We came to give the advance to the caterer and guesthouse. Then we said, we might as well make the full payment for your wedding venue. It's such a beautiful place, I can't tell you. You will love it.'

'Why did you do that? Take that money back.'

'What? It's not refundable. How does it matter?'

'It's just . . . *so* much money,' I said.

'Don't be silly, Manu. You're our only daughter. We've been saving for your wedding since you were born.'

Indian parents. They make it impossible for their daughters to call off their wedding.

I took a deep breath. I remembered my childhood friend Malini, who had cancelled her wedding two years ago. The gossip and scandal that followed had forced her parents and her to move out of their building. Malini had stopped being invited to parties or weddings as her mere presence was considered unlucky. This was our Indian society. The window for a woman to decide whether or not she wanted to marry a man closed once the wedding date was fixed.

I would have to go through with my wedding. I could not let my parents down.

When Rahul texted: 'What?????? Why cancel???? What happened????' I texted back, 'Just kidding!!!!!'

I put my head back on the pillow. Was I even thinking straight? Was I even capable of it right now? I didn't know. But I knew then that I had chosen a certain way of life that would involve me living alone with my truths. This wasn't who I was. But it was who I'd have to become.

That's when I heard loud sobbing coming from the bedroom. Suneet was crying! Slowly, I got out of the tub. It was now safe to assume that he was preoccupied. I could dash out the front door in a second. I opened the bathroom door carefully, trying not to make a noise. I peeked into the bedroom on the way out. There he was. On the bed. Holding himself in a foetal position and howling loudly. I had never seen a man cry like that. I stood at the bedroom door, transfixed. When he looked up, I made a move to run. This made him cry more loudly.

'I'm so sorry,' he said. 'This will never happen again. It was a one-time thing. I swear. I love you so much, my Manu. More than I've ever loved anyone. Don't leave me. I'll be left alone. Please. I beg you, jaanu.'

He held out his arms.

It was over. I could see it in his eyes. I wouldn't have to dash out the front door.

I went to the kitchen and drank a glass of water.

I could hear his voice: I'm sorry, I'm sorry, I'm sorry.

I went towards him. I sat down next to him, an empty shell of a body.

He spoke the whole night about how much he loved me. How he couldn't wait to marry me. I was all that he had. He was the luckiest man on this planet. After an hour I began to console him. After four hours I brought him dinner. He said he didn't deserve to eat. I fed him with my hands.

It was the strangest thing. He was acting like the victim whom I had to tend to and console. I accepted that as some form of repentance. I couldn't think straight.

But over the next few days, as my body ached, he tried hard to mend my heart. He cooked for me. He patted me dry after my bath. He massaged my shoulders and feet. He smiled at me whenever our eyes met. I accepted his guilt without a word. I threw myself into my studies. I didn't speak to anyone about anything.

On the day of the exam, which I failed, five days after he had first hit me, he came to the exam centre with me in the morning and waited outside in the cold. During the break, he fed me a cucumber sandwich that he had made himself. He put two almonds in my mouth for good memory. He kissed my cold lips with his cold lips and told me that he loved me.

As we were walking back from the exam centre, I stopped. I looked at him and said, 'Suneet—' I was trembling like a baby bird on a slab of ice '—I couldn't talk about this earlier as I was focused on the exam. Our wedding is around the corner. I am not sure of it . . . of us . . . anymore. Do you think it makes sense for us to postpone the wedding? Don't you think we need some time?'

Even in my decision I needed his permission. He stopped. There were already tears in his eyes. 'Don't even say that, my jaanu. I love you. I want to marry you. You cannot call off the wedding.'

I knew that. I'd accepted that. But the clamour in my heart refused to quiet down.

'I'm not calling it off. I—we—just—maybe need more time.' I looked straight into his eyes. 'Look, this is not an easy conversation. But we don't know each other very well. We've only met during holidays. Are you sure that you want to get married to me? Should we wait till you finish your MBA?'

'Jaanu,' he turned to me and hugged me. 'Your teeth are chattering. You're so nervous. So uncomfortable. Why? Are you forgetting that we're meant to be together? Have you forgotten all the signs? Don't you remember how we met?'

Of course I remembered how we'd met. It was 2005. I had quit my post-MBA corporate job in Switzerland and decided to come to New York for a vacation before moving back to Mumbai. I was going out for lunch with two of my childhood friends who lived in Newport. As we were circling the streets looking for parking, I spotted my family friend Jay outside a Starbucks. I got out to say hello and he introduced me to Suneet, his family friend, and Suneet's parents. Suneet's parents said that they knew my mother from Shimla, and asked me to join them at their son Samit's house for evening tea. I saw the way that Suneet was looking at me—he was tall, dark and handsome— and I said yes. Two days later, when we kissed on the 4th of July, under the fireworks on the Hudson River, we marvelled at how many worlds had to collide to make us meet. I was down from Switzerland, he was down from Boston, his parents were down from Dubai and Jay was down from Mumbai. The fact that we all ended up at the same spot outside a Starbucks in New Jersey had to mean something. It was design, not coincidence. Like

Einstein, we knew that God does not play dice. The universe had contrived to make us meet. Wasn't that the beginning of every true love story?

'We're meant to be together,' Suneet repeated. 'You mean everything to me.' He stopped walking and made me sit down on the steps of an art-deco building. He held me. There was a moment's silence. Then he said softly, 'I haven't ever told you this, but I was waiting for the right girl to lose my virginity to, and you were worth it.'

'Virginity?' I said, confused. 'You told me that you've slept with many women before.' He had, in fact, made himself out to be quite promiscuous.

'I didn't want you to think that I was a loser,' he said, raising his voice a little. How was he making this my fault? 'I thought you wouldn't understand that I was saving myself for the woman I would marry.'

I knew that men multiplied their sexual partners the way that women divided them. But isn't multiplication with zero still a zero?

'What about your scar?' I asked. There was a scar on his penis that he claimed was from a woman who'd bitten him while giving him a blow job.

'Yes, I've done everything possible with hundreds of women. But I just couldn't have sex with them. Call me old-fashioned, but I only wanted that with my future wife. With you. And it was worth it. You're the most amazing woman I've ever met, an angel, a goddess, a—'

'Suneet—'

'I swear. I'm not lying.'

'This is ridiculous. This is exactly what I'm talking about! I don't know your truth.'

'Please don't embarrass me. I just opened my heart to you, and you're mocking me?'

I looked at him. Was it true? Was I mocking him?

'Don't break me,' he continued, taking my hand in his. 'If you don't marry me, I will become nothing.'

I didn't say anything. His lies kept stacking up. Was this the way with men?

'Look, our parents have spent lakhs on the wedding already,' he said. I wanted to correct him saying that mine definitely had. We were paying for everything except the groom's guests' accommodation in Delhi. 'Our relatives have booked their tickets. Our trousseau is ready. Your jewellery has been bought. It's too late to cancel what's already set in motion.'

Did that matter? Or were our lives already too mixed?

'The whole world knows that we are getting married. If we cancel at this point it will be really bad for everyone.' He paused. 'Especially you. You know how our desi aunties talk about girls who call off their weddings.'

I knew this. Malini could not stop talking about the number of people who'd told her that no one would marry her now.

'Look. I love you, Manu. And I know that you love me. I can't wait to begin my life with you. Isn't that all we need?'

I shut my eyes.

A week ago, before all this, before my reality unravelled, I had gone shopping for groceries. On the way back I'd seen a small bird, possibly a chickadee, trembling on the pavement. She had fallen into a puddle and was freezing to death. I knew that the next gust of cold wind would be the end of her. So, I picked her up gently and put her in my purse, where at least she'd be warm. By the time I was home, three minutes later, the bird had shat all over the inside of my purse. She flew out of my purse and all over the house, banging into the lamp, the blinds, the TV. 'Quick, close the window,' I told Suneet. 'If she flies out she won't survive for two minutes.' I ran into the kitchen and got water in a bowl. I tried to keep it in front of the bird. But the nearer I went to her, the more frightened she became. 'How do you know it's a she?' Suneet asked me as I emptied out a shoe box and put cotton in it, a warm bed for the bird to rest in. 'Shh,' I told him. 'Let's place this near her, so she'll know it's home.' We placed the box in the middle of our living room and stepped away into the kitchen, hoping the bird would drink the water and nestle in her new home till she was strong enough for a new day. But all we heard was the thump of the bird banging against our walls and windows. Suneet turned towards me, 'Your intentions are great, Chikni, but the bird will die of shock in here quicker than it will die in the cold outside.' I sighed. He was right.

Reality was allowing things to come to us naturally, and we enjoyed what drifted in. But what could we do with what drifted away? We had to let it go. Because sometimes we don't recognize a good thing when it comes to us, or know a bad thing when it goes away.

I opened the window and let the bird go.

Today, deciding my fate on the steps of an art-deco building, I understood why I'd assumed that the bird was a she. Because I was that bird. Because I'd accepted the known over the unknown. I had stopped seeking.

'It's going to be fine. We are going to be fine,' I heard Suneet saying.

'You're right,' I said. I got up.

Because we don't select our partners. They are given to us. And I knew Suneet would change into the partner I needed him to be. My love still had hope.

'Fuck it. Let's do it,' I said. 'Let's get married.'

I walked down the steps. I walked into the snow.

'Worst-case scenario,' I added, 'we'll get divorced.'

'Indians don't get divorced,' I heard him say, behind me. He chuckled.

When he caught up with me and held my hand, I didn't let go.

I didn't call off the wedding.

That day on the steps of the art-deco building I made the worst mistake of my life. Because, as any divorcee will tell you, divorce is *not* the worst-case scenario in a bad marriage, living with your own stupidity is.

CHAPTER FIVE

LIKE ANY new bride, I didn't know what to make of my in-laws.

The day before our wedding, Suneet was bitten by a stray dog in Khan Market. As he took his anti-rabies shots, I held him and took care of him. I asked my doctor father-in-law if there was anything else I could do for Suneet. My formerly charming father-in-law, Manjrekar Sodi, who had also stated that he loved me like the daughter he never had, retorted, 'It's between you and your husband. Don't ask me to interfere.' I stared at him, shocked and hurt. His face was like the bark of an oak tree that's never been watered, drooping and withered. But he was a charming man. He had been incredibly loving with me before the wedding. We would go for meals together. We would talk on the phone. We would crack jokes. I had even told Suneet jokingly that I was marrying him for his father. What was the reason for this volte-face? My mother told me later: the guesthouse where the groom's guests were staying had sent my father-in-law a bill. My father-in-law was upset that he'd been asked to pay anything at all for the wedding. After making such a show of not asking for dowry, he expected dowry by way of the bride's family footing all the wedding expenses. Forget emotions and relationships and so-called daughters; ultimately, to him, everything boiled down to money. I didn't know then that this was all he measured anyone by. It was not a coincidence that he had made Jay's wealthy father his best friend, a friend he used for his generosity. I didn't know then that this was just the beginning.

Back at Newport, we were walking back home after seven long hours. This included a three-hour Skype session with Suneet's father, where the family tore apart some apology email that Kamini had sent Samit. I hadn't asked why Samit was sharing a private email between his wife and him with his family. And another four hours cooking dinner with my mother-in-law, serving the dinner and then cleaning up. I hadn't asked why the men didn't help.

It was an excruciating start of a marriage. I needed fresh air.

'Why did you tell Maa that you didn't want to stay over?' Suneet asked me.

I said simply, in surprise. 'You do remember that I just flew across the world on a plane for thirty-six hours? That I haven't slept in two days?'

'That doesn't mean you can make faces when talking to Dad.'

I stopped in my tracks. Why was my husband picking on me? Why was he criticizing his new wife, who had just landed in a new country and spent the day cooking for his family? What kind of a man was he?

'I wasn't making a face, Suneet.' I didn't tell him that my father-in-law had been brusque with me on Skype, as he had been in Delhi. I couldn't tell him that their three-hour conversation had been like pulling each strand of hair out of my scalp. Men don't see the humour in their own family. 'Look, I'm exhausted. All I want to do is sleep—'

'Whatever.'

'Fine, if you really want to find faults, then tell me—why you didn't give me a heads-up about Samit's divorce? Why would you hide such a big thing from your own wife?'

'Don't change the subject. I've always known that you're selfish, Maneka. Today you've proven it. You could've spent more time with my family, but you're too much of a princess to care about anyone but yourself.'

'Selfish? Suneet, what is wrong with you? I spent hours in the kitchen today to make one meal while you sat around watching TV. I told you before we got married that I don't cook. You insisted I learn some basic cooking—dal, chawal, sabzi—because we're not in India. I agreed. But cooking for hours non-stop to make one meal? Serving you like you're a maharaja? Picking up your plate? Cleaning your dishes? All while you chill. Am I your servant?'

'You're worse than a servant. You're unemployed. Do you have anything better to do than cook and clean?' he snapped and stomped off, leaving me alone in the muddy puddles.

I stared at his vanishing figure. In one sentence he had reduced my degrees, my education, my scholarships and my hard work to nothing. I had known I was marrying an unreasonable man. But I hadn't known what this would entail. That I'd always have to give more than I'd get. It was 2008. Women like me, educated, modern and independent, were still living in the shadows of our foremothers, who were told that women must know their place. It was not a shock to give more in a marriage. It was a necessity, no matter what women said publicly. Perhaps it *was* fair that I ran the house alone till I started making money. Perhaps it *was* fair that I did everything for my husband's family while my husband made no effort with mine. I would have to accept that this would be the way forward. *What choice did I have?*

I took a deep breath. Fine. Love is a simple negotiation. We love the people who love us. We measure the give and take. I would do what I had to do. This was adulthood.

The next day Suneet curiously changed his mind, as if a shot of empathy had been injected into his heart while we slept. He decided that he wanted to spend time with me. He teased me about the masalas and dals that I had packed in my suitcase. I giggled as I told him how I'd flaunted my chooras during check-in to avoid paying for excess luggage (back then airport staff were kind, unlike today). He counted the cash gifts from our wedding.

'This will cover rent for two months,' he said, thrilled. The money would go into the joint bank account we had opened when I'd moved here.

I smiled, relieved that we were finally behaving like a newly married couple.

'And see what my parents gave us,' he said. He pulled out a steel knife from a golden sheath. It was curved and embossed with gold trimmings. I saw the blade glint in the morning light. For some reason a shiver ran down my spine.

'It's a kirpan,' he said.

'What are we going to do with it?' I asked slowly.

'Well, it's decorative, so we can hang it above the TV. Or—' he said, bringing the knife to my throat '—I can use it to kill you when we have a fight.'

I took a big gulp. He laughed.

His phone rang. 'It's Maa,' he said. He said the word Maa like some long-forgotten pain. 'She has hurt herself.'

'What?' I said, genuinely alarmed.

'Her leg is cramping.'

How did this family turn a cramp into an injury?

'We have to go help her,' he said urgently, like a superhero on a mission to rescue a damsel falling off a building.

I'd spent the previous day with my mother-in-law. I still hadn't unpacked.

I looked at him and said, 'Sure.'

When we reached his brother's house, his mother was lying on the sofa, groaning. Her hips, thick like tumours on a slim neck, were being held by her twig-like hands. It struck me, with a heavy sadness, that this was the worst acting I'd ever seen. Her behaviour was as confusing to me as her husband's and son's. What they had shown me before marriage was completely different from what they were showing me now. I couldn't reconcile their public image with their private truth. Who were these people?

'Get her a hot water bottle,' Suneet barked at me.

I got the hot water bottle.

'She needs nimbu pani with salt. Make that quickly.'

'Add half a spoon of sugar to it,' she said.

I made the nimbu pani.

I spent the day in the same loop as the prior one: serving, supporting, listening. My in-laws were ensuring that no attention was given to the new bride. Was this a bid to keep me in my place? The thought crossed my mind unexpectedly and stayed there.

The next day my mother-in-law came to our house unannounced.

'I got up at six in the morning to make food for my daughter,' she said in front of Suneet. She had made his favourite dishes.

'And to help her settle the house. In India she has maids, in the US she has me.' I could see her horse-like teeth, large and protruding, through her fake passive-aggressive laugh.

I blinked, unsure about whether to be affronted by this mockery, and then ignored it. I could only handle one asshole at a time. Plus the food looked delicious. Even more so because I didn't have to cook it. Fifteen minutes later Suneet left for college, and I spent another day with my mother-in-law, 'settling the house', as she called it.

Fortunately, when he got back, Suneet seemed as tired of her as I was. We spent the next two days alone. She called on the second day to say that she was making fresh chapattis, if we wanted to come over. Suneet said no, he had homework. 'Your loss,' I heard her say on the phone. On the third day he got another call from her. It was a new drama this time.

'She's stepped on some knitting needles and can't move,' he said. The superhero voice was back. I really must learn how to play the damsel in distress, I thought.

When we reached Samit's house, she—of course—had no marks on her feet.

'I thought you were hurt, Maa,' I asked, trying not to make it sound like an accusation.

'I was,' she said, her snake-like plait swinging on her back. 'But when I heard you both are coming, I became okay. Now, let's cook. It's almost lunchtime.'

What could I say? I was too busy wondering how long it took her to plan her schemes.

'I made chapattis for you, Maneka. I know you don't know how to make them'—another insult—'but you should learn from me,' she continued, as I followed her to the kitchen.

A jolt ran through me. My mother-in-law spent all day in the kitchen since she loved cooking and had nothing else to do. Surely she didn't expect the same of me?

I couldn't stay quiet, as I normally did with her taunts. 'I'm afraid I'll never be as good a cook as you, Maa,' I said. 'I find cooking annoying.'

She turned to me and said, 'I'll slap you if you say that. The men of this house like good food. You will have to learn.'

I couldn't hide the shock from my face. She sounded . . . barbaric. Where was the woman I'd met before marriage, the mother-in-law who had promised me friendship, love and respect? How did I go from being adored to being scorned just because I was now her daughter-in-law?

'Anyone can cook well,' she continued. 'You just have to try, Maneka. The way you do with your writing.'

She took dahi out of the fridge and told me to beat it. I took a deep breath. I didn't tell her that you cannot teach a fish to climb a tree. I wanted my new family to like me.

While another elaborate lunch was being made by the women of the house, Suneet played Halo 3 and Samit watched *Chak De India*. Neither of them offered to help. Instead, Suneet told me to get him a glass of water.

This was all very new to me. My parents had never once demanded I cook for them or serve them. My father would not even let me pick up his plate. My brother was equally involved with household responsibilities. The men of my family didn't think women were beneath them.

As I chopped coriander, I placated myself. This is the real India. Women do the housework while the men chill. Your husband and in-laws expect it. Get used to it.

I smiled as I laid the table.

Lunch was followed by another long Skype chat with my father-in-law. The four of them discussed lunch in excruciating detail. They bitched about Kamini. They planned dinner. Between the long silences, they stared melancholically at each other. All this happened as I cleared the dishes, loaded the dishwasher, cleaned the kitchen and made them tea.

As we were leaving, my mother-in-law said, 'Tomorrow is Monday. Samit will be at work. I will come to your house to stay.'

Samit looked relieved.

'But wouldn't Bhaiya's house be more comfortable, Maa?' I asked, genuinely. Samit lived alone in a three-bedroom duplex. We lived in a small one-bedroom apartment.

'I'm happy where my sons are,' she said. A tear rolled down her cheek. I wished someone had told her that the role of the impoverished, long-suffering mother had already been enacted much better by Nirupa Roy. 'But, don't worry, Samit beta,' she turned to him and said. 'Maneka and I will cook every meal for you. You'll eat with us.'

Men weren't expected to grow up even after their wives had left them.

I heard my father-in-law shout from Skype. Had he been on it the entire day? 'The boys will be tired, bahu. Make them something nice to eat. Give them a drink when they come home. There's a bottle of Black Label . . . '

Was I a servant? I looked at Suneet. He didn't say anything. Suneet was showing his family that he controlled me, because controlling women was of paramount importance to the men of this family. No wonder my mother-in-law was so conniving.

Or, perhaps (I hoped), they were all acting out because of what had happened with Kamini?

Only time would tell. I would have to be patient.

So, Maa came to stay with us. She took over our room, while we slept on the second-hand futon in the living room, which tilted to one side. I found myself cooking and cleaning all the time. If I tried to watch TV, she'd play bhajans on her laptop so I wouldn't be able to hear a word, or she'd sit next to me and talk throughout the show. If I tried to write or apply for jobs, she'd keep interrupting me with some inane thing or the other. She'd talk for hours on Skype with her husband about asinine things, like the price of tomatoes in the US versus Dubai, or how much jeera to add in dal. She called him Raji, and the whole day I had to hear: 'Raji this' and 'Raji that'. If she saw that I wasn't cooking or cleaning, she'd force me to join those calls. Her tears would roll on cue every evening, when Suneet came home from college, as she discussed the sad plight of 'poor' Samit.

After two weeks of this, I'd had enough. A part of me was being slowly choked. I was sick of this drudgery and sullenness. I was resentful that I hadn't had a moment to be a newlywed. So, after dinner one night, when Suneet seemed to be in a good mood, I told him that we should go out for dinner, or a movie, or take a half-day trip somewhere nearby in Samit's car.

'Great idea, jaanu,' he said. He snuggled in beside me on the futon. 'I'll tell Maa. She needs an outing.'

Some men should marry their mothers.

'No, I meant just the two of us, baby. It would be nice to do something like a newly married couple, no?'

'What do you mean? You want to go without Maa?'

I held my tongue and said, 'It's been almost a month since we got married. I've barely had time alone with you, jaanu. We can take her the next time—'

Before I could say anything more, Suneet got up from the futon and began shouting, 'How can you ask for something when my family is in a crisis? How can we leave my mother alone during such a tragedy? I can't believe how selfish you are!'

I missed the man who had fucked me in an aeroplane toilet.

'Shhh! Maa can hear you,' I said.

'It doesn't matter. Maa will agree with everything I have to say,' Suneet said. He had the look of a jockey flogging a tired horse, drunk with his own power. 'We all know the kind of person you are.'

Ouch! As he continued criticizing me, I blinked back the tears collecting in my eyes. Why was my husband so irrational? Why were things so black and white with him? How would I tolerate his family and him for a lifetime, when four weeks felt like too much?

'You know what,' I said finally, getting up from the futon as well. 'I've done more than anyone else would, for each and every one of you. I have compromised my marriage for the sake of your family. I have proven I'm a good wife without a single thanks from you. Despite everything I've done, all I've gotten is criticism. If you don't appreciate what I've done, stuff that *you* would never do for me, then you're nothing but an ungrateful brat.'

'Fine. Fuck off then. Get out of my house.'

'Excuse me? This is not your house. Not only is my money paying the rent, but I'm also running the house.'

'The lease is in my name, bitch! So get lost!'

'Why don't you get lost?'

In response, Suneet jumped on the futon and lay across it, so I couldn't get in. He pulled the blanket over himself for good effect. Where could I go? The bedroom light was on.

My mother-in-law was awake, listening keenly to our fight, I imagined. I couldn't stand the sight of her at this weak moment.

'You know what?' I said, raising my hands in surrender. 'I *will* get out of this house. At least I'll finally have some time to myself!'

I grabbed my coat and keys, and went for a walk.

I reached the promenade overlooking the Hudson River, and peace descended upon me. I had truly not enjoyed a single aspect of the US until now. The many messages from my friends asking me to meet them, asking to come over, had gone unanswered. I had done nothing but be a good bahu and yet, here I was, being treated like a terrible one. I walked around for forty minutes and went back home feeling much better. I opened the front door to find the two of them sitting in the living room with one single lamp on.

'I am going to give you one tight slap!' my mother-in-law yelled at me in Hindi. 'Why did you storm out of the house at two in the morning?'

I hadn't realized it was that late. I looked at the clock on the wall. It was half past one. I didn't correct her.

'Sorry, Maa. I didn't realize it was this late.'

'What if something had happened to you?' She began crying. By now I had seen her cry at least twice a day, which amounted to over fifty times. I made no move to console her like I used to earlier. 'What would we have told your parents?'

'I'm sorry. I just went for a walk around the building. I'll go change now. My pyjamas got dirty. Then we can all sleep.'

I went to my room and shut the door. While putting on my nightie, an overwhelming sense of grief and loss gripped me. I missed my mother, father and brother. I missed my friends. I missed my city, Mumbai. I missed who I used to be even two months ago. I missed the uncomplicated life I'd led. I missed the love I had expected.

Maa entered the room without knocking. She saw that I was crying.

'Don't worry, beta. Even though you've hurt me badly today, your secret is safe with me,' she said.

Hurt *her*?

'What? What secret?' I said, wiping my cheeks. She didn't care that I was in tears.

'This one . . . of a young girl . . . destroying her husband's peace . . . misbehaving in front of her mother-in-law . . . vanishing from her marital home at two in the morning. What will people think when they hear about this?' Why was she acting like I'd burnt down my 'marital' home, whatever that was? 'Eesh, your generation of women. What can I say? We would not have dared behave like this in front of our in-laws.'

I looked at her quizzically. How did she transform from playing Nirupa Roy to playing Lalita Pawar in one hour? It would be fascinating if it weren't so evil.

'I promise you, beta. There is no need to feel ashamed,' she continued. I really wasn't feeling shame. 'I've spoken to Suneet as well. I have calmed him down . . . for now. No need to thank me.' She took my hand in hers. 'And I promise never to talk about this horrible incident to anyone. After all, the reputation of my bahu is at stake.'

The only way to avoid getting scrutinized under a microscope is to stop wriggling. I stopped crying. I mumbled good night and went outside to the living room. Suneet stomped off on seeing me and went into the bedroom. I heard Maa weeping inside as Suneet consoled her. Why was she making this about herself when I was upset? Why was she always pouncing on me? I couldn't hold back my tears. These people were all so strange.

Suneet came in after a while and saw me crying. He said nothing. He lay down on the futon, careful not to cross the wedge between us.

We never spoke of this again. Just like we never spoke of that cold December night again.

Time passed by. My mother-in-law was still staying with us. It had been a month. I was beginning to lose my mind. Then came a twist in the tale. After all that melodrama, Samit decided to get back together with his wife. Suneet was furious. 'Don't be a coward,' he told his brother. Maa and Dad too went into a frenzy, calling Samit weak and naïve. Samit stopped coming over to our house to eat. Kamini was now cooking for him, finding ways to move back in with him.

Somehow, this changed the dynamic between Suneet and me. To him, his brother's marriage working out meant that he had to make his work. We began to live like a somewhat normal couple. Suneet started being nicer to me. He began to help me load the dishwasher. He started doing the laundry. He stopped finding faults with everything I did. On Valentine's Day, he brought me flowers and cooked me a lovely dinner. I was so grateful for these small gestures that, through our entire marriage, I would circle back to them as his greatest acts of kindness.

I assumed that our testing times were over and he had finally changed. After all, what punishment of God is not also a gift?

It was time to start getting out of the house. We met Farha, Sherna and her husband Baizad for lunch. Suneet's face fell when the bill came. I squeezed his hand so he wouldn't create a scene. But then he jumped at the chance to join them at a carnival near South Street Seaport. We went. For the first time since coming to the US, I was having a good time. Being with my friends was like coming up for air after being underwater. But I could see Suneet beginning to sulk again. I ignored him. After two hours there, I wanted to buy a hot dog. He told me to stop wasting *his* money. The hot dog was $2. My friends were getting uncomfortable. I told him I wanted to leave.

As we headed back home in the PATH train, Suneet said, 'Don't you hate the way your friends flaunt their money?' I thought of my friends with all their 'money' I hadn't noticed earlier. 'Why do they expect us to spend as much? They want to order beer with their lunch. They want to take taxis everywhere. Don't they know I'm a student?' I thought of my friends, most from middle-class families like mine, who'd worked hard as first-generation immigrants to be able to afford $40 lunches and $20 taxi rides. 'They clearly don't care about you, Chikni. They're not sensitive to your situation. I told you, baby. It's just you and me,' he finished.

Why was Suneet always trying to isolate me from everyone and everything I loved?

I knew he detested Sherna because she'd once planned to meet him for lunch in Manhattan, but was unable to get out of a work meeting on time. It didn't matter to him that she had apologized profusely, or thrown a big party for us when we announced our nuptials, and made several efforts to be friends with him. My husband was not a forgiving man. She had made one mistake and was now irredeemable in his eyes. But why would he try to poison my mind against *all* my friends? They were the only people in this country who were making me happy. I let it be. There are only so many battles you can pick in a marriage and mine already had much larger ones.

I squeezed his hand and repeated, 'Yup! It's just you and me, Charsi.'

And your entire family, I wanted to add.

Fortuitously, I soon got a job offer from an Indian news organization to work as a reporter at the New York Stock Exchange. I would begin in two weeks.

To Suneet this was a sign that I finally deserved a honeymoon. We had to go before I began my job. So, after some quick research, we decided to go to Jamaica, where—as Indian passport holders—we wouldn't need a visa.

In a week's time our tickets were booked and we were on our first trip as a married couple. During the four-hour plane ride to Montego Bay and on the way to our hotel, we couldn't keep our hands off each other. We laughed non-stop. We were inseparable even if someone came in front of us.

More than two months after my wedding, I was finally celebrating my marriage.

When we arrived at our hotel and I saw the seven-mile Negril beach in front of us, I felt that who we'd become didn't matter. The last few months didn't matter. Our story began now.

Within ten minutes of check-in, a bellboy offered us a doobie for $10 a stick.

'Time to smoke the snake,' Suneet said, thrilled as a toddler with candy. 'And, I have more.'

He opened his suitcase.

'You don't? Are you crazy, babe? This is America! We'll get deported!'

'No chance! I'm too smart for that. Watch!'

I watched as he opened his toiletries bag.

'Oh no, the shampoo has spilled all over it!' I said.

He smiled. I watched as he took out his aspirin bottle. He emptied it and pulled out a bag from it. He had triple-bagged his stash and hidden it among the tablets!

'The super-scented shampoo is a decoy,' he said and grinned. He was enjoying this, this fooling the system.

'Seriously, Suneet! You'll get arrested for this one day. You're crazy!' I said.

'Only about you,' he said and kissed me.

I smiled. Something about travel made Suneet a different person, like he could escape whatever armour he otherwise lay trapped under. I realized then that, during our courtship, I'd only ever met him when he was travelling, a time when he was at his most wonderful. No wonder that in our day-to-day life he was so different from the man I'd thought he was.

We spent the next five days in bliss. Our first adventure was to go parasailing, where we were harnessed to a parachute and towed behind a boat over the turquoise water. With the world beneath our feet, we were like birds in the open skies, flying and laughing. We ate a lot: jerk chicken, fried callaloo, fresh hot coco bread, curried goat and conch bits, luscious star apples and mangoes that tasted like bits of heaven after North America's tasteless, genetically modified fruit. There was a live reggae show on the beach every night, where we ate two-for-one lobsters with bowls of melted butter and drank free beer. The south side of the beach had a large Bob Marley venue with huge murals of the legend on stage. There we danced amid the cheers of drunken spring-breakers. Everywhere we went Suneet was greeted with a joyful, 'Hey brother!' There were bands playing reggae on drums. There were bursts of fraternity dances. Locals were playing dominos and there were fire dancers everywhere. This place was sheer happiness.

One night, after drinking many papaya daiquiris, we were walking along the moonlit beach, whispering sweet nothings into each other's ears. That afternoon we had gone snorkelling, holding hands, saving each other from coral reefs that touched the water's surface and laughing so hard that there was salt water in our nostrils for the rest of the day.

'Captain Kirk's boat was fun,' I said.

'Ya, it was,' he said.

'And we didn't let each other get screwed by reef burns.'

Suneet stopped and turned towards me. I'd had my hair braided with colourful beads in medusa-like dreadlocks. My head looked like a soccer ball. He ran his hands through my dreadlocks and said, 'I've always trusted you, Chikni. A lot more than I'm used to trusting people. So don't worry about getting screwed by me. I'd never do that to someone I love.'

I held up two fingers with the middle two put down. It was the Jamaican hand sign for love that a local drum-maker had taught us the day before. Suneet smiled and put my head on his chest. I smiled till my eyes grew blurry. This was all I'd ever wanted from marriage: trust and a little bit of romance. The land of Bob Marley, incense, rasta fashion and reggae drums, so far from everything we knew, had brought us everything we wanted. Because to meet each other, we sometimes have to separate from ourselves. From now on we were going to be just fine.

CHAPTER SIX

WHAT I didn't know then was that love is a play and we are all actors in it.

We returned from our honeymoon to find my mother-in-law in our apartment.

'I stayed here while you were gone,' she said. 'Samit needed a break from his Maa.'

I thought of the sea urchins we'd seen in Jamaica, porcupine-like creatures with long black spikes, out of place with the red seaweed and orange starfish. Because bottom dwellers live where they're not welcome.

I touched my mother-in-law's feet. There's nothing you can do about what happens to your life when you're not looking. I went to my room, hoping I'd kept my diary under lock and key. She wouldn't want to read what was written there.

'Don't worry. I'm leaving now,' I heard her say, though I hadn't said a thing. 'I made Himachali dishes for you: mahni-mandra. Suneet told me that even though you're half-Himachali you don't know how to make a single Himachali dish. Plus he's sick of wasting money on outside food.'

There it was again: them versus me. Another reminder that I was an outsider to this family, no matter what I did. I told her I'd bring out the souvenir we'd got for her, an expensive box of Blue Mountain coffee, which cost more than our food bill for the entire trip.

When she left, after dinner, Suneet turned to me and said, 'Maa said that the bathroom was stinking while she was here. Are you not cleaning it properly?'

I looked at him, sadly. The honeymoon was over.

I began unpacking, hoping to make the good feelings linger a little longer.

'I asked you something,' he said.

I asked him back, 'Have you ever cleaned the bathroom?'

'I pay the bills. I do the laundry. I do more than you.'

'How do you do more, Suneet? Bills are paid once a month. Laundry is done once a week. That's not even five-six hours of housework a month. Cooking is four times a day. Cleaning is every single day. Grocery shopping is every week. I do all that. I do five-six hours of housework every day, not every month. So, don't even compare.'

'Are you keeping score? Is that what this marriage is to you? Keeping tabs? You're so immature.'

Responsibility kills relationships. So does lack of logic.

'Why do you keep coming after me?' I asked him simply.

He looked taken aback. He had been ready for a fight. 'I told you the day I married you that I want to see growth in you,' he said. 'This is how you'll grow. Through criticism.'

'*Over*-criticism kills confidence, it doesn't build it.'

'Nah! You're *over*-sensitive because you're used to everyone around you praising you all the time.'

'Suneet, no one praises me all the time! I'm not surrounded by sycophants. This is all in your head because you choose not to like my family or friends for no fault of theirs.'

'Please. You live in your own world. I'm the only one honest enough to tell you who you really are. I give you advice because I care so much about you. No one else obviously does. You should thank me for making you a better person.'

'I don't need other people to praise me or insult me to know who I am. I may not be perfect but I'm honest, responsible and as mature as I can be at twenty-seven.'

'Oh, please. I'm the only one who knows who you really are. I thought you would become a better person after marrying me but you've clearly not.'

'If I'm so awful then why did you want to marry me?'

'I never wanted to marry you.'

I couldn't believe what I was hearing.

'You're the one who proposed, Suneet!'

'I never proposed to you!' he said with such confidence that I almost reeled backwards.

His proposal in the Air Deccan flight had made me believe in his love for me. There was little else to go on. I was grasping at straws. How could he snap that without a thought? In an attempt to be right, to make me feel small, he would go to any extent, including marring beautiful memories.

'How can you just deny something that happened?' I asked him.

'Let's look at the facts, shall we? You sent me those alphabet chocolates. You made me meet your friends. You were desperate to get married because your parents were putting pressure on you.'

I stared at him with my mouth open.

After Suneet gave his MBA admission exams, KMAT, in 2006, I'd flown to Boston to celebrate his birthday. We were in his bathroom, getting ready to go out for a walk, when he asked me again if I would marry him. I'd told him that he couldn't ask such a question while seated on a toilet. We'd laughed. To lend the proposal some romance, I'd gone back to India and, with the help of various friends, including Sherna, and some major transnational coordination, I'd sent him alphabet chocolates that spelt out: YES I WILL. He'd said it was the most romantic thing that someone had done for him.

Now he was using that against me. *Why?*

'Suneet, if anything, I was the one who was thinking of calling off the wedding after . . . '

I couldn't even talk about that cold December evening. It was a Bermuda Triangle in our marriage, where all things went to vanish.

'Please! You have a really bad memory, Maneka. We all know that.'

'It's not a memory you can twist, it's a fact.'

'Who's going to believe you anyway? My family knows you're a liar.'

'Liar?' I looked at him quizzically. I was many things but I was not a liar. I was, in fact, too honest for my own good. The truth dawned on me. They had said the same thing about Kamini. I didn't know the term gaslighting then, but I did know that stripping a woman of all her goodness was a narrative that suited his family and him. It made the woman small. It kept power over the daughters-in-law of the household. It helped them believe that they were always right and the woman was always wrong. How convenient and how trite! I'd never met people like this. There was no need to believe them.

'This is the first time in my life that someone has called me a liar,' I said, gathering my thoughts. 'No one outside your family and you would ever think that of me.' I sat down on the bed. It was all too much. Every day Suneet would either criticize me or go into a long sulk about some issue or the other. Everything I did was wrong and not enough. He was slowly chipping away at my confidence. I was alone even while being married, drowning in expectations I could never meet. 'I really don't understand, Suneet. If you didn't like anything about me, why marry me? Why stay married?'

'Oh, so now you want a divorce? For no reason? I can't believe you'd just say something like that so casually.'

'That's not at all what I'm saying,' I said. 'All I'm saying is that ever since we got married, our focus has been on your parents, on Bhaiya, and not on us. We haven't been able to build a foundation. Isn't it time we did that?'

'How dare you say anything about my parents?'

I looked at him. 'What's wrong with what I'm saying?'

'It's not what you're saying, it's your tone.'

It doesn't matter if your words are soft as roses when they fall on ears with thorns.

'What I'm saying is right, as is my tone,' I said firmly. 'You are not ready to listen. You don't want a discussion. You only want to pick fights. Suneet, you're entitled to your own opinion but you are not entitled to your own facts, okay?'

'Really?' he said, looking at the kirpan hanging on our wall. 'Well, the *fact* is that sometimes I feel like there's a simpler way to just end it all.'

I took a big gulp. Was he threatening to kill me?

He stormed out of the house.

I let him go.

Prior to this we'd had a few fights, almost always immediately after his parents made some snarky remark about my cooking or cleaning. At one point he'd come at me with his fist raised. I'd challenged him to hit me and he'd stopped. I told him I'd call the police if he ever hit me again. He knew that.

The truth, I realized, wasn't that his parents made sure that we focused on them. The truth was that he was letting them. When a man lets outsiders decide the fate of his marriage, do we blame the outsiders or the man?

Suneet didn't talk to me for a week. For the first time, I made no effort at reconciliation. I didn't want his constant prickliness to alarm or diminish me. I had understood that he was the kind of man for whom being a good son was more important than being a good husband, the kind of man who thought that a man could only be either. So, I stopped minding that he spent more time with his mother than with me. That we never went out for a meal or a movie, unless his brother came along, because then he would pay. I didn't mind that I didn't have a husband despite being married.

Fortunately, the 'honeymoon' was over and my job started. Work was salvation, my life raft. I could control it. I could be rewarded for it. It kept me away from home. It helped me meet new people. Work gave me positive consequences, unlike my marriage, which seemed like a dark tunnel that would never see the light. I found Americans charming with their 'world's craziest story' and 'world's biggest chocolate'. I walked non-stop, discovering New York.

I began to ignore my in-laws' constant interference and snide criticism of me.

I didn't even mind when Suneet didn't let me subscribe to a newspaper, which I needed in order to tell the news at my new job.

'We can't spend $90 a month on anything you feel like. I'm a student, remember?' he said. Suneet had hacked into a neighbour's internet connection as he didn't want to 'waste' $20 a month on 'frivolities'.

'I'll pay,' I said. 'I'll make extra money writing freelance articles.'

'Don't throw your money at me.'

You can't argue with an angry lion. You can only become its prey. So, I'd get up at 6 a.m., scramble to my front door, glance through the peephole to make sure that no one was around, and then scamper down the corridor to read *The Wall Street Journal* lying outside my neighbour's front door. I'd carry my notebook and jot down the points I had to make for my newscast three hours later. I'd pray that no one opened their door. I never took the newspaper. I always placed it back as neatly as I had found it. It was a fearful fifteen minutes I spent every morning. That paper was a reminder of how low I was falling. For don't our private humiliations taunt us more than our public ones?

Despite my resilience, over time, like Suneet, I began to blame myself for everything that went wrong in our marriage. If you pluck a rose and end up being pricked by the thorn, you can't blame the thorn, can you? You get pricked because you don't know how to pluck the rose correctly. I knew that I had picked the wrong man to marry. It was my fault. I deserved whatever was happening to me.

I also knew that his mother was a shroud on our marriage. But I was not the kind of woman who blamed her problems on other women. I'd always been greatly loved by mothers—my own, my friends', my neighbours', and even my ex-boyfriends'—

so I held on to the hope that it was only a matter of time before I won my mother-in-law over and broke archaic traditions that demanded sordid daughter-in-law-mother-in-law relationships. So, I focused on the fact that my mother-in-law was a great cook, that she had once cleaned my cupboard because I didn't have the time, that she had told my husband to buy me flowers for helping him with his MBA applications, and the warmth she had shown me before my marriage. So, when she finally left in April, almost four months after coming to the US, I dropped her to the airport, something I'd never done for my own parents. It was me—and not her beloved son—who wiped her tears at the gate and hugged her.

With my mother-in-law gone, I felt that the Suneet I'd known once would return to me: loving, attentive, caring and fun.

It didn't happen, of course. Things were already far too broken, and my husband was not a man of optimism. I had to face the fact that in this marriage I was like the step of a temple. A part of the temple, but not the temple. A tree's shadow but not the tree. I was not my husband's first love. Or his priority.

My nani had taught me that when a sweater is torn it's better to mend it than to throw it away. It was not in my nature to let go of things I held dear. I decided that I would fight this pall that had descended on my marriage. I would make my husband love me. I would make my in-laws love me.

They'd gone through a bad phase because of Samit's almost-divorce. After all, some families make tragedy their friend and not acquaintance.

The bad marriage wasn't Suneet's fault, I told myself. In 16,000 years of patriarchy, men had never taken responsibility for their actions, then why would Suneet apologize for his? Like most Indian men, he'd been raised on a pedestal as a *ladla* beta. He had to live with this incredible idea of himself that didn't let him be human, it didn't let him be sensitive. After all, a family without daughters is a family without love for women. Was it his fault that he'd been born into a misogynistic family? Was it his fault that he'd been put in a cage where he wasn't allowed to feel? No.

Adoration of a man is not love. I would show Suneet the right way to be loved. I would let my love change him. I would cling to him with my last thread of hope. No matter how strong the urge, I would not leave my husband. I would not get divorced. No one else in my family or friend circle had ever got divorced. The handful of acquaintances—both men and women—who had, faced bruising stigma. As a woman I knew it would take a bigger toll on me than it would on a man. Divorces happened to bad people, I told myself. And I was a good person. I was not worthy of scandal or taboo or derision. I would stay married no matter what happened. I would show him that I was worthy of being loved.

I told myself these things, and in telling myself these things, I turned myself into a statistic. A woman, among millions of women over the world, who tolerated anything at the hands of men in the hope that they would change.

*

'So—your ex-husband, apart from being physically abusive, was also emotionally abusive? Most likely bipolar. And you didn't think there was something wrong with him?' Anmol asks.

'Of course I did, DCP Sahib. But I didn't know what exactly I was dealing with. Unlike today, we didn't grow up knowing what mental health issues were. Nobody addressed personality disorders, or acknowledged people who were schizophrenic or bipolar. There were no discussions with parents, teachers or friends. All we were told about people who didn't behave normally was that "*woh pagal hai*". You were either pagal or normal. Since Suneet was neither pagal nor normal, I didn't know what he was!'

'But the abuse was obvious in his actions.'

'I know. What Suneet was doing was obviously wrong, but I was too naïve to recognize that it was a textbook example of abuse. Don't laugh.'

Anmol's shoulders stop shaking. 'I'm not laughing. I'm just in shock. You are smart, educated and well-read. I don't understand how you did not know you were being abused!'

He is not the first person to say this to me. 'Sir, to know you're in an abusive relationship, you first have to recognize abuse. Emotional, physical or financial. I didn't know that the man I married was abusing me. When the man I trusted the most in the world convinced me that what he was doing was normal and something was wrong with me, I believed him. I thought that I was the crazy one. I thought that I was imagining things. I didn't know my own truth. Should I have doubted myself? No. But what you see of me today is not who I was then.'

I have been a dot my entire life. Bold, assertive and definitive. Marriage had turned me into a comma, something that was always bent, uncertain and easily overlooked. To understand me now, Anmol has to understand me then.

Because even glass has to crack before it breaks. And my time to break was still to come.

CHAPTER SEVEN

IF A mother elephant and her baby are tied together, the baby elephant will be tied with a thick chain because he will try to escape. The mother elephant, on the other hand, will be tied with a thin chain, because she'll never escape without her baby. That's what marriage felt like to me. I was the mother elephant who had made peace with her entrapment.

But things were better after my mother-in-law left. Samit had distanced himself from his family who would, of course, poison his reconciliation with his wife. That made Suneet realize that wives could not be dismissed for the sake of one's parents. He'd also finished the first year of his MBA course and was doing a summer internship with a big media firm in Connecticut. This left him little time to find faults with me. Before we knew it, it was July, more than six tough months of our marriage. According to sage advice, these months were the most difficult for a couple due to teething issues. I prayed that the worst was behind us.

My birthday was coming up. I wanted to throw a picnic party at Central Park for my friends. When I told Suneet this, he once again became belligerent and accused me of wasting *his*

85

money. He demanded that I tell my friends to bring their own food and drinks. I couldn't do that, not after their many birthday celebrations that we had attended. In retaliation, Suneet neither talked to me for a week nor did he help out. I remembered how for his birthday the previous year I had quit my job and flown halfway across the world to surprise him. How I had spent two months' salary to fly to Boston two years ago to celebrate his birthday. Forget it, I told myself. Any joy I got in my life would have to be outside of my husband. This was the way with many marriages. So, I organized everything by myself.

At the picnic, Suneet was withdrawn and peevish. He made snide remarks about everyone to Samit. He didn't participate in any of the fun we were having. I didn't know what to do. I tried to be playful with him, hoping it would put him in a better mood, but he remained standing alone in a corner, glaring at everyone. Once again, my friends noticed that something was amiss. I told them it was nothing.

Suneet didn't talk properly to me for weeks after the picnic. He began sending me perfunctory emails about our bills and my chores. I found it odd, of course, but the truth was that Suneet didn't communicate well face-to-face. Emails were the only medium he expressed himself in. Maybe that's why our long-distance courtship had worked.

My sorrow began to find solace in food. I began to eat. A lot. There was a Duane Reade store below our building, where cheap and delicious Entenmann cakes were available. I'd always had a sweet tooth and began to indulge in their 1-kilo chocolate fudge cake, sometimes scarfing down two a week. I would eat America's mega-sized Cheetos packets for dinner. I'd stand in long lines during lunch to eat unhealthy $3 falafels. I put on 7 kilos in two months. I began to feel lethargic and dull. My skin

stopped glowing. I stopped laughing. My smile turned inwards.
There was nothing to be happy about.

Finally, I sent Suneet an email explaining how unhappy I
was and why.

He didn't reply, but at least he began communicating with
me in monosyllables.

Then, at the end of August, my mother called to tell me that
my beloved masi had passed away from cancer. I was miserable.
I couldn't imagine never seeing her again. It was unfortunate
that I couldn't even afford to fly down to India for her funeral.
I lay crying in bed for hours. Finally, Suneet came up to me and
hugged me. It felt good to get some show of humanity from
him.

'Wait, I have something to make you feel better,' he told
me.

He left our bedroom and came back with his laptop. He
showed me the screen. He had logged on to a porn site!

'How is that going to make me feel better?' I asked him in
shock.

'Doesn't sex make everything all right?' he said.

This man was crazy. Whether it was in happiness or grief,
my husband would never do right by me. I told him to leave me
alone in my mourning.

He came to me the next day and said, 'Jaanu, I've been
thinking. The last few months have been rough. Let's take a
break. A second honeymoon. It's my belated birthday gift to
you.'

I could never reconcile Suneet's stinginess in day-to-day
life and his lavishness on vacations. Everything about him was
a binary. It was like being married to two people. I was about
to tell him this when I remembered Jamaica. When we were

there, we'd gone to Rick's Café, a restaurant popular for its 40-foot cliff from which tourists and locals jumped off into the Caribbean Sea. Despite rumours of broken spines, cracked tail bones and even death, the place was packed. Without a thought, my otherwise prudent husband had run forward and dived off the cliff. I had watched in fear and awe, marvelling at what I couldn't place as his courage or foolishness. I wanted to see that wild side again, to lay privy to the man Suneet could be when only I was watching.

I would have to fix that sweater and not throw it away.

We went to Hawaii.

CHAPTER EIGHT

ON THE Hawaiian island of Maui lies the Haleakalā National Park. Inside the park is a dormant volcano, which is open for viewing from the summit. Watching the sunrise from this summit is said to be a once-in-a-lifetime experience. Suneet and I decided not to give this a miss. On our last day before heading back to New York, we woke up at 2 a.m. and boarded a tour van to the mountain top. We reached the summit in temperatures below freezing. People from all over the world were around us. Despite the crowd, there was complete silence in the area. No one wanted to break God's spectacular spell. The only sound was of the wind in our ears as we walked to the observatory. My jaw dropped when we reached there. For ahead of us was a valley, barren and pock-marked, dotted with cinder cones that seemed to be glazed with golden mud. As we admired the volcanic moonscape in front of us, Suneet wrapped the blanket we had taken from the hotel around us and whispered into my ear, 'This is the closest we'll ever get to heaven.' My man was back. He held me as we gazed in awe at the stars twinkling in the night sky. I had never seen so many stars in my life. I kissed him through my chattering teeth. Not long after, thin orange streaks began to break through the darkness. People cheered, some cried, some took photos. We were on top of the world's largest dormant volcano and it felt like the beginning of time itself. For the second time in our marriage, after Jamaica, being in Suneet's arms seemed to beckon a fresh start to our relationship. I was filled with hope.

An hour later, as we were walking down the observatory steps, back to the parking lot, we saw lava rocks.

'These are awesome. Free souvenirs! Let's take one as a memento,' Suneet said.

'Let's take two so they're not lonely,' I said. I wanted us to be a team at last. I picked up two crescent-shaped brown rocks. I put them in our knapsack.

At the parking lot, our tour operator was giving out bicycles for our next adventure. I heard him say, 'Whatever you do, do not take the lava rocks from the mountain.'

Someone asked why.

'Because they're sacred and *cursed*. By taking them away from their home, you are messing with nature, with the way things are meant to be. This will anger Pele, the goddess of volcanoes and fire, and bring you bad luck. The park receives hundreds of returned rocks every month from people who've taken them and suffered. It's not worth it.'

Suneet and I looked at each other and sniggered. In our culture anything fun—sex, adventure, dating, singledom, childlessness—was marred by superstition and apocalyptic warnings. We were not going to be scared by some old wives' tale. After all, we'd done all the touristy things in Hawaii. We'd navigated the hairpin bends on the highway at Hana, taken scenic walks through cascading waterfalls and rainforests in the Garden of Eden, cheered for hula dancers while scarfing down a traditional luau dinner, and watched turtles lay eggs at the Big Beach. Now we had a piece of history in our hands, a survivor of time, stronger than memory, and we were not letting it go. We kept the two rocks.

Our next adventure was to bike down the volcano for 23 miles. Bundled up in thick rain jackets and motocross helmets, Suneet and I navigated the switchbacks, the wind whistling in our ears like a happy tune. The mountain road had no streetlights or guard rails, just nature at its finest. An hour later, we found ourselves alone, overlooking the valley.

'Where's the bad luck, huh?' Suneet asked, as we stopped among the eucalyptus trees to have a sandwich from our backpack.

'Seriously. If this is not paradise I don't know what is,' I said. 'I swear the spokes on my bike are singing.'

'The singing spokes,' Suneet laughed and broke into a song: *Zindagi ek safar hai suhana, yahan kal kya ho kisne jana.*

We rode past pineapple and cane fields, ate mango plucked freshly from a tree, took multiple photos, and decided that we were having more fun than we'd had even in Jamaica.

It was 13 September 2008.

When we got back home, everything was fine. Samit was back with his wife and in his own world. We spoke to my in-laws once a week on Skype. We began to call my friends over or go to their homes. Suneet was less frosty with them. He began the second year of his MBA course and was inundated with deadlines. I became super busy at work as Lehman Brothers had fallen, the banking and housing industries were collapsing, and there was blood on Wall Street. Life was routine. We were finally a normal married couple.

This lasted for exactly two weeks.

One night, Suneet woke me up at three in the morning. He held up his laptop.

'Who died?' I asked—about to comment on his warped notion of death and online porn—and stopped.

He looked like he had.

'What's wrong?'

He began to cry. 'I got an email from KMAC, the company that owns KMAT.' KMAT was the entrance test he had taken to get into his MBA programme. 'They've accused me . . . of . . . of cheating. They . . . they're saying that they've . . . that my KMAT score is cancelled.'

I looked at him open-mouthed. Was he joking? This made no sense.

I sat up and rubbed my eyes. I knew Suneet was a lot of things, but he was not a cheater. He had excelled in his KMAT exam, scoring 770 out of 800, a fact that he was rightly proud of. I held him till he stopped crying.

I read the email. Random words popped out at me: posted KMAT questions . . . fraudulent comments . . . unethical activity . . . ongoing investigation . . . breach of conduct . . . cancellation of score . . . informed university . . .

'I don't understand, jaanu,' I said as he sat slumped next to me.

'They're saying that I logged into this illegal website . . . knowing that they posted real KMAT questions . . . under a section called Jungle Juice. Therefore I've cheated. Apparently there was a . . . a legal investigation of this site. Since I paid with my credit card . . . they managed to trace me. How could I have possibly known all this, baby? I logged in to practise KMAT questions before my exam . . . like any other student.'

He began to cry. I began to cry.

'What's going to happen now?' he asked, sobbing loudly. 'What if they throw me out of university? Out of this country? My life will be ruined!'

'Don't worry. You've done nothing wrong. They won't throw you out.'

'We don't know that. The dean has also been sent an email about this.'

I took him in my arms and said, 'Everything will be fine, baby. You're already in the second year of your MBA. The dean will not do anything now. Just continue your classes as if nothing has happened. Forget about this email.'

I wiped the drool from his mouth with my bare hands and kissed him.

As we stayed awake the whole night, with our future up in the air, I remembered Pele's curse. I looked at the lava rocks on our windowsill and knew that we had unwittingly invited a tragedy into our lives. How could superstition be stronger than certainty?

And what would this do to our marriage? We were so precarious anyway. So many things had been thrown at us over the last ten months that we'd rarely had a normal phase in our marriage. What would become of us?

Our relationship was not unlike the mountains we crossed to get to Shimla, the place where we were both born. The landslides in our lives kept destroying us. We kept tumbling and falling, shifting shape due to the erosion. But what we didn't know was that the real danger was yet to come.

CHAPTER NINE

ON MONDAY Suneet went back to university as usual. No one stopped him. The next day, after he had finished his last class, he got called into the dean's office. Afterwards, his phone call to me at work was one of the worst I'd ever received.

'They've thrown me out ... expelled ... just like that ... no explanation.'

I made an excuse at work and rushed home. Suneet was lying in bed howling and in complete shock.

I would not let my man drown.

Over the next two weeks, I lost count of the days and hours as I worked relentlessly to help Suneet find a way back into university. I called up thirty lawyers a day at a time when work was at its busiest because sub-prime mortgages were leading to a global meltdown. I spend nights and days trying to find a case for us against KMAC. I sent back the cursed lava rocks. I cooked for him. I cleaned for him. I bathed him. I fed him with my hands. I coddled him like an infant till he fell asleep. I barely slept or ate.

If two people are shot in the leg, one will focus on the pain while the other will make new friends in the hospital. Suneet lay around all day, watching TV, playing Dead Space on his PS3 or talking to his parents. I told myself it was okay. He had been wronged. He needed time to heal. He was a good student with good prospects. I was certain that his university would take him back, just as I'd been sure that this marriage would work out no matter what. My problem in life had always been that I was too optimistic for my own good.

'Babe, don't worry so much,' I told him one day as I was feeding him his dinner. 'We will fight this together. Whatever happens, we'll be okay.'

'My future is destroyed,' he said, not letting me put the spoon in his mouth. He gazed into my eyes. 'Will you leave me now?'

I looked at him and smiled. This was the most vulnerable Suneet had been with me. It was one of the few times he'd shown me that he cared about me. 'Never,' I said. 'I'm with you through anything. Just let me in.' I was happy we were fighting a problem together as a couple, instead of turning on each other.

I continued talking, 'I've spoken to many lawyers to ask about the appeals process with KMAC: how we can get your posts from KMAC, how we should respond to the expulsion letter, if we can subpoena KMAC, if we can get a judicial review with your university. We can mediate or arbitrate, whatever is the best solution. We can go to the student council. But I think the meeting with the dean will resolve everything. He'll realize you're a person, not a statistic.'

I'd sent the dean an email, as had Suneet. We'd both written that cancelling Suneet's scores was a drastic action by KMAC. We clarified that Suneet had not knowingly committed fraud nor indulged in wrongdoing. We'd asked for a meeting so the dean could hear us out. He'd called us to his office next Tuesday.

'You have to come with me,' Suneet reiterated. 'We'll tell him that we're planning a family . . . he can't do this to us.'

I smiled at him. We had discussed children, of course: our Chintu and Chutki. I was twenty-eight. He was twenty-nine. We wanted to start a family by the time he graduated next year.

'Manu, you know that if the dean doesn't help me, we'll lose 30 lakh?' Suneet said.

It was a huge loss. But his brother had paid for his tuition and our savings were paying for our living expenses. At least we wouldn't be in debt, like most students in the US.

'If that happens, we'll hire a lawyer. In fact—' I pulled out a folder from my purse. 'Here are the notes I made with each lawyer. I've shortlisted four lawyers out of the hundred I've spoken to. They match our needs and our price range. See who most appeals to you.'

'How will we afford a lawyer?' Suneet said. 'Some of them charge $600 an hour.'

'We'll figure out a way. I'll sell my jewellery.'

Suneet knew that I loved my jewellery. He smiled at me. 'That's really sweet of you. Very 1980s *Mother India* type.'

'That movie is from the fifties,' I laughed. I hugged him. 'Now don't worry. Any decision we take will be after meeting the dean. I'm sure it'll go well.'

The next day, when I got back from work, my in-laws were sitting on the sofa in my house! I took a step back in surprise. I had no idea that they were going to be here! That too both of them together. Fuck!

I bent down to touch my mother-in-law's feet first.

'What happened to my son?' she said, wiping the copious tears falling down her cheeks. Nirupa Roy was back. 'He doesn't deserve it! How could God do this to me? Who has brought him such bad luck?'

She looked pointedly at me. Was she implying that I'd brought him bad luck?

I looked at Suneet. Why hadn't he told me they were coming?

'Maa and Dad cancelled their trip to Australia to be with us,' he mumbled, as if reading my mind. 'Mom has even quit her job. They took the first flight out from Dubai. It all happened so quickly.' I could see his eyes tearing up.

I didn't know that jobs could be quit, trips cancelled and flights from Dubai taken so quickly.

But what could I do? I went to touch my father-in-law's feet.

'How are you, Dad?' I asked him. I put down my purse and sat down beside him.

'How do you think I am?' he said gruffly. 'I need ice for my drink. Get that and then you can help Maa in the kitchen. We'll take our dinner in seventy-five minutes.'

Once again he reduced me from a human being to a slave. He didn't care what I was going through or that I'd just returned from work. I still couldn't reconcile who this man pretended to be in public with who he was in private. Was it heavy to wear such a mask?

It had been a long week. I had been looking forward to eating leftovers and going to bed early. I was exhausted. I contemplated asking Suneet for help. But he wasn't cooking or cleaning, even though he was home all day, and he would certainly not do so in front of his parents. I was tempted to remind him of the first day of our married life here, when he had told me I had to take care of the house because I was doing *nothing*. Now he was doing *nothing*, while I was working and running the house. But who was I to fight patriarchy single-handedly? Who would even listen to me? So, I washed my hands and began chopping and cleaning, listening to the men discuss my husband's future, my future, our future, as if I didn't belong in it.

My weekend was spent cooking, cleaning and serving Suneet and his family. I tried not to cry. When I asked Suneet about the lawyers he told me we'd talk later; he was spending time with his parents. I once again ceased to exist.

He's going through a phase, I told myself. I took many deep breaths.

On Monday, at work, I got a call from my father-in-law.

'There's been a disaster. The dean is not budging.'

'What? But—'

'Maa is not well. Someone needs to make lunch. Leave your work and come home.'

Was that a priority after what he'd just told me? I was not going to leave work to make dal-chawal for this man. I made an excuse and didn't go home. I called Suneet. He did not answer. I left him a voice message: 'What happened, babe? Why did you go to the dean today instead of tomorrow? Why didn't you take me with you as we'd planned?'

When I got home that evening they were in our living room, in tears. I sat beside Suneet. I wanted to hug my husband and cry in his arms. I wanted to curl up in bed and weep till nothing was left inside me. 'Khana. Seventy-five minutes,' my father-in-law said sharply. 'Maa is too emotional today, so cook alone.' They didn't care what I was going through. My emotions were subservient to theirs. I let myself be reduced. I was too exhausted. I went about on autopilot till his family left and only then did I sink into his arms. We both began to cry.

'I'm so sorry that the dean was so stubborn, babe,' I said softly. 'We will fight this. We will go to the student council and demand a disciplinary hearing. Everything will be okay.'

Other universities had also received KMAC's email about a few of their incumbent students. None of them had rescinded their MBA programmes. I wanted to keep that sliver of hope alive in Suneet. His family was incapable of hope, and I couldn't watch him fall further.

He didn't reply.

'We always have the option to sue them,' I continued, putting my arms around Suneet. 'I spoke to the shortlisted lawyers again today.' I must have researched at least two hundred of them by then. 'I think I've found the perfect one for us.'

Suneet wriggled out of my arms and said, 'Don't bother. My father's cousin has a contact who's agreed to help us. We'll use him.'

We? Who 'we'? A jolt ran through my body. How was Suneet suddenly making important life decisions that affected both of us, that until three days ago we were making together, without as much as talking to me? How could he dismiss my efforts like this just because his parents had come into the picture?

'Is that fair to me, Suneet?'

'Stop making this about you,' he replied, his standard reply every time I said anything.

We seek to love someone who makes us fall in love with ourselves. This man was making me hate everything about myself.

'I can't believe you're using this lame argument again, Suneet. Nothing here is about *me*. It's all about *you*. It's always about *you*. We were doing great and now you've thrown me away like trash. You know how hard I worked on the lawyers. You know how long I took to compose that email to the dean. A decent man would've had the courtesy to tell me that he's going without me to the dean, or that he prefers another lawyer.'

'Stop being such a drama queen! Do you want an award for helping your husband? I do more for you than you do for me. Should I ask for a bigger award?'

It was at that moment that I thought of what Suneet *had* done for me. There had been a few instances of kindness he'd shown me over the last three years that we'd been together, but these didn't even add up to five fingers.

'Suneet, since the day we met, I've been doing everything for you, from booking your tickets to Goa to your college applications to *this*!' I replied. 'At least acknowledge that!'

'Please. All you did during my applications was to fight with me and chew my brain.'

In 2005, a few months after we'd met, Suneet had been fired from his job with a Fortune 500 company in Boston. No one would hire him, so he went to work at a small tech firm. He hated his new job, his new boss, his new colleagues. Far away in Mumbai, I didn't take these feelings seriously because he'd despised everyone at his old company as well. Perhaps the American work culture made it impossible to like your colleagues, I'd reasoned. For good measure, he wasn't on talking terms with his Chinese flatmate in Boston either. I should've seen the hate that coloured every aspect of his life. But I was too busy being in love.

I vowed to help the love of my life get back on his feet and be happy again. So, in 2006, when he began applying to schools for an MBA programme, I scheduled my entire life around helping him with his applications. I'd wake up at 4 a.m. and drive to my office. It was the only window I had to make long-distance calls to him, since people began coming into the office by 6.30 a.m., and he said he didn't have the money to call me. Mumbai was safe, but not that safe. I drove alone at night for love, risking not only my safety but also my job. When I was on a family vacation in Lucknow, I stayed up till 3 a.m. every day writing his essays, till my parents got annoyed with me. I went to a consultant and spent Rs 10,000 of my own money, one-fifth of my monthly after tax salary back then, so his essays could be edited professionally. He didn't miss a single deadline for his coveted colleges and got into one among his top three choices.

When he came to Mumbai a few months before our wedding, I celebrated his achievements with a surprise. I went to pick him up at the airport dressed in a nun outfit borrowed from Maganlal Dresswala. I walked up to him as he was coming out of the airport. He didn't look at me, as he was busy searching for the real me. I gave him a pamphlet that had Jesus on the cover. He took it but didn't look. 'Look at what's in your hand, son,' I said to him in my most sombre voice. He looked at the pamphlet absent-mindedly. He turned it over and saw his photo on the back with a caption saying: 'Welcome To Mumbai, Agent 770!' It was his KMAT score. That's when the truth dawned on him. He hugged me so tight that I was lifted off the ground.

There is no value for sacrifice. Our yesteryear mothers, who forsook their ambition and identity to make hot chapattis for ungrateful husbands and children, would know this. I wished that instead of fighting with me this time, Suneet had said a simple 'thank you'. But gratitude is what turns a meal into a feast and a house into a home, and it is the kind of acceptance that some men are simply not capable of.

'I think you're delusional, Suneet,' I said slowly. 'It's taken me a long time to realize this, but nothing you ever say is the truth. I don't think you even know what the truth is.'

'How dare you?' Suneet said and raised his hand. I took a step back in shock. I was not looking at a man but a barbarian.

The love of a good man can save your life. The love of a bad man can destroy it.

I walked away.

The next day he messaged me at work, 'I am your body; when you feel pain, I feel pain. This hurts me as much as it hurts you.'

There was no apology. I didn't respond.

Ten minutes later he sent me an email. 'i already told you, you will be hurt by me at some point. probably more than a few times and so will i. i don't know anyone, married or not, that doesn't get hurt by someone over time. i obviously can't predict how we'll hurt each other but i am not worried. i've been hurt enough by people who didn't give a damn about me that being hurt by someone who loves me has a sweetness to it. i've hurt people before and i really don't want to put people through it again, so just believe that anything i say or do is taking your feelings into account.'

I didn't reply. A man who cared would talk to his wife, not email her.

At this point, if I got over my fear of divorce and restarting my life, I had enough reasons to leave Suneet. But I wasn't sure if Suneet was acting out because of his brother's almost-divorce and then getting thrown out of university, or whether he was actually an asshole. He had been different when we were dating; moody, sure, but not a psycho like this. Yet, I reasoned, it had been a bad year for him. Was this a bad phase in his life? Could I leave him if it was just a matter of time before he was back to normal? Could I leave him when he was at his lowest? No, weak and cowardly people left their loved ones in their time of need.

Not me. I would stand by my man through thick and thin. He would eventually notice my sacrifices and love me again. I just had to be patient. If even bad people had good marriages, didn't I deserve one? Yes, I did. It was just a matter of time.

Maybe, deep down, he was still a good guy.

When I got home that evening after work, he was not there. I called him. There was no response. I went to the bathroom to find a Post-it note stuck to the mirror. It stated that he was going to stay at Samit's place for the night. I was being punished. He was trying to tell me that if I ignored him he would retaliate by abandoning me. I wouldn't let it work this time. I couldn't let it work because a part of me was exhilarated. It was good to have the house to myself. Finally, I was alone. I decided to have a blast. I took off my clothes and walked around naked. I danced to *Like A Virgin* and *Desi Girl*. I ate leftover dal-chawal on the bed. I drank two glasses of chilled vodka with coke. I watched *Jab We Met* on my laptop. I was light.

Life is infinitely better when you find a way to who you are again.

CHAPTER TEN

IT WAS his mother's leg. It had cramped again.

It was also election day in the US. 4 November 2008. I had to be on call, live on my television network, the entire day. I asked for a work-from-home, so I could look after my mother-in-law, and went to Samit's house. As she lay on the pillow listening to bhajans, I massaged her legs. There was hair on them. And warts. But still, I massaged them. I gave her a hot water bottle. I found her medicines and administered them.

I thought I'd make a nice lunch for the family, but work got more hectic. Suneet refused to help; his father and he were watching *Pardes*. A working adult had to cook for three non-working adults because she was a woman. I didn't protest. But I also didn't have the time to soak basmati rice for thirty minutes before cooking it, the way they liked it. I didn't have the time to cook lauki or make raita, as Dad had asked me to.

We sat down to eat. The air was sullen.

'There is less jeera in the dal,' my father-in-law said. 'And you added haldi before the lal mirchi again, didn't you?'

'Sorry,' I replied, insincerely, I admit.

Dad criticized my food every time I cooked, so I'd stopped trying to impress him.

Suneet glared at me. Again. This seemed to be his de facto face with me when his parents were around. A face designed to show them that their ladla beta controlled his wife. I was past the point of caring. I wasn't superwoman and didn't intend to be one.

They were discussing Kamini and her move back to Samit's house next week. She would be joining us for dinner today. They had held a separate 'family meeting' with her the previous week, sans only me, on the condition that she apologize to them for having broken their trust and brought grief to their family. An email had found its way to my inbox as well, apologizing for the toll her actions had taken on my marriage. I hadn't asked for an apology nor needed one. She wasn't the reason there was a toll on my marriage. But this was their 'condition' for letting her back into the house, into *her* house.

I was just glad that I would no longer be the only outsider in this hell of a family.

Later that evening, when we were cooking dinner in the kitchen, Maa turned to me and said, '*Aaj toh main tujhe ek thapad marne walli thi* (I was going to slap you today).'

Again, I recoiled at the use of such language.

'Why, Maa?' What had I done now?

'Where were you when my leg was cramping?'

I looked at her in confusion. Maybe she was suffering from the onset of Alzheimer's?

'I was with you, remember? I didn't go to office to look after you. I gave you medicines. Rubbed your legs.'

'Yes, and then you locked yourself in the room to sleep.'

I rubbed my neck. In the last two months, I'd had a constant throbbing at the base of my neck. My shoulders were always stiff. My back was in perpetual pain. It was as though an iron mould had been cast inside my body.

'I wasn't sleeping, Maa. I was working,' I said slowly, as if talking to a three-year-old child. 'I had to be on live television today, remember? I locked the door so that no one would walk in by mistake. I had told you this?'

'Is your work so important that you ignore this family? Is it worth it? You're hardly even making money!'

There it was. First, they wanted a working wife for their son, who also cooked and cleaned. Now, they wanted a *rich* working wife, who also cooked and cleaned. Did they think that their unemployed lazy son was such a good catch?

'You left me alone for an hour when my leg was cramping,' she continued. Was her leg cramping a performance we had to witness? 'That's not how family behaves.'

There was no way to win with this family. I mumbled an apology.

Maybe the strategy was to divert the discussion to more positive topics. Like Dad's upcoming sixtieth birthday.

'So, Maa,' I asked, carefully adding one-and-a-half *katoris* of water to the dal, the way they liked it. 'I had sent all of you some ideas to celebrate Dad's birthday, but I didn't hear back from anyone. What do you think?'

'Why don't you ask him yourself?' she snapped.

'I . . . I thought it would be a surprise. I was thinking of making him a cartoon strip about his life. I had told you all about this a month ago, I think. Let me know if we should do it, otherwise it will not be ready in time for his birthday.'

'Are you threatening me?'

'What?'

'How dare you? You threaten me in my own kitchen?'

Saying this, she walked out of the kitchen. I stared after her. She was walking straight towards Suneet to complain about me. Once again, I had no idea what I'd done wrong. I realized that finding faults with a person does not require the actual presence of faults in that person.

I held back my tears. It was difficult. This was a rare time in my life when I was crying all the time. Sometimes, I was so overwhelmed by my own unhappiness that I would cry in public. The first time I did this, a few weeks ago, was while carrying two heavy bags of groceries home. I was so embarrassed about crying in front of people that I wore my sunglasses, even though it was winter and there was no sun. The second time, and all the times after, I felt no shame in crying openly when the desire seized me. I once cried all the way from my house to my office. Fortunately, this was New York. No one stared. No one interfered. Somehow this made me feel better. I realized that it was okay to show the world that you were sad. It was okay to be vulnerable in front of others.

But here, in front of my so-called family, I couldn't cry. I knew that my tears would be met with derision or heartlessness. It was safer to cry in front of strangers.

Kamini arrived. Dinner was served. Dishes were washed. I barely spoke.

The same boiling water that softens the potato also hardens the egg. It's about what you're made of and not your circumstances. I would not let myself harden, I decided. I would hang on to some thread of happiness, I promised myself.

When we were leaving, Suneet's father came down to see us all off.

As we stood in the lobby, I asked him, 'Dad, your special birthday is coming up! How would you like to celebrate? I've thought of some plans.'

'Celebrate?' he turned to me and said. 'Only a selfish and immature girl would think of celebrating at a time like this. We know you Bombay girls walk out of the house at two in the morning, but that's not how we do things in this family.'

I looked at Suneet. His mother had broken her promise to me. How else would Dad know about Suneet and my fight ages ago, when I'd walked out of the house? And why was his father using our personal life to humiliate me in public? But Suneet turned away and walked off.

His father continued shouting, 'Why don't you focus on Suneet and your future instead of thinking of frivolous things like birthdays?'

With that he stomped off towards the elevator.

I felt like I'd been lynched. I looked around. The doorman was staring at me, along with two strangers. I blinked back my tears. This was embarrassing! I turned around and noticed Kamini looking at me. Ugh, I thought to myself, expecting another mean comment about how awful I was. But Kamini said nothing. Instead, she looked at me with a deep understanding. I gave her half a smile in surprise. After all, when a person is dying of thirst even seawater looks alluring, doesn't it?

Then I put on my jacket and walked out into the cold, back to my life, alone.

CHAPTER ELEVEN

'HE IS a murderer,' she said. 'Didn't your mother tell you? The whole of Shimla knows.'

I shook my head and shut the dishwasher. My father-in-law had been previously married to an anaesthesiologist with whom he had worked at AIIMS hospital in Delhi. This was before he moved to Dubai. Samit was born to them a year after marriage. His wife had committed suicide by inhaling a deadly dose of propofol that she was supposed to administer to a patient. Samit was just six months old then. This fact hadn't bothered me before marriage. I'd ignored the rumours about how my father-in-law had pushed his first wife to suicide. Now that I knew what he was like, I wasn't surprised. There are people who feel big only by making others feel small. He was that kind of a person.

Kamini turned to me and asked, 'Forget him. How are you doing?'

We were in the kitchen, alone. Kamini had moved back in with Samit. Our mother-in-law had gone into a sulk about something or the other, so the two of us now cooked and cleaned all the time together.

'How do you think I'm doing?' I said slowly. Kamini had met me prior to my marriage. She knew I was now a shell of the person I used to be.

She said, 'I didn't think they'd do to you what they did to me.'

I didn't know what they'd done to Kamini, but I knew what they were capable of.

'Well, they have,' I said evenly.

She smiled at me. She touched my back and said softly, 'I'm surprised. Maa loves Suneet more than Samit. I thought she would spare you so at least her real son would be happy.'

I couldn't remember the last time someone had spoken gently to me. My eyes welled up.

'My family thinks that I'm crazy to get back with Samit . . . to come back to this horrible family. You have no idea how much I have suffered with them. You can't even imagine how bad it gets. It's been ten years, and it just doesn't stop.'

'I—'

'Wait, I think she's calling me,' Kamini mumbled. She snapped her head around. Her eyes darted all over the living room. No one was calling her. They were all upstairs, watching *Biwi No 1*. 'Let's not talk here,' she said. 'It's not safe.'

'Why not?' I asked. I was ready to talk in the kitchen.

'They'll be listening,' she whispered. Her nose ring quivered. What had they done to make her so fearful? Kamini seemed like a confident and strong woman. An Indian-American raised in the US, she had attended one of the best universities in the country and worked as the vice-president of sales for a pharmaceutical company. How had they managed to break her? 'Take my number,' she continued. 'We'll talk on the phone. It's safer.'

I entered her name and number on my mobile.

'Wait, save my number under some other name,' she said.

'What? Why? That's ridiculous!'

'It's not. Because they'll spy on you.'

I laughed.

She grabbed my hand, 'It's not funny, Maneka. Trust me. You have to swear that you'll not repeat anything that we discuss to them. Not even to Suneet. Promise me! If they find out that we're talking, we'll both pay, trust me.' Her large eyes became larger.

A chill ran up my spine. Was this going to be me ten years into my marriage?

'Remember,' she added, 'we have to keep this quiet. I'll find a way for us to have a proper conversation, but you'll have to delete my calls and messages the minute you get them. Now go up and act like nothing has happened. I'll follow you after two minutes. We can't go together or they'll get suspicious.'

I had witnessed such odd behaviour over the last year that nothing surprised me anymore. I went up to the loft. I saved Kamini's number as Sherna 2.

The opportunity for a conversation came soon enough. I got a call from Kamini a few days later at work.

'Sorry, can't talk. I'm busy,' I told her.

'I know,' she said. 'But we can only speak when we're at work.'

I sighed.

'Dad's second cousin, Biru Uncle, has called them to his house for dinner this Thursday. Make an excuse that you can't go.'

'But they always force us to go to relatives' homes,' I said. 'They have to show how united we are as a family to everyone.'

'Not for Biru Uncle. He's not very well off, so they don't feel the need to impress him. They'll buy any excuse you make.'

'What should I say?' I was terrible at making excuses.

'I'm saying I have a late meeting. You can say that you're not well.'

'Okay.'

That Thursday we met at the PATH station downtown. Kamini's office was in midtown but she travelled all the way downtown so we could talk. I could see the desperation and eagerness on her face. It was sad. On the train ride back, she told me.

'Maa and Dad have the boys under their thumb. And they want us there too. I don't know what hold they have over them, especially her, but from what I understand she threatens to commit suicide if they don't listen to her.'

'Like the first wife?' I asked.

Over the sound of the train, I heard her say, 'I've told you before. That wasn't a suicide. She had told her family that it was better for her to die than to live with him. He drove her to suicide. He was horrible to her. Physically abusive and, as is obvious, emotionally too.' I shuddered. Had Suneet seen his father hit his mother too? Is that why he thought it was normal? 'Many people say that he gave her that fatal dose of propofol.'

I looked out of the window and let this sink in.

'Afterwards, he spread a rumour that she suffered from post-partum depression so that no one would blame him. To save his own ass he actually told everyone that Samit was responsible for his own mother's death! Can you imagine?'

I couldn't. My heart went out to Samit. To believe that the story of your life began by ending your mother's. What a dreadful burden to carry. No wonder he walked around like his soul had left his body.

'Deep down, Samit knows that they're not nice people. That's why he went straight from boarding school to college in the US. He never wanted to live with them. But his father emotionally blackmails him. He tells him all the time that I have cut my stomach open to pay for your fancy boarding school and American college. That I lost a wife because of you. I had to remarry so someone could look after you. Samit feels such guilt that he does whatever they say.'

Kamini paused. She was gripping the pole and her knuckles had turned white. 'Everyone's parents have sacrificed to give their kids a better life. They don't use that to manipulate us.'

It was true. I thought of my parents who took the bus to work every day till they were almost forty. They didn't have a lot of money when we were growing up, but they never made my brother and I feel like they were doing us a favour by educating and feeding us. They never rubbed their sacrifices in our faces.

'How come Suneet didn't tell me all this?' I asked.

'You know the boys will never say a single bad thing about their parents. They think that being honest is being a traitor to them,' Kamini replied. 'Samit hasn't even told me about his mother. I heard the truth from her family and other relatives. They've told Samit this, obviously, but what's he to believe? That his own father drove his mother to her death? That he made her so miserable that leaving her infant child was better for her than staying married to a monster?'

I stared at a poster of a mother and child pasted on the train wall. The whole world's love was in that photo. No, I couldn't imagine a mother doing anything that would harm her child.

'After his wife's suicide, Dad couldn't handle raising a child alone. So, he went looking for a bride. Even though he was a doctor working at AIIMS, which was a big deal at that time—tall, dark and handsome—no one would marry him. His reputation as a terrible husband had spread far and wide. It was then that his eyes fell on his friend's sister, Anju. She was odd-looking: dark with protruding teeth. She was known for doing black magic. People called her *pagal*. She had no marriage prospects. And he had no choice. He had got a job offer in Dubai. He needed someone to look after Samit and his house in a foreign country. So, he married Maa.'

I'd heard about my mother-in-law's notoriety from various people: relatives, cousins and friends from Shimla, where my mother was born and raised, and where I too was born. But I never believe rumours about any woman because I know what easy targets women are. Seeing my mother-in-law's behaviour, though, left no room for doubt.

Kamini continued, 'Somehow, she convinced Dad to send Samit to a boarding school when Suneet was born. He was only five then. Maa gets her way with the men each and every time for each and every thing. She's a master plotter. Everything she does and says is contrived. Even her tears are not about her getting emotional. She times them carefully so she can make up imaginary grievances against us.'

'What?'

'Yup. It's all part of a bigger plan to make sure that she remains the only woman in the family who the men love and trust. She'll never let any other woman in. She hates me so much that I'm scared she'll poison my food one day.'

I laughed, but I could actually see Maa doing it. Slyly, of course, without getting caught. I wondered if she had always been this way, or if marrying a terrible person had made her nasty. I knew how carefully Dad cultivated his public persona, especially—I guessed—after the rumours of murder surfaced against him, but Maa was not as discrete. Who had marred whom? Or were they two marred people prancing in sync?

'Everyone hates Maa. I haven't heard a single person say one nice thing about her, except maybe in Dubai, where no one knows their truth.'

How many unseen layers did people have? Peeling off one raw skin for another, showing their harshness only to those who could bear it.

We reached Newport station.

Kamini turned to me and said, 'Come home for dinner.' I looked at her. 'Don't worry. I won't make you cook and clean. I'll roast a salmon steak, and we'll be done.'

We laughed.

'Okay.'

'But don't tell anyone, not even Suneet, that we had dinner together.'

'Okay.'

As we walked to her building, all I could think of was what I'd gotten myself into. How could I have been so gullible that I'd ignored all the telltale signs? How could I have been stupid enough to discount people's warnings about this family?

We reached Kamini's house. It looked bright and happy without the in-laws in it. She put two salmon steaks in a frying pan and continued speaking, 'It's taken me ten years to figure all this out. Samit and I met in college, and we've been together for seventeen years! If I'd known his parents were this way, I would've never married him.'

'But he's a nice guy.'

'He's nice, but he's also spineless.'

I understood what she was saying. It's easy to be nice when you have nothing to lose. A person's true nature is revealed only by how they act under duress.

'But isn't that why you guys reconciled after—'

'After what?'

'After, you know—' could I say it? '—your . . . well . . . ehm . . . wavering?'

Kamini turned towards me, 'My cheating on him? Don't judge me. You know how you're told to rest between intense yoga asanas? This was my rest from my marriage. You'd do the same if you were married into this family for this long.'

I smiled. At least she was honest.

For cheating doesn't reveal cracks in a person, it reveals cracks in a marriage.

'Samit's parents were decent to me before we got married,' she continued. 'They did a complete U-turn when I became their son's wife. They found fault with everything I did. They'd call Samit and talk about how I wasn't living up to my responsibilities. They said I was selfish and self-centred. They'd keep accusing me of disrespecting them when I wasn't. They'd say *ki puchti nahin ki kya khaya* (she doesn't ask what we ate) hours after I'd cooked for them. They'd ask Samit, "What has she ever done for us?" even when I was doing everything I could for them. I didn't know how to respond. All they did was to ruin the beautiful relationship that Samit and I had.'

I wanted to laugh. My in-laws' attacks were following some kind of bahu torture template that we'd missed the memo on.

We sat down to eat.

'The reason I'm telling you all this, Maneka, is that you have to watch your back.'

'What?'

'Look. Their criticism is not just criticism. It's an age-old ploy used by north Indian families whose sons have had a love marriage. This relentless taunting not only undermines the bahus, but also makes the sons doubt their decision-making skills. This keeps everyone under check. You understand?'

'I don't think so.'

'I'm saying, watch yourself even with Suneet. What you see of your husband is just the tip of the iceberg of what's going on.'

'What do you mean?'

'Look, I don't know him well. He kept to himself when Samit and I were dating. All I knew about him back then was that he was good-looking, due to which girls found his sullen behaviour attractive. But you are too innocent for him, for these people.'

'In what way?'

'You're not aware of the shit you're in. I've seen that you let Suneet be alone with his parents. They wait for this chance to fill his ears bitching about you. They make things up when they can't find anything. Then they all gang up and each one attacks you in their own way. Maa will taunt, Dad will bark orders and Suneet will keep criticizing you. That's how they operate. You make one mistake and they will throw it in your face forever. I think they keep a journal of everything they think we've done wrong.'

'Yes, I once went out at 2 a.m. . . . '

'And they couldn't reach you. They've told this story to everyone who'll listen from the moment it happened. You should've seen how thrilled Maa was to have something on you. She thought it proved her point that you were a karamjali who needed to be tamed.'

I laughed. 'I'm not even surprised.'

'You know this will not stop, right? This is who they are. It's all some kind of sick power trip for them.'

The earth beneath my feet seemed to be shaking. We can prepare ourselves for a change in the weather, but can we ever be prepared for when the climate changes?

'Why don't you talk to Bhaiya about all this, Kamini?'

'Have you tried to talk to Suneet about his parents and their mind games?'

'Yes,' I said.

'And?'

I shrugged. He had become angry and belligerent.

'Exactly,' she continued. 'I've never said anything because there's no point. All four of them only see things from their perspective. They don't care about what you're feeling. They never give you a chance to voice your opinion. They'll tell you to talk and then find a way to shut you down.'

What kind of marriage was it when you couldn't trust your husband with your feelings?

'Why do the boys let their marriages be destroyed?' I asked her.

'Because it's convenient for them to listen to their parents,' she said. 'I'll give you a small example. I have to do all the housework even though my job is as demanding as Samit's. We're living abroad and not in India where we can get help. But the rules don't change. This is because his parents have told him that a boy shouldn't lift a finger in the house. They've told him that they'll manage the bahu so she does the housework quietly. This is convenient for him, isn't it? If someone told you don't vacuum for two hours but watch a movie instead, what option would you take?'

'But the boys have lived abroad for most of their lives now. Who did their housework before they got married?'

'They did everything themselves. But it's beneath them to help their wives.'

'Sad. What kind of parents destroy their kids' lives to make their life better?'

'Crazy ones, like them. And look, those stupid eek-mails they keep sending you—'

'Eek-mails?'

'I call their emails eek-mails, for obvious reasons.'

I smiled.

'Well, these are not as innocent as they look. They are not impulsive or in isolation. The four of them sit down and consult one another. Then one person writes a draft. They send this draft to each other, edit it and then decide from whose account they'll finally send it.'

'What are you talking about?'

'Haven't you ever checked Suneet's email drafts?'

I hadn't.

'You don't know his passwords?'

I'd asked him once but he'd never told me, even though I gave him all of mine. She was right . . . I was naïve.

'Go home and check his drafts folder. You'll find many versions of every email you've ever received from them or him, discussed and analysed. They have weekly family meetings with us, but they also have separate and secret ones with their sons. This year, of course, they've become—'

'DFM's . . . daily family meetings. I know.'

We looked at each other and laughed. *What had we both gotten ourselves into?*

'Why do they send so many emails . . . I mean . . . eek-mails?' I asked.

'They want to maintain a record of everything. Have they made you send an eek-mail against your wish?'

'Not yet.'

'They've made me do it. They're collecting evidence to show people. That's why every eek-mail criticizes us, and if we ever reply we are called . . .'

'Liars. So convenient, right?'

'Ya. And this way they build up a nice collection of eek-mails that shows them in a good light while dissing us. I'm scared to know for what purpose they're using these.'

I let this sink in.

'Why are they like this?' I asked.

'I don't know. They would've been better off marrying their sons to village girls.'

'I don't think girls from villages will put up with this,' I said. 'They're smarter than us.'

We smiled at each other.

'Doesn't all this make you angry?' I asked her.

'Very. That rage has turned to bitterness, but what can I do? Kill my in-laws?' She smiled at me. 'Look, Maneka. I thought that they would've learnt from the mistakes they made with me, but they haven't. They seem to thrive on screwing over their daughters-in-law. All I'm saying is, don't be so innocent. Don't be naïve. This is all a game to them and they'll win it at your loss. If you want your marriage to work, then you'll have to become smarter than them.'

'Kamini, this sounds like too much. I'm not built for tricks and manipulation.'

'If you want to stay married you'll have to, otherwise . . .'

I knew.

'Look. Samit is easier to manage for me than Suneet will be for you. Samit has been away from them for longer. He is financially independent. He has been with me for longer.

So, he has some objectivity left. I know that eventually I'll make him see things my way. I'll make him realize how awful his parents are. I know that in the long run he will see why they deserve to be hated. But my time is not now. Your time is. If you don't stop them now, you'll never be able to. You have the power to control the situation before it gets worse.'

I held her hand and said, 'Thanks for telling me all this, Kamini. I've been so lost.'

Our meal was done. 'Do you need help?' I asked her.

'Please, all we dirtied were two plates and one frying pan. After the huge effort that feeding our husbands' parents involves, this feels like a breeze.'

It did. I got up to go.

'Look. You're really shaky. Nothing like the bright and happy Maneka I'd first met. We don't know each other, but I thought you deserve the truth. Especially now, when you're clearly struggling. But don't break my trust. Don't tell anyone about our conversation.'

'I won't. I promise.'

But I did. And I would never forgive myself for it.

CHAPTER TWELVE

I WENT home. Suneet wouldn't be back for another hour or so. I had time. I opened his laptop, something I'd never done before, and was surprised to find it was not locked. I guess he never expected me to snoop because it was not in my nature. My hands shook as I clicked on the Gmail app icon and his account opened. I hadn't expected it to be so easy to spy on my husband. The first email in his inbox was from his university friend Tammy. I had met her once when she'd called us to her house for Halloween. I hadn't thought much of her: rich little white girl with the kind of face you saw and immediately forgot. After he was thrown out, Suneet mentioned that she was paying him to do her homework by supplying him weed. I hadn't asked for details because they seemed unimportant. But here was an email with just two lines: I'm amped to do naked night again. It was such a blast!

The last leg holding up the chair of our marriage broke. Was Suneet having an affair with Tammy? It wouldn't have surprised me. He had begun vanishing for nights on end without telling me where he was going. I had assumed it was Samit's house. He often came back drunk, and most times he was baked. Should

I have asked more persistently? Could I have lived with his answer?

Maybe it was innocent. Maybe it was some American slang I didn't understand, I reasoned. I couldn't fathom cheating on someone. I'd never done it and knew instinctively that I would never do it. Was he capable of it? Could he be the cheating spouse after spending the past year berating one? No. But then, who knew with that man?

I had to move on. I had more important business to attend to.

I went through his email drafts, as Kamini had recommended. There they were. Dating back to a year and more. All the emails I'd received from his family and him. Sent back and forth between them. The edits were highlighted in yellow. The comments highlighted in red. There was another eek-mail being framed, saying nasty things about me. It was written by his mother and edited by him. His father had recommended copying my parents to make them aware of their 'daughter's actions'. His brother had deleted some lines and adjectives about me saying they were too harsh.

It was a family lynching.

I felt like I'd been kicked in the stomach. Was I really such an awful person? Was I really what these people were saying I was? Maybe I was. Maybe my family and friends shielded me from who I really was. Maybe I deserved all this. Maybe it was me screwing all this up. Hot tears rolled down my cheeks. I shut the laptop and took a deep breath. I couldn't weaken. Not now. I had to know my husband's truths. This was the only window I had, and would most likely get. Better to know the devil you married than to pretend he's a saint.

I opened the laptop again, slowly, and went back to his inbox. I scrolled down and found an eek-mail from his mother dated ten months ago. Back then I used to talk to his mother openly and with love. One day she had sensed that I was upset and asked me what was on my mind. I had not said anything. 'This is just between a mother and daughter,' she had goaded me. 'I will never repeat it to anyone, so tell me whatever is in your heart, beta.' I had then spoken to her frankly about my fears of not finding a job in the US without a green card, how Suneet was not pulling his weight in the house, how the family could do with more cheer, etc. Every line from that conversation had been sent to all three men. Each line had been discussed and analysed.

Kamini was right. They'd been ganging up against me from the beginning. It had always been them versus me. I had never stood a chance. I had never been a part of their family. I had failed to see who they really were.

I went back to the drafts, and stumbled upon the early draft of an eek-mail that his parents had sent to my family and me a month ago. My in-laws had decided to make a pro-and-con list of Suneet and my personalities to 'help these two *children* with the problems they are having in their marriage', they wrote. It had come out of the blue. When my parents had panicked on reading it and called me, I'd assured them that there was nothing to worry about; my in-laws were the children. Fortunately, the proof of that was in the pudding. Their eek-mail sounded childish and petty, as they were. They had been harsh with me, as expected, while Suneet's personality had been described with the finesse of a job interview—where they ask what your drawbacks are and you state them with a positive spin. He had an anger issue, but it was because *I* provoked him. He was being misunderstood because *I* was not communicating with him. I saw that the eek-mail, which claimed to be an objective assessment of Suneet and my personalities, had been composed and edited by Suneet. I laughed in shock. What was this hypocrisy? How could I trust a word this family said?

Then I found a Gmail chat conversation from two days ago between Suneet, his father and his brother. It seemed to have happened after Suneet had called my mother, after we'd had a small fight, to bitch about me. He had recounted their entire conversation in the chat. Apparently, my mother had told him I was not the way he was describing me at all. He obviously had not liked that my mother stood up for me. Her opinions didn't fit the narrative they were building. So, Suneet wrote: 'I am tired of these sick fucking immature people. I can't take it any more. Her father doesn't want to get involved. Her mother is useless. She just passes opinions.'

His father had egged him on: 'It must be because she is frustrated with her daughter.'

She wasn't. She was frustrated with them.

Samit had typed: 'Kamini is here. I can't let her know I'm having this conversation. She can't know she's being excluded in all this. Gotta go!'

What a spineless man!

After all the times that Suneet had censured me for saying something as innocent as, 'Let's spend time alone,' which he construed as anti his parents, or the number of lectures I'd received from them telling me I could not question them, this was a revelation. Not because of what Suneet had said. He'd made no effort with my family from the beginning. He'd said the same things about Kamini's family. It was a format and not the truth. I was surprised by the way his family reacted: with sympathy and agreement, egging him on in his misunderstanding of things. I couldn't say anything against my in-laws but my husband could bitch about his, for no reason. The rules of engagement never applied to them.

I read more email drafts.

I found that Suneet had forwarded all my private emails, from the time we were dating to now, to his mother! My love declarations, my dirty sex talks, my disappointments, my most private feelings, were presented to her to be picked apart, like a dead body for vultures! How humiliating. How could Suneet breach my privacy like this? Why was he so obsessed with his parents? Why would a man do this to a woman he loved?

Unless he didn't.

I shut the laptop. This was all too much for me to process. I couldn't understand why this family composed long emails to write trash about the women whom their sons were married to. I'd never heard of anyone doing such things. Early in our relationship, Suneet had written long emails to me as well, but I'd thought those were a necessity born of distance. Now, despite the fact that we were all currently living within a two-mile radius of one another, they were still using email. They were wasting all their time to character-assassinate their daughters-in-law. Why were they letting Samit, with this long working hours, waste his downtime ripping apart his wife and sister-in-law? And Suneet? He had done nothing for months now. Instead of planning his future course of action, they were busy poisoning his marriage. What kind of parents were these?

Just then, Suneet entered the house. I turned to this man, whom I knew intimately and also not at all, and told him quietly that I had seen his emails.

He was at once driven to fury. 'How dare you?' he shouted. 'They were upsetting emails.'

'Your emails are no better, Maneka!' he shouted.

'So, you've read my emails? When?'

He didn't reply. Kamini had been right about everything. He had been spying on me.

'Suneet, at least I had the decency to tell you. How long have you been monitoring my emails? Why did you never tell me about this?'

When he didn't reply, I added, 'I will still not lock my laptop because I have nothing to hide.' My parents had no time or intention to destroy their children's marriages. 'But you, Maa, Bhaiya, Dad? How could you lie so much for so long?'

'How dare you say anything about my family? Who are you? Nothing but a stupid, lying bitch!'

Every time I confronted him about something, he would mirror the accusation.

'Stop it, Suneet.'

'My whole family says that. Are all of us wrong and only you right?'

I told him quietly that I wasn't looking for a fight. 'I just wanted to let you know that I would appreciate it if in the future, you do not forward my private emails to your family. These are my innermost thoughts. It's a sacred line that no one should cross.'

He shifted on his feet. He didn't know what to do with his anger.

'And if you're *all* composing the emails you send to my family and me, then at least have the decency to say that. There's no need to sneak around so much.'

'I'm not going to change anything. Except creating a password to lock my computer.'

'Okay. End of discussion. I've said what I had to. You can do what you want with it. I know I have no control in this matter.'

I was in the double helix of being so tolerant that I tolerated intolerance.

I turned to go and then looked back at him, 'By the way, I read that last email from Tammy.'

His eyes became soft. He thought I would ask the obvious question. I didn't. I was too exhausted. I went into my room. Kamini's words echoed in my ears. There was going to be no end to this. The realization that this was happening simply because my husband didn't love me fully dawned on me. It had been staring at me the entire time. How could I have been so dumb? The least I had expected of marriage was love. Even when it was so obviously not there. Suneet was right. I was a foolish woman.

I cried the whole night, softly, gently.

Suneet did what he always did. He vanished.

I didn't go to work the next day, or the one after that. I was exhausted. Of them, of my life, of myself. My emotions weighed down so heavily on me that my body couldn't move. What kind of a man had I married? What kind of a family had I entered into? How had I turned my beautiful life into a nightmare within one year? How had I willing let myself get here? How had I made so many wrong choices? What the hell was wrong with me? Everything I had imagined myself to be was obviously false. I was the biggest idiot the world had seen. I was, in fact, nothing. I was useless. I was a piece of trash. I'd gone so far from everything I used to be that I couldn't even reach out to my friends or family. How would I explain to them the train-wreck that I'd made my life? Because to tell them of my failure was to remind myself of my failings. And, if I was so ashamed of myself, how ashamed would they be of me?

For the first time in my life, I began to hate myself.
I was all alone. I had nothing to live for.
All I had was blackness.

*

Then, one Thursday night, Suneet and his mother showed up at the house with their bags.

'Kamini's house is making me claustrophobic,' his mother said to me as she went into my room. 'I'll stay here for a while.'

Pigs always find a way to the garbage, don't they?

I didn't say anything. I went into the kitchen and began to cook.

CHAPTER THIRTEEN

I WALKED into the house.

It was shrouded in darkness. The lights had been turned off. A lamp in the living room flickered like a scared lamb. They were sitting in silence; still, like a tiger waiting for its prey.

Oh god, what had I done now?

'I have shown you so much love and respect, but today you have crossed all lines,' his mother said to me. 'You are selfish . . . irresponsible . . . immature . . . we are getting tired of this behaviour.'

Maybe I could gift her a thesaurus, so she'd have new adjectives to describe me with.

'Sit down,' his father said.

I sat down. I didn't remove my shoes. I didn't put down my purse. I slid down the chair like a deflated balloon.

'*Ek tamacha lagane ka man ho raha hai* (I feel like giving you a tight slap),' Maa said. I flinched. She was red in the face with fury. 'We have been at your house the whole day, and you have not once called us to check if we had lunch or chai.'

I looked up, surprised. The three of them had obviously spent the entire day planning this showdown. Couldn't they have made up a more plausible reason than chai?

I opened my mouth but didn't say anything. There was no point.

'Look at this rude girl. I am talking to her and she is not replying,' Maa said, looking at Suneet.

Suneet looked at me. I took a deep breath and said, 'I'm sorry, Maa. My new show on TV started today and I was busy.' I paused to hear a little congratulations; there was none. 'I messaged you on Gmail chat to ask if you guys had eaten. You told me that everything was fine.'

I waited for her to tell me that I was lying, as usual, but she was smart enough to know that I could produce evidence in a matter of seconds.

'Chatting is not calling,' she snapped. 'You must call us every few hours to check.'

'Should I call every three hours or would you prefer every hour?' I wanted to ask, but she was really furious. I didn't understand this.

'I did call Suneet, twice, to check,' I said, not sure what I was defending, 'and he also said that you were all fine.'

'Why call Suneet? You should've called me!' Something had to be said for the over-confidence of someone clutching at straws. 'You should've called me to ask what we want for dinner,' she continued. 'Instead you waltz in here at seven o'clock with no care in the world!'

This was infuriating!

'Maa, I got a little late today because I was working.'

'That is your priority, eh? Have you even noticed that there are no tomatoes at home? Who will buy them? Me?'

'Tomatoes?' I asked. Is that what this was about? Tomatoes? I took a deep breath. 'Suneet could've gone down to the store and picked them up.'

This really enraged her.

'You want him, this poor boy, to keep suffering for your immaturity? Why should he buy tomatoes? Is it your responsibility to run this house or his?'

I looked at Suneet. I swear I saw him smirk. Why do Indian parents do this to their sons?

'Your in-laws have come to stay with you and you don't have the decency to be at home? You've been out the entire time we have been here!'

I had to be a memory keeper of my life. I had to recall every sentence, every action, every phone call, every single word I uttered or they would twist things and throw them in my face.

'Maa, that's not at all true. I've been at home every day since you got here. I didn't cook today's meals yesterday because you told me not to! You said you wanted fresh food.'

This was all so trite and meaningless, like some outdated saas-bahu serial. As the default villainess, I should've been wearing grey lenses and heavy make-up, ready to defend my every move.

She couldn't argue with logic, so she added, 'There are other problems as well.' Great! 'When I call you at work you sometimes don't answer. Do you have no respect for me?'

I looked at her incredulously. 'Maa, I don't answer the phone only if I'm in a meeting or live on TV! And I always call you back.'

'Suneet used to answer on the first ring no matter what. His priority was always family, not some *faltu*, low-paying job.'

No wonder he got fired, I thought.

'Beta, you will have to buck up. You are very irresponsible. We expect more from our bahus,' my father-in-law added. Their minds were already made up. This was not a death-by-trial but a death-by-judgement. Death actually began to feel like a better alternative than listening to them.

'What do you have to say for yourself?' she asked.

I had to say something.

'Maa, I am doing more than anyone else is. I have been since the day I got married. I am doing more for you guys than I've ever done for my own family. Yet, I feel like you are all always criticizing me. You're all finding the same faults in me as you do in Kamini. Is this really going to help anyone?'

Hearing Kamini's name triggered something in her. She lost it. She began to shout at me like I had murdered someone.

'You are talking like this because you have become friends with that Kamini . . .'

'I have not.'

'Really?' She turned to Suneet as if he was a judge in a court hearing. 'This Saturday, in the kitchen, I heard Maneka tell Kamini that I don't make my sons cook! Can you imagine spreading such vicious lies about your mother-in-law?'

The difference between the truth and a lie is a lie.

'I didn't say sons,' I said. 'I told Kamini that men are so lucky that they don't have to cook, and that I wish I was a man. It was a joke.'

'How dare you! Are you calling me a liar?'

'No. I'm just clarifying what I said, Maa. You can cross-check this with Kamini.'

'Do you think I'm deaf? I heard the two of you making fun of me the next day as well.'

'When?'

'I heard both of you giggling. Obviously you were talking about me!'

She wasn't even in the kitchen. How did she hear us? Was Kamini right when she said that they were spying on us?

'We weren't, Maa. I told Kamini that I didn't need help in the kitchen and she could sit outside with all of you. She said, "I'm going up a level". It was a joke. We meant no harm.'

'I will deal with her later. She has just rejoined this family. She has no *right* to be talking like this.'

'Right?'

'And you should keep quiet if you know what's good for you,' she said.

I closed my eyes and took a deep breath.

'Let her talk,' I heard my father-in-law say. 'Bottling up emotions will only lead to resentment.'

But I'd had enough. I refused to speak.

My mother-in-law continued to complain. 'Bahu is just taking my love for granted. My love is unconditional, but only if I am shown love and respect like a mother. I want to love her, but at what cost?'

I stopped listening. I finally understood what the issue was. This wasn't about chai or tamatar. They had somehow figured out that Kamini and I were becoming friendly. This made them very cagey for some reason. What were they trying to hide? And what could I do? I zoned out. Half an hour later, it looked like my mother-in-law had finally run out of breath. There was a pause. We all looked up from the floor we had been staring at.

'Tell me, am I wrong Raji?' she asked her husband.

'No, you are not wrong,' he said.

'What say, Suneet? Am I not right?' she asked her son.

'You are right, Maa,' he said. 'Maneka is immature and selfish. I don't even respect her anymore.'

I felt like I'd been slapped. No love, no respect. What had I done to deserve this from my own husband? I held back the sob that was rising in my chest. It's true that we can be without food for forty days, without water for four days, without air for four minutes, but we can exist only four seconds without being loved . . . that's why love is so important in this world.

'Tell me what my son is doing wrong?' I heard Maa ask me. 'Why are there problems in your marriage?'

I had told them several times and each time they had found a way to make it my fault. What was the point?

'You don't have any serious issues with Suneet because he's a good boy. Yet, you both have so many problems. Who should we blame for them?' said his mother.

'You have to grow up, my girl, and admit that if the problems in your marriage are not because of him, then they are because of you. Suneet has told us what all you are doing. But you . . . you don't think about things properly. We didn't say anything all this time because we didn't want to interfere,' said his father. I almost laughed. This was them *not* interfering? 'But how long can we stay quiet?'

They kept talking. Every word felt like a stone digging deeper into a fresh wound.

I looked at Suneet. He was still staring at the floor. He didn't say a word in my defence as his parents attacked me. He didn't once tell them to stop. This was what Draupadi must have felt like during her *vastraharan*. I held back my tears.

Finally, I heard my father-in-law say, 'Go and buy tomatoes.'

'What?' I looked at my watch. 'Dad, it's 9.30 p.m. All the stores are shut.'

'Morton Williams is open for another thirty minutes. Run and go there. Then quickly make dinner for us.'

'But it's so dark! And cold. Are the tomatoes really necessary?'

'Trust a woman who doesn't know how to cook to ask that,' he said. 'We are all hungry. Do you not care?'

What could I do? When a tree is struck with an axe over and over again, it will fall at some point. I got up and went out in the biting cold. I felt infinitely exhausted.

'You are a useless and selfish girl,' I heard my mother-in-law's voice in my head, as I tried to run on the snow-filled road. I slipped. A shooting pain ran up from my tail bone to my neck. Tears were rolling down my cheeks. My stomach was growling. I hadn't eaten since lunch. But I got up. God knows what they'd do to me if I didn't buy those bloody tomatoes. Was this the way to treat a human being? I reached Morton Williams just as the shutters were coming down. I slid under them. I grabbed a packet of tomatoes, begged the cashier to let me pay for them, and ran back home.

Back home the air was still sullen. I quickly made dal and bhindi, both dishes that didn't really require tomatoes. The three of them sat in stiff silence while I was cooking. Not one of them offered to help, even though I had been at work all day and they had been home. My anger and resentment were at their peak. My in-laws had crossed all boundaries. No one had ever spoken to me like they had today. They treated me like some filthy and dangerous wild animal that had to be tamed. I was angry with myself as well. Why hadn't I defended myself? Why hadn't I spoken back to them? What was the point of being cultured with uncultured people?

I spat in the dal. I had never done something like that before, but it felt good. A small redemption. They were getting what they deserved. I took out plates to serve them.

They ate without once mentioning that the food had no tomatoes. It had all been a ruse.

None of them asked me to sit down with them and eat.

I heard my mother-in-law laugh. She was now pretending to be in high spirits. Like their harsh words to me didn't matter. Like I didn't matter.

Maybe I didn't.

She came into the kitchen a little later, while I was washing the dishes.

'Give me a spoon,' she barked.

I didn't make a move. There were spoons in the cutlery stand right in front of her. She was doing this to show me how much control she had over me. I'd had enough.

She stormed out of the kitchen.

'This bahu is too much!' I heard her shout. 'She is refusing to give me a spoon now. I hope she hasn't poisoned the food.'

I wished that I had. I left the remaining dishes in the sink and went into the bathroom. My in-laws were not even pretending to be nice anymore. I didn't want them to see me cry. After some time, I heard knocking on the door.

'I wanted to say that I shouldn't have become so angry with you,' I heard her say. 'I should have said things calmly. After all, I am fifty plus, and you are half my age.'

Suneet must have told her to apologize. But this was no apology.

'We shout at you because you are family,' she continued. 'We treat you the way we treat our sons. Would you prefer we treat you like a bahu and not daughter?'

I didn't respond.

'She is soaking in the bathtub,' I heard her say angrily. 'Imagine! While I am trying to talk to her. I have been humiliated enough by this woman. Let's go to our room, Raji.'

I heard the bedroom door slam shut.

Moments later, there was a knock on the bathroom door.

'They've gone,' I heard Suneet say. His voice was soft. 'Please let me in.'

I opened the door. He entered the bathroom.

'No matter what's happening, things will be okay, baby. We'll work it out because we love each other, no?' he said. Every time he pushed me to my farthest edge, he would speak to me like this. And today he'd come to talk to me only after his parents were locked in the bedroom, so they wouldn't know what he was doing. This was pure hell.

'And don't blame Maa. She didn't mean it. She loves you.'

Suneet touched my face. I felt like he was poking a hot pin into my cheek. It was too little, too late. I turned away from him.

He went away.

After some time, when I could no longer separate myself from my sorrow, I came out of the bathroom. I took off my shoes, changed into my nightie and lay down on the futon. I hadn't eaten in twelve hours. My head was pounding. My body ached. Suneet was saying something to me. I looked at my husband but realized that he was of no greater significance to me than the tomatoes I had just bought. I shut my eyes.

When he was asleep, I went into the kitchen and took a knife. I went into the bathroom. I held the knife against my stomach. Too bloody. I sat down on the toilet and held it against my thighs. What damage would that do? The only thing I wanted was to tear my skin. To feel something beyond the pain that was throbbing inside me like a ticking bomb. I brought the knife to my wrists and made a cut. It was all going to be okay.

CHAPTER FOURTEEN

THE CUTS were not deep. I wanted to kill myself but not enough to die. I couldn't understand this complex misery. But there were two cuts on my left wrist and they were throbbing in pain. I went and lay down next to Suneet. I told myself the pain would go away because my mind was in more agony than my body.

It didn't. I needed medical aid.

'I cut my wrist,' I said softly to Suneet. 'Can you get some Dettol?'

He woke up with a start and blinked in confusion. He didn't comprehend what I was saying till he saw my wrists. 'Oh my god! What have you done?'

'It's nothing. It was very stupid.' He frowned. 'Can you get gauze and Dettol? And something sweet for me to drink? I can't stand up. I feel like I'm going to faint.'

Suneet stood up, and the words that came out of his mouth were, 'What the fuck, Maneka! You know we don't have insurance!'

I stood in the middle of an ice-cold highway, facing an ice-cold storm, and this man was throwing an ice-cold bucket of water on me.

139

There was no panic in his eyes. There was no empathy. He didn't hug me. He didn't console me. He didn't shout at me for being foolish. He didn't even get what I asked for.

My husband really didn't care whether I lived or died.

'I'm going to call my parents and you call yours. Let's tell them what you've done,' he said instead.

What the fuck was wrong with this man?

'Please. Don't. Tell. Anyone.' I said empathically. 'Don't. You. Dare.'

But Suneet ran to the bedroom and within seconds his parents came out. Fuck! Now I really wished that I'd killed myself.

His father sat down beside me on the futon. His mother stood next to him. I cringed. This was the weakest moment of my life. These were the last people I wanted to see. If, at that point, anyone had asked me if I recommended falling in love, I would've told them 'Run!' Because here I was, with my chest cut open, my heart cut open, allowing people to get in and break me so wide open that nothing inside me could live again. All because I'd let myself love.

'Why did you call us for this nonsense, Suneet?' I heard his mother say. 'What drama is this? Cutting her wrists? If she really wanted to kill herself, she would've done it properly!'

The anchor pulling me down into the deep sea now sank me completely.

'She's doing this so I look bad . . . our family looks bad. Don't go by her innocent face. She'll do anything to get everyone to take her side. She's doing all this for attention, and you are giving it to her.'

'Maa, please!' Suneet finally said.

But it was—again—too little too late. It dawned on me that Suneet had called his parents here for entertainment, as if I was a circus performer, and not to help. How deep is the absence of love?

I got up, slowly. I would not let myself fall further than I had with these awful people. I had to save myself. None of them would. I hobbled to the kitchen, holding the wall, and drank a few sips of Coke so I wouldn't collapse. Feeling slightly better, I went into the bathroom and began to put Dettol on my cuts. It singed.

Suneet came up to me and said, 'I've called your mother. She's on the phone.'

What do you do when you ask for the cool of the moon but get burnt by the scorching sun?

I took the phone and shut the bathroom door. I heard my mother's voice. She was in a panic.

'What's going on, beta? Are you okay?'

Are you okay . . . that's all I needed to hear.

I wiped my tears. I cleared my throat. I forced myself to say something.

'Mom, I really can't talk right now.'

'Beta, please. Tell me that you're okay. Tell me you didn't do what he's saying you did.'

I took a deep breath. There was only so much I could process at a time.

'Mom, I don't want to talk right now. But I'm okay.'

'Suneet said something about you . . .'

She couldn't even say it. How could she when I couldn't say it either?

'I don't know what's going on there, Manu,' she added, 'but if you want to come back to Mumbai, take the next flight and come here to us.'

I wanted to sob. There was nothing I would've liked more. But going back to Mumbai was to admit defeat, to admit my failure. I wasn't ready for that. My mother had raised me to be a strong woman; I didn't know then that being strong could also mean being vulnerable.

Suneet knocked on the door and entered.

'Are you done?' he asked, as if I'd stopped at a green light.

'I'll talk to you later,' I told my mother.

'But—'

I cut the call and looked at Suneet. This had been the worst night of my life, after that cold December night when he had hit me. Both times it had been his fault. He was giving me his worst instead of giving me his best. How long was I supposed to put up with it?

'All I asked of you today, Suneet, was to hug me and tell me that I'd done the stupidest thing ever. To tell me never to do it again because you love me,' I told him. 'Instead, you made a spectacle out of me. You punished me more than I had punished myself.'

He looked down at the floor. He knew that I was right.

'Whenever you shed a single tear, Suneet, if you as much as frown, I am by your side, holding you, comforting you, being there for you. And today, when I'm at my lowest, you haven't had the decency to even ask me if I'm okay. I'll never forgive you for this, as long as I live. No matter what happens, don't ever forget that.'

He stepped back. So far in our marriage, I hadn't pushed back or stood up for myself like this; annoyingly so. Now, at my weakest, I was.

I went into the living room and lay down on the futon.

'Did you speak to your mother?' his father asked.

I looked at him with dead eyes and replied formally. 'I did. Thank you for asking. Now I'd like to sleep if you could all excuse me.'

I pulled the blanket over my head.

I didn't bother about their whispers, or that my husband came to bed at some point and lay at the farthest end, with his back to me.

I closed my eyes.

I didn't sleep, of course. I wept softly the entire night. I tried to tell myself that I wasn't in pain, but the body shows what the mind knows. When morning came, I didn't want to go to work. But they were home. It was my father-in-law's sixtieth birthday. I got ready, still crying, wore a long-sleeved sweater so my cuts wouldn't show, and I wished my father-in-law a happy birthday. I gave him his gift. I went to work. I have no clue how I got to office, what I did at work or whether I even ate that day. My colleagues had been telling me for months that I looked sad. I'd joke with them that I wasn't sad, I was married. I have no clue if I spoke to any of them that day. I went about my workday like a plane on autopilot. In the evening, I met the family for a Broadway show. Till today I don't remember the name of the show or what it was about. Suneet and his mother ignored me. I ignored them as well. They still hadn't asked me if I was okay. They sat next to each other during the show. They walked hand-in-hand like a couple. It was them versus me.

The cuts on my wrist still hurt. No one could see them. I wouldn't let anyone see them.

I touched my wrist gently, to soothe the itchy feeling, and ignored the pain.

I had done something foolish and irresponsible. A woman should never kill herself over a man. No man is worth it. Especially not one who's a monster.

It was only after the show that my father-in-law finally asked me if I was okay. He gave me a hug. He was a doctor. He would've known what to do last night. But he hadn't done it. I didn't hug him back.

As we were walking back, Kamini asked me why I was in such a bad mood. 'Are you all right?'

No, I wanted to shout. I'm not all right. I tried to kill myself. I tried to slit my wrists. But that's not the worst part: I feel like I'm losing my mind.

'I'm in hell,' I said instead, dying to say something honest to someone.

'I'm not surprised. I had warned you. Have you spoken to Samit about this?'

'No.'

'Go to him. Tell him that as your brother he has to support you.'

I looked at Samit. 'I don't think so.' I thought of all the times that I'd called him, thinking of him as my own brother, and he hadn't answered. The way he had taken sides by remaining silent. The way he had participated in those eek-mail drafts.

'Look, he doesn't like getting involved, but whatever you're going through looks serious,' she added. 'I never thought I'd see you in such bad shape.'

'I'll see when the time is right,' I said. Samit wouldn't remember what I'd done for him when he was at his lowest, earlier this year. He wouldn't bother about the right thing to do. He was a weak man, and weak men are insignificant. He was insignificant in my story with Suneet.

We saw Maa approaching us and left it at that.

Three days later, at home, his mother said to me, 'I know you think you have a right to be angry with me, but I've done nothing to deserve this. I have only come to you with my love.'

Love. There it was again. A word they used so flippantly and so often, only to win arguments. Before them I'd never known such a wide distance between what people said and what they did. This chasm, I realized, is what the world knows as hypocrisy.

I ignored her. We were in the kitchen. I continued to chop onions for our dinner. I told myself my tears were because of that.

'I am so depressed,' she said, to a woman who was suicidal. Because she had to have first rights to whatever I was feeling. 'It's tough for me because I have to work in both the bahus' houses. I have got stuck because of this "*tera ghar, mera ghar*" (your house, my house) love I have. I ask you, is it fair?'

I looked at her. The only reason I was spending hours in the kitchen, in *both* houses, was to please her.

I didn't dare say this to her, of course.

'You are twenty-eight years old, beta, so you don't know a lot of things,' she continued. 'It is my job to guide you as a mother. You should not show your weakness to others because they will take advantage of it. So, listen to my advice, woman to woman. Always hide what you're really feeling. Don't be so open, so transparent. It will make your life a lot easier.'

Who had done this to her? Who had fucked her up so badly? She had everything going for her. She lived a luxurious life in Dubai, driving a Lexus and attending kitty parties wearing her gold necklaces. She worked for fun as a teacher and not out of necessity to make money. She had few responsibilities as a mother, since her children had not lived with her for more than twenty years. Her health was perfect, except for her imaginary cramps and headaches. She travelled around the world. She was an incredibly blessed woman. Where did this self-inflicted victimhood come from?

Or is happiness not about having but accepting what you have?

'I want to say this as a twenty-eight-year-old who knows nothing, Maa. A woman does not kick another woman when she falls,' I said slowly. My wrists were tingling.

I had never pushed back with her like this.

'I—' she said.

'Please let me be. You've won. You can keep your son.'

Some women should marry their sons.

The next day she packed her bags and moved back with her husband to Samit's house.

I was alone with Suneet, at last.

I didn't know then that this was the worst thing that could happen to us.

CHAPTER FIFTEEN

IT BEGAN with a silly argument. We both were eating dinner in front of the TV. I had cooked curd rice. He said it tasted awful. I agreed with him. The quality of my cooking was declining as rapidly as my mental health. He told me to make something else. I decided to push back, as I had with his mother. I told him he could make his own food since he was at home all day watching TV. This made him furious. He started shouting about how I was ill-treating him.

'You even made a face when I asked you to talk to Dad in the evening,' he said.

'Suneet, I was in the middle of writing an article so I can pay for this rice,' I said, 'and then I was in the middle of cooking the damn thing. I've been working the entire day!'

'This is why we have problems in our marriage. Because you have no respect for my family,' he continued. 'You are so—'

'Suneet, stop! Just stop! Stop blaming everything else for what's wrong in our marriage. Fuck your family. Fuck the food. Fuck the university. This isn't about them. This is about us.'

'How dare you? How dare you say "fuck your family" to me. After all the love they've given you. You're nothing but an ungrateful whore.'

'Don't you dare speak to me that way,' I said, completely losing my temper. 'I am sick of you treating me like shit. Talking to me like I'm garbage. You cannot do this to your own wife. Don't you have any shame?'

'If you're so traumatized, why don't you do something about it?'

'What can I do?' What could I do? 'I'm married to you. I'm stuck. It's not some college romance where I can break-up and carry on.'

'You're not stuck. Leave me. It's easy.'

'How can I leave you when you're like *this*?'

'Like what?'

'Down and out.'

'Are you staying married to me out of pity?'

'Oh my god! Is that what you want to hear, Suneet? That I'm staying because I pity you? Not because I love you?'

'I cannot believe you would say that to me.'

'Say what? Suneet, I don't get it. Why do you play victim in every possible scenario? Why do you think everyone is out to get you?'

'It's a cruel world.'

'No, it's not. You choose to see things that way. You've had a great life. You've gone to the best schools in India, Dubai and the US. You've had great jobs. You're good-looking and intelligent. You have a family and wife who love you. You should be happy! Instead, you're always angry! Why do you find reasons to be miserable? Why do you twist facts to your convenience when the truth is good enough?'

'Like I did with the university?'

This guy was frustrating to talk to!

'I don't know what went down with your university because you suddenly left me out of the process, remember?'

'Are you saying that I deserved to get expelled?'

'I don't know what you deserved! I don't even know what happened!'

'I cannot believe you'd say that! You're so——'

'You know what, Suneet? Maybe you did deserve being thrown out of your university. Maybe you should've also been thrown out of this country. But how would I know when you never talk to me about anything?'

'I don't talk to you because you don't talk sense, Maneka.'

'I can't do this anymore! I am not a robot made to service your family and you. I have feelings and emotions, and I get hurt. I've tolerated too much. Fuck this shit.'

I got up from the sofa and the bowl I was eating in broke. Shards of glass fell near his feet.

'Are you trying to hurt me, you bitch!' he shouted. He stood up.

Instinctively, I knew what was coming next.

As he came towards me, like a raging bull, I warned him, 'Suneet, don't you dare do what I think you're going to do.'

He didn't stop. His eyes had turned sinister. His nostrils were flaring. His fist was in the air. I stood my ground. This time I would not be submissive. This time I would fight back. For women everywhere. When he came near me, I held out my hands to stop him and pushed his chin. I couldn't go any higher. He was 6 feet tall, I was 3 inches above 5 feet. But I was too furious to care.

'You bitch! Your nails! You've scratched me!' he shouted.

He pushed me back and punched me hard across my face. Everything turned black for a moment. My glasses flew across the room. My skull shook. My cheeks were burning. My entire face felt like it was on fire.

I didn't care how much it hurt. Not after everything that had gone down. There was a blur of red dots when I opened my eyes, but I still shouted, 'You think I can't hit back? I can, you bastard.'

I raised my hand. I was ready to beat the crap out of him. To show him how much it hurt.

But he grabbed my hand tightly and told me he would break all my fingers.

'I'll begin with the thumb,' he said menacingly and caught hold of my thumb, twisting it backwards. He was serious.

'Stop it, you're hurting me,' I yelled.

He didn't stop.

'Suneet, stop,' I shouted at the top of my lungs. 'You're about to break my hand!'

Suneet got startled and let go of my hand. I quickly ran into the bedroom. The same room where he had first hit me. I was suddenly afraid: what if there was a repeat of what had happened the last time? I locked the door. I sat down on the edge of the bed. I took a few deep breaths and let the tears come out in a sob. I felt so helpless. Why weren't women build to be physically stronger than men?

That's when I saw the doorknob turning. He was opening the door! How could I forget? He knew a way to open the locked door from the outside, something he had done many times before. I should have run to the bathroom, I realized. How stupid of me to come here instead! But what could I do now? The only escape from him was through the window. I looked at it. We were on the fifth floor. Could I? No. It would mean certain death. Facing him at least gave me a fighting chance.

I wiped my tears. I went to the other end of the room. I looked around and picked up a shoe that was lying there. I remembered the kirpan. The way he had brought it to my neck.

I hoped he didn't remember. He stormed in. He had curd rice in his hand. Thank god it was only rice.

'Stop,' I shouted, lifting the shoe. 'Or I'll throw this at you.'

'I challenge you to.' His face was red with fury.

I threw the shoe at him. I missed. He laughed.

Then he pursed his lips and charged at me.

'This is the crap you wanted to feed me, right? Here, now eat it yourself!'

He threw the rice on my face and rubbed it all over. I couldn't breathe as the rice got stuck in my nose and mouth. I spat it out.

'You bitch, you're spitting at me,' he said.

He pinned me down on the bed and began to choke me. I tried to kick him. I tried to push him. It was pointless. He was much stronger than I was. His grip around my neck tightened. I thought my tongue would pop out. My head began pounding. My face was on fire again. There was no escape. I became absolutely still. *Wouldn't death be better than this?* I closed my eyes and let myself go. My body became light, as if I were watching myself from the outside.

No! No! What was I doing? I couldn't die at the hands of an asshole.

I took a deep laboured breath, gathered all my strength and heaved with both my hands. I managed to push him away. I caught the flicker of surprise on his face before it turned to rage. Shit. That's when he lifted me and flung me across the bed. My head hit the hard floor.

I don't know what happened next, but when I came to my senses, he was no longer in the house. I gathered myself. I got up slowly, holding the frame of the bed, and lay down on the bed for a few minutes. What the hell had happened? Had my husband left me for dead?

It didn't matter. I was alive.

I walked slowly to the bathroom and splashed water on my face. I watched the blood, tears and rice flow down the sink. I checked my body in the mirror. I looked like a ghost, but everything else was intact. Thank god!

I came out of the bathroom, searched for my phone and called his brother.

'Bhaiya, please come and get me. Suneet hit me again. He may come back and I don't know what he'll do.'

My hands were shaking. My body was trembling.

I needed to get out of this house as quickly as possible. Samit was my only chance. I couldn't think of anyone else. My family was not here. My friends lived far away. Kamini had gone to her mother's house for the weekend and I remembered her telling me to reach out to Samit.

His brother said he'd be there in ten minutes. I went downstairs and waited for him in the lobby. I tried not to, but I kept crying into a towel. It was late. No one was in the lobby. I could cry without being ashamed.

We drove in silence.

'Where are we going?' I asked, still in a daze.

'My place. You can rest there,' he said.

'What about Maa and Dad? I need to be alone right now.'

'They'll be sleeping. Don't worry.'

When I entered Samit's house, Suneet was sitting in the living room with his parents. Another trap. Fuck, these people were evil.

'I'm going to go,' I said. I was furious. With Suneet. With his parents. With Samit for not telling me that Suneet was at his house.

'Sit,' his father said.

I was all alone with these people. I turned to go.

I heard his mother say, 'Suneet is saying that you attacked him? You scratched him? You threw a shoe at him?'

I turned around. I looked at Suneet. He was sitting coyly next to his mother, looking down at his feet like a wronged child. I shuddered. I could still feel his hands on my neck.

'I came here to be safe. I do not want to talk right now,' I said slowly.

'Beta, this is shocking to us. We are going through so much already,' his father said.

'You should be there for him instead of creating all this drama,' his mother said.

'We need to keep calm, especially you, beta,' his father said.

'I'm going to go,' I said.

I didn't care what they thought of me anymore.

'Well, this is a family meeting, so you have to talk,' said his father. 'You never talk.'

'What happened needs to be discussed between Suneet and me,' I said.

Despite everything, I didn't want to embarrass my husband in front of his family. I didn't believe in airing my dirty laundry but keeping it safely in the machine where only I could wash it.

'We are a family. We don't keep secrets from one another,' his mother said.

'With all due respect,' I said, as gently as I could, 'what I say will not be dealt with objectively. I understand you are his parents, but I don't deserve this. Especially not now.'

'Excuse me! We've been very objective with you, Maneka. We've given you more leeway than we should have,' his mother said. 'You walked in right now and didn't even touch our feet.

Did we say anything to you? Should we keep tolerating your disrespect?'

I blinked and looked at Suneet. He didn't dare meet my eyes.

'Anju,' his father said, 'Let her speak.' He turned to me. 'Whatever you want to say, beta, say it in front of everybody.'

They were playing good cop, bad cop. I turned to go.

'You're leaving us no choice, bahu. We are going to call your parents and tell them that you attacked our son because he told you not to talk trash about us,' I heard his mother say.

Did I mention that these people were pure evil?

I turned and I glared at my mother-in-law. I had never looked at her this way.

I saw her squirm.

'Please, beta,' his father said. 'Be sensible. Let's close this incident here and now. Do you really want your parents to get worried . . . again?'

Was he threatening me? I shook my head in disbelief. I didn't want my parents to worry more than they already were. I'd already spent the last few days assuring them that I was fine. What was the point of telling them the truth? They couldn't do anything sitting in India. In fact, what was the point of telling anyone the truth? No one would be able to help me until I was able to help myself. They'd tell me to fuck social taboos and leave him, and I wasn't ready to make life-changing decisions right now. I didn't trust anything happening around me. I didn't trust anything I was doing or thinking. My in-laws obviously sensed my weakness or they would've never pushed me like this. I was nothing but a puppet in their mastermind hands.

It was a choice between telling them the truth, or letting them tell my parents a lie.

'Fine,' I said. I took a deep breath and sat down on the nearest chair. 'The truth is that he . . . Suneet . . . he . . . hit . . . me.'

'Beta,' his mother said, as if talking to a criminal, 'we already know what happened. These lies will not help you.'

'Maa,' Suneet said. 'You know she says anything to prove a point, na?'

'I know, beta. She's a writer, na? Her imagination is wild. She can't help it,' she said.

I was in the middle of another lynching. Each thing they said was a stone hurled at me. But no, this time I had to be strong. They could gang up all they wanted; I would fight back.

'He hit me,' I said slowly and more confidently, more to myself than to them. 'And this is not the first time. It's happened once before.'

I had finally acknowledged it to someone outside my frightened mind.

'She's lying. She threw a bowl of rice at me and then scratched me. She threw a shoe at me. I was trying to protect myself from her attacks.'

If you throw a squirrel into a room full of eagles, it takes time for the squirrel to learn how to save itself. I would save myself.

'How can you lie while I'm right here, Suneet?' I said. 'Your version doesn't even make sense. Have you seen your size and mine? It's physically impossible for me to attack you.'

'You pushed me!'

'I pushed you because you were hitting me. You punched me and choked me. You threw me across the bed. I was defending myself against you. You could've killed me!'

'I would never kill you.'

'That's what every wife-beater says.'

The word 'wife-beater' really riled up his parents.

'How dare you call him that!' his father shouted.

'My son would never do such things,' his mother shouted. 'He's a good boy. I have raised him well.'

'Haven't you put him through enough already?' his father asked me.

'I've done nothing but be amazing to him,' I said. I had.

'Please. *Ek haath se taali nahin bajti* (it's not one person's doing). Obviously you provoked our son,' she said.

'Why are you acting surprised, Maa? This isn't the first time that he's hit someone, is it?'

When Suneet was at boarding school in India, he told me he'd beat up many of his schoolmates because he hated school. One day, he beat up a boy so badly that the guy had to be hospitalized. He missed two semesters. The school wanted to expel Suneet, but since he was in the tenth standard, the principal allowed him to finish that year. They didn't let him finish his eleventh and twelfth there, though, like Samit had. Suneet had told me this rather proudly one afternoon, when we were lying down under a tree in a park in Boston. God knows how many other such incidents there were. God knows why I'd brushed them aside as childhood skirmishes.

'You've done a lot of nonsense since we got married, Maneka, but I never thought you would stoop so low,' Suneet said. 'Do you know what it does to a man's reputation when a woman accuses him of hitting her?'

'Suneet, do you know what it does to a woman when a man hits her?'

They went silent. I saw his father look at his mother. I saw his mother look at her feet. What was going on there?

I turned to Samit who had kept quiet throughout.

'Bhaiya, I am asking you as a sister. Would you ever raise your hand on a woman?'

His brother looked around sheepishly. He had not lived with his family for the last twenty-eight years. If anyone in this family still had an iota of humanity left, it was him.

'No,' he said softly.

'She hit me first!' Suneet shouted.

I continued looking at Samit, 'Tell me, Bhaiya. Kamini and you have been together since you were, what, sixteen years old? I'm sure you've had many fights. Have you ever hit her?'

'I don't want to get involved,' he said. 'This is between the two of you.'

I looked around the room. 'It's not anymore. Remember, when you were in a bad place earlier this year, Bhaiya, and I supported you through everything? You owe me the truth!'

Samit looked at me. It was a fact he couldn't deny.

'I'm asking you to be honest. Have you ever hit your wife?' I asked again.

'No.'

'Has she ever hit you?'

He looked straight into my eyes. Finally, a family member who saw me.

'She slapped me once,' he said, shuffling in his seat.

'Did you slap her back?'

'No. I would never do that.'

At least one man in this family had a moral compass.

'Why did you do it then?' I turned to Suneet and asked. 'Not once, but twice now, and with many threats in between that.' I should've asked him this after the first time he hit me, but I hadn't dared. Here, in a crowd, even among his people, I knew I could. He would have to give me an answer.

'You must have provoked him, obviously,' his mother said.

I looked at her. Why do women do this to each other?

'If a doctor gives chocolate to a sick child, he'll be loved by the child,' Suneet said softly. 'If he gives the child medicine, he'll save the child. That is generosity. That is what I'm doing with you. I'm saving you. And this is the only way.'

'I am not a sick child, Suneet. I don't need to be saved.'

'Of course you do. Look at you. You're a terrible wife. You cook badly. You're fat. You're barely making money. You have no career prospects. Your family is far away. Your friends are floozies. You're a failure. I'm all you have. Isn't it time you accepted that?'

Ouch! Was that what he thought of me? Or was that who I'd become?

I didn't know what gaslighting was back then. I wish I had. It would have changed my life.

I fumbled for a minute before I found my voice again. I couldn't let him get to me. Not today.

'Even if that's true,' I said, 'does it give you the right to treat me like shit, Suneet? To raise your hand? To call me names?'

I didn't tell them what names. Whore. Bitch. *Randi*. Slut. Faltu. *Nikami*.

'You said "fuck your family", Maneka. You said that I deserved to get thrown out of university and this country. You said you're with me only because you pity me.'

'Don't quote things out of context, Suneet. If I wanted you out of the country, I wouldn't have put you on my visa. I wouldn't have supported you.'

'Are you saying that I'm lying? Nice try. Everyone in this room knows that you're a liar.'

'Am I the liar in this marriage? Really, Suneet?' I said. 'Don't make me open my mouth.' Whether it was his virginity or his 'friendship' with Tammy or his brother's marital status or his checking my email—if anyone was a liar, he was. 'If you're denying saying the things you said and still doing the things you did, that means you know they're wrong. You're doing these things knowing how wrong you are. What does that make you?'

Suneet fumbled, then turned quickly to his parents and said, 'Now that I don't have an MBA degree from a fancy college, she wants to get out of the marriage. She's making things up.' I stood up in shock. I was the one who'd been trying to help him, who'd been taking care of him. Was it so easy to dismiss my efforts? 'I never choked her. Or punched her. She threw rice at me and attacked me, so I defended myself,' he continued. 'She lies, she is immature, she is stupid. She will pay for what she has done.'

Neither his father, mother or brother thought there was anything wrong with this last sentence. Apparently, they all agreed that women should pay for what others perceived as wrong. Pity that, at some point, I had believed them when they said I was their family.

'If I attacked you, Suneet, then why did you throw me over the bed and then leave me there to die instead of calling an ambulance?'

Suneet laughed. He kept looking at his parents. And then I heard him say—he actually said—'Why is she complaining about me trying to kill her? She wanted to die anyway, right? Just last week. Why does she care so much about her life now?'

Of all the cruel things that Suneet had said to me, this was the cruellest. Would he have been happier if I'd succeeded in my foolish attempt to kill myself?

My legs gave way. I sat down on the nearest seat.

His mother turned to the three men and said, 'Does bahu even know what hitting involves? Did my son send her to the hospital? Did he cover her in wounds? Has he left scars on her? She is up and about, with the energy to fight some more. Who will believe her?'

'You're right. I'm a doctor and I've seen real cases of violence. This is all drama,' his father said. He turned to me and added, 'No one is hitting you, beta. Hitting is a serious issue. Women break their necks. Their noses get displaced.' His voice lowered. 'They get killed.'

He continued, with the voice of a jockey taming a wild horse, 'Married couples get into these kind of scuffles once in a while. Things are said in anger. A little bit of slapping here and there happens. It's normal. No need to make a big deal out of it. You'll look like a bloody fool.'

What?

'That's not true, Dad,' I said. 'My friends are married. My parents are married. They don't hit each other.'

'You don't know what they do because *ghar ki baat har ladki ghar pe rehne deti hai* (every girl keeps these things a secret). Trust me, as a doctor I know all this. What you think has happened, has not happened.'

Was that even possible? There was so much going on in my mind and body. I had barely processed what had happened. I couldn't cope with this as well.

'She makes up things anyway,' his mother said. 'I have seen it with my own eyes when that day she didn't get the tomatoes—'

'Anju,' his father interrupted her. 'Let's not bring ourselves into the kids' problems. It looks like they had a fight, and because of what they're already going through, Maneka exaggerated it in her head. Bas!'

'Beta,' he turned to me, with the pleasant voice he used with me before I got married. 'As a woman, you must not provoke Suneet. You have to learn to control your temper. No man will tolerate a wife who behaves the way you do.'

'I—' I tried to say something in my defence.

'It is your duty as a wife to bring your family together. You should be the glue, not the axe,' his mother said. 'I have cut my stomach open so that my husband and sons are united. You think it's been easy for me?'

'Anju, I just told you. Let's not bring ourselves into this. That's for later. These two have had a silly fight and they're trying to get us involved. Let them figure it out when her temper has cooled,' his father said. 'It's very late. Let's wrap this up.'

They all looked at me. I didn't know what to say. Their collective voices were drowning out my voice.

My father-in-law continued. 'But first, she must call her parents and tell them about her lies, so there's no misunderstanding. She must tell them she's sorry for what she said and did.'

All he wanted, even in moments of distress, was to maintain his public persona.

'Please don't, Dad. We can't keep emailing them and calling them every second day. Imagine how worried they'll get.'

'This is how things are done in our family,' my mother-in-law said.

'Please. Don't.'

'Let's agree to disagree.'

'I cannot talk about this to anyone right now, Maa. Especially not my parents.'

'Don't worry. I will speak to them. I will tell them what really happened. If tomorrow something happens to you, we don't want them to blame us. *Tauba, tauba!* We have a standing in society. People respect us!'

I looked at Suneet in fear. I didn't want to drag my parents into this. They knew I didn't lie. They would know that I had been hit. But, already, he was dialling my mother's number. It was morning in India. My parents would be having their chai before going to work. The phone rang. He put it against my ear. I heard my mother's voice and began to cry. Her voice was like an embrace that I longed to be in. Suneet yanked the cordless phone from my ear and passed it on to his mother. She glared at me and locked herself in a room. When she emerged, after a few minutes, I heard her say, 'I don't know how to control her. She is taking advantage of how much love I have shown her.'

Her voice was so weepy that *I* felt like consoling her. How did she do that?

'Your mother wants to talk to you,' she said.

I took the phone and heard my mother say, 'Are you okay, Maneka? What is Anju saying?'

I took a deep breath. There was no point saying anything. The truth would be a burden on my parents, not a release. More than that, I was simply too exhausted to talk, to say anything. 'Nothing, Mom,' I mumbled. 'It's nothing.'

'Tell her it's just drama,' my father-in-law told me.

They were all listening to what I was saying. Surrounded by hawks even a sparrow forgets her own truth.

'You fell off the bed and passed out?' she asked.

I closed my eyes. I took a deep breath. 'It was silly. I slipped off the bed accidentally. I got up in a second. It's no biggie.'

'Are you sure? I'm getting really worried for you. Do you want me to come there?'

'No! It's all just a misunderstanding,' I lied. 'I'll talk to you later.'

When I hung up, my father-in-law said, 'Now forget all this. Go home and send us an email apologizing for lying about our son. We want your mother, father and brother cc'd on it. Till then Suneet will be staying here.'

I was being punished for being hit and daring to speak about it.

And the man who hit me? His mother was hugging and consoling him. He was being rewarded for hitting me.

My mother-in-law glared at me. 'Think about your actions. Suneet and you are standing in front of an avalanche. Instead of helping him, you are harassing him?'

I stared at her. She was holding Suneet's hands. My own were throbbing with pain.

None of them had once asked if I needed help.

Suneet said, 'I want to love you but you're making it impossible, Maneka.'

I went home alone. Samit didn't offer to drop me. Suddenly, they were okay with letting their young daughter-in-law roam the streets at night. Maybe they did want me dead.

But I wasn't scared walking alone in the dark. I didn't notice the silence of the night. I didn't dread the empty streets. Something inside me was so numb that I was incapable of feeling even fear. I'd already faced the worst in myself, in my life. If someone murdered me, it would be a mercy.

Once again, I didn't move from my bed the next day. Not to go to work. Not to put a morsel in my mouth. Not to answer my phone that rang laced with worry from my parents. I couldn't speak to anyone about what had happened. I was in so much pain, physically and emotionally, that I couldn't share my pain. My heart had broken to such an extent that it would never again know where to reside.

I didn't hear from Suneet or my in-laws for six days. They had left me alone in this foreign land so I could learn that women should shut up and not fight back.

Their voices became my reality. Everyone had lied to me all my life by telling me that I was good. I was not. I was a horrible person. A loser who was good at nothing. I was impossible to love. I was a selfish, immature, stupid girl who deserved everything bad that was happening to her.

A good person would not be forced to suffer this way.

On the sixth day, I sent an email to them apologizing for my behaviour and admitting it was all my fault, and my husband was returned to our house.

CHAPTER SIXTEEN

TODAY IS the day. The day that he will finally kill me. I hear the doorknob turning. I push my hand under the pillow. I feel the edge of the kitchen knife I've begun keeping under my pillow in case he attacks me. I tell myself to use it. To not be afraid. To kill him before he kills me. He enters the room.

'My parents are leaving tomorrow,' I heard him say. I didn't move. I had to be close to the knife. 'They no longer feel welcome in our house.'

I didn't remind him that their tickets had been booked for this return date even before they had arrived. But I sighed in relief. There are some people who bring joy only when they leave.

'You know they hate you now, right?' he said.

Was he going to kill me over that? I thought of the kirpan. I should've thrown the damn thing out of the house. It was more dangerous than my kitchen knife.

I said I was sorry. I didn't want to, but it could save me.

I heard him come closer. We know our abusers well. We know the sound of their footsteps. I put my hand on the handle of the knife and slowly turned my head around. My only chance at coming out of this alive was the element of surprise.

He was holding a cake in his hand. The chocolate fudge cake from Entenmann that he knew was my favourite. On it was a lit candle.

'It's our one-year anniversary,' he said.

I let go of the knife. I had completely forgotten the date today.

'Despite everything,' he continued. 'Despite all the shit that has gone down this year, I thought we deserved a moment to enjoy.'

I got up from bed slowly. I couldn't believe we'd been married a year. Every moment of this year had been a century in itself.

'We should celebrate by going to my university campus and throwing toilet paper at it,' he said. He smiled.

I almost smiled back. I was so relieved. He was being nice. Was my man coming back to me? Was his bad phase over? Was he falling back in love with me? Was my patience paying off?

I'd been through so many unpleasant surprises that year that a pleasant surprise was something to accept, not question. Because getting curious about your own happiness was to watch it withdraw like a touch-me-not flower.

My relief turned to an overwhelming sense of guilt. What was wrong with me? Why was I so unhinged that a smile from him would make up for his emotional and physical abuse? Was it because what he was doing to me was not abuse? Maybe my in-laws were right. Maybe slaps and punches and chokeholds were normal in a marriage. Maybe people didn't talk about it. What way was there to even know? I'd never been abused and never seen abuse in real life. No one had ever spoken to me about it: how to recognise it or how to fight it. I had no idea what to think anymore.

Suneet was still talking: 'And we have those tickets from our Hawaii trip.' On our way to Hawaii a few months ago—which seemed a lifetime away—we were given free air tickets after being off-loaded from an overbooked flight. 'We can use them to go somewhere, maybe San Fran to meet Bharti?' Bharti was his cousin sister, and the only person outside his immediate family whom he cared about. 'We could stay with her. She really wants us to visit.'

He sat down next to me and blew out the candle. He cut a piece of cake with his hands and put it in my mouth. I looked into his eyes. His eyes were the colour of earth after the first rain. The colour of hope. Of the future.

'Hello?' he said, his eyes hardening. 'I'm talking to you.'

If I didn't respond quickly to his peace offering it would scare him off and I'd lose him again.

I didn't trust my own decisions. Maybe I could trust his?

'Great idea,' I said cheerfully. 'San Fran sounds awesome.'

My voice seemed alien to me. I'd stepped into a time machine of love and fallen from its ferocious spinning into a life where I couldn't recognize myself.

'Great,' I heard him say. 'Book our tickets. I'll speak to Bharti.'

I didn't dare ask him what had changed his mind. Suneet was probably being normal because his parents were no longer here.

I didn't care. I also wanted to feel normal again.

Then, I heard him say, 'You know that I still love you, right?'

I was startled at this unexpected confession. What was there to love about me? I looked the way I felt: horrible. My lips were curled down. My neck was always throbbing. My skin and hair were listless. I wore shabby clothes. I'd aged ten years. I was lower than the faeces in a worm's ass.

I had completely lost faith in who I was as a person.

I glanced in the mirror across my bed. I didn't recognize the unhappy woman staring back at me.

'I love you too,' I said. I walked over and hugged him.

'Let's make a resolution to end this awful year on the right note, okay?' he said. 'Let me begin by telling you my future plans. I know you've asked me and I've not given you a reply.'

We finally discussed our future. He said he would retake his KMAT exam while looking for jobs. Since there was a global meltdown, he was not likely to get a job in the US, and was considering moving to either Dubai or India. This would mean us living close to his parents, or even with his parents. I balked at the idea, but what choice did I have? I told him I would move to wherever he wanted. He added that he wanted to get a fake MBA degree made for his job applications to companies in India. I balked again. But Suneet had been sitting at home for four months now doing absolutely nothing. Men needed to work. It was good for them. And it was especially good for their wives. I was desperate for him to get back on his feet. I was desperate for the kind of husband he'd be when the gloom and doom was over.

'I'll do anything that makes you happy,' I told him.

But, despite that, the knife remained.

Like I said, I knew then only passion and none of its consequences.

That evening, while he was at his brother's, I cooked him a romantic dinner of his favourite foods: bharta, rajma and bhindi. I didn't want him to accuse me of wasting money, so I was careful with the celebration. I bought a cheap bottle of wine from Trader Joe's. I made a heart out of pink Post-it notes in the living room. I used cheap tea lights instead of roses, which were expensive in the US. When I heard the key turning in the front door, I put myself in the middle of the Post-it heart.

'Happy anniversary!' I shouted when he entered.

His face fell for some reason. But he walked towards me and hugged me.

'Wow! This is amazing, baby! You are amazing.' He looked around. 'Maa was right. It's in a woman's nature to forgive. But I don't deserve this.'

To stop the truth ringing in my ears, I kissed him. 'Stop it. You do.'

He ran his fingers through his hair. 'It's just . . . you're always making these big romantic gestures. I can't—'

'What? I thought you'd like it.'

'I do. But you are . . . this is . . . too much. Every time you do something and it's just . . .'

'Just what?'

'It's just too romantic, okay? I can't keep up. I'm not creative like you. You dress up as a nun, you send alphabet chocolates, you fly across continents for my birthdays . . . you make all these grand gestures. And yes, you can feel good about yourself, you can tell everyone how great you are. But do you realize how small that makes me look?'

He was still measuring love. I wasn't going to let him bring me down.

'Don't say that,' I hugged him. He didn't know what he was saying. 'We both have different ways of expressing love. It's not a competition. I do what I can and you do what you can. I'm not expecting anything in return.'

'This is my last big romantic gesture. I promise,' I said, and snuggled up against him.

He purred like a kitten. 'You know I love this, right? I love us like this.'

'There's no need to change then,' I said. I smiled and kissed him.

*

'No,' says Anmol.

'Yes,' I say. 'Women are truly fools for men.'

*

'How does Sherna know about the email my parents sent you?' he asked me one Saturday afternoon when I was writing a short story in bed.

'Huh?' I replied. My mind was on my story.

'Sherna sent you an SMS right now that said "When will the internet in Dubai die so we don't have to read another eek-mail from Maa and Dad?"'

I had left my phone in the living room. Kamini must have sent me that SMS. Her number on my phone was still saved under Sherna 2.

Shit.

I should've asked him why he was going through my phone, when his was always locked and inaccessible. Instead I said, 'I have no idea.'

I hoped he didn't hear me gulp. I was a terrible liar.

'Really? Do you mind telling me why Sherna's number is the same as Kamini's?'

Fuck. We'd been caught.

'I thought we were trying to make this marriage work,' he shouted.

We were. For New Year's we went to my colleagues' party and had a blast. He carried me to the subway because my boots hurt. On 10 January 2009, he celebrated the No Pants Subway Ride that New York was famous for. He sent me photos of himself without pants while I was at work. We laughed about it. I had booked our tickets to San Francisco and planned our itinerary, happy to finally have something to look forward to. I had got in touch with people from Dubai and India for his job. I had forwarded him job resources. I'd spent endless hours researching his idiotic scheme of a fake MBA certificate till he dropped the idea. For some time everything seemed great. He seemed to be getting better. I didn't want this to end.

'You're ganging up with that horrible Kamini? You know Maa hates her! You know I hate her! Why would you betray us like this? Why would you two plot behind our backs?'

I took a deep breath. 'There's no conspiracy, Suneet. Just some girl bonding!'

'Bonding or bitching?' He turned around and walked to the bedroom door. 'Just when I began to trust you again, Maneka, you went and betrayed me. *You* told me we have to share things and now *you're* hiding things. Everything I thought about you earlier was right!'

I'd have to pay big time for this.

'Tell me the truth,' he said. 'Prove with whom your loyalty lies. Her or me?'

So, I told him. The truth. It went against everything I believed in, yet I did.

'I want to know how the conversation started,' he asked, like he was breaking down a mathematical equation. 'Who spoke to whom first? That is what is most important here.'

I realized my faux pas. *What had I done?* He was not the kind of man to dismiss this as harmless gossip. What had I done in a desperate bid to get close to him?

'I . . . I really don't remember.' I genuinely didn't. 'Look, I was in a bad place and I wanted to talk to her,' I admitted. I didn't want to stir up a hornet's nest more than was necessary. 'She's known your family for ten years, while I seem to be getting everything wrong with all of you. It didn't mean anything.'

'And . . .'

'And . . . you know, Suneet . . . I needed to vent. Ok? Unfortunately, I didn't think I could do it with you. Another part of me was pissed off. You know I've been feeling that you all ganged up on me. I sought her out thinking she'd give me neutral advice.'

'I'm telling my parents right now. How dare she? We just allowed her back into the house and she's already talking shit about us.'

Allowed? Did these people know this was the twenty-first century? If his brother was big enough to forgive his wife, who were they not to?

'Suneet, please don't tell your family. It'll become an issue when it doesn't need to be.'

'I have to.'

'I'm begging you! Can't you keep anything between us as a couple? Why does every discussion we have . . . everything we do . . . have to be broadcast to your entire family?'

He didn't reply.

'That bitch broke my kirpan the last time she was home,' he said after a minute. 'This is my way of getting back at her.'

While we were in our room, Kamini had said that she'd taken the kirpan down from the wall and was admiring it by the window, when it had slipped out of her hand and fallen to the pavement. Suneet had run down to salvage it and found the blade broken. He had cursed her behind her back for weeks. Now he used the hollow of the kirpan's sheath to store his drugs.

'Please, Suneet, promise me you will not say anything.'

He promised, but of course, told his folks anyway. They had a 'family meeting' with her, where she obviously denied saying anything. This was exactly what Suneet was looking for.

'She said you're a liar,' he said gleefully when he came home after meeting her.

'I'm sure that must have pleased everyone,' I mumbled. I was feeling awful for having opened my mouth. I should not have betrayed her trust like that. I should've been smarter. I could have had one ally in that family if I'd kept our conversations private. What a mistake!

'She said you came to her and told her that everyone is ill-treating you in this family, especially Maa and Dad.'

I didn't say anything.

'We've called for a family meeting tomorrow. Bhaiya's place. 6 p.m. Four of us.'

I couldn't think of anything less agonizing.

'Are you crazy? I'm not going for that. I shouldn't have said anything in the first place. It's my fault.'

'Are you admitting you lied?'

I sighed. He knew I was on thin ground.

'If you don't come tomorrow, Maneka, you will look like a liar.'

'How is that different from what you guys keep saying I am anyway?' I asked him bluntly.

He changed tactic.

'Babe, I need you to come for my sake. I need Bhaiya to see how manipulative his wife is. How evil she is. Remember the time she broke Dad's water-heating rod?'

I remembered. Samit and Kamini had taken his parents to Egypt two years ago. Instead of being grateful, they apparently kept telling Kamini to make them hot water for tea using a heating rod they'd brought. After three days, Kamini said that the rod had slipped from her hand and broken. The family repeated this incident ad nauseam to anyone who'd listen. But I knew she'd done the right thing. My in-laws asked us to make several cups of chai a day. But the chai was not chai. It was an execution. We had to use a precise amount of tea leaves, milk and sugar, an exact time for boiling the water, a specific spoon for stirring the sugar, a specific *chalni* and a 'right-sized' cup. They didn't hesitate to send tea back and ask that it be remade if it wasn't to their exact liking or specification. At last count I was spending one-and-a-half, sometimes two, hours a day making and serving tea! I empathized with Kamini's frustration at being treated like a servant by them, even during her vacation.

'We hated her from the beginning,' Suneet said. But you guys hate every daughter-in-law, I wanted to say. 'Remember, she didn't serve them dinner the night before they left? Who does she think she is?'

As someone younger, with more world exposure, Suneet should've made up his own mind, but he only thought of us what his parents thought of us, through a redundant 1950s trope of what a bahu should behave like.

'She had a migraine that day, Suneet,' I replied. She had told me about the fit our in-laws had thrown over this. 'Even maids get time off, so why not us?'

'Why are you defending her?' he said slyly. 'She did not defend you. She had some nasty things to say about you. She hates you.'

'Of course she hates me. I hate me right now.'

'Babe, this is a golden opportunity to show Bhaiya her true colours,' he added.

'I don't want to show anyone anything, Suneet,' I said. 'I shouldn't have said anything in the first place. I wouldn't have if I'd known it would become such a big issue.'

'Don't you love me?' he asked.

I blinked. Did I? I must for putting up with this.

'Of course I do.'

'Then do this for me. It will give a whole new meaning to our relationship.'

'How?'

'Trust me.'

'How will this help anyone, Suneet? What purpose will it serve? Why would Bhaiya believe me over his own wife? They've been together for seventeen years. He's always given her the benefit of the doubt, even when she cheated on him. He loves her. Can we respect that?'

'No. We can prove to him that he shouldn't love her.'

Suneet was becoming his mother.

'Suneet, I am the only person who'll lose in this. Bhaiya and she will end up hating me. What's the point?'

'I will come to your rescue, babe. I will defend you tomorrow,' he said. Fat chance of that. When had he ever stood up for me? He held my hands, as if begging me to save his brother's life. 'Even if he doesn't believe you, he'll know his wife is bitching about his family behind his back.'

Why couldn't they just leave her alone?

'How does it matter, Suneet? She isn't the first woman to hate her in-laws.'

'You are too naïve to understand family politics, baby. Maa told us all along that Kamini is not capable of honesty. That she'll back-stab us the minute she gets a chance. Meanwhile, Kamini has been claiming that she loves my parents. She lied to reconcile with Bhaiya. Now, Bhaiya will know she's a liar. He'll lose respect for her. It will prove Maa's point.'

And achieve her goal of breaking another son's marriage. If these boys were too dumb to see their mother's shrewdness, then they deserved the unhappiness in their marriages.

'Have you thought about the fact that they've just gotten back together, Suneet? Maybe Bhaiya doesn't want to deal with another issue? Maybe he doesn't want to acknowledge his failure in once again putting his faith in her? Even if he's convinced she said those things, he'll not do anything about it. Frankly, if Kamini doesn't admit that she's said anything, then there's nothing he can do. So—let it go. Why do you want to get caught in the crossfire?'

'She told him that she's changed but she hasn't. That's all I want him to realize.'

'Have you thought about how that might be traumatic for him, not helpful?'

What was Suneet trying to achieve with all this? Was everything a power trip to him?

'Please, jaanu. If you love me, you have to come tomorrow. This is your chance to show that you care about this marriage. I know it will be unpleasant, but it'll mean everything to me.'

He looked into my eyes like he hadn't in a long time. I took a deep breath. I knew he was manipulating me. Every time I told him I'd leave, every time he pushed me too hard, his tactic was to cry. Every time he wanted his way, his tactic was to use force or emotional blackmail. Now he claimed that our marriage depended on me having a showdown with my sister-in-law. Would his brother see who was manipulating whom?

'Fine, whatever,' I said.

My relationship with Suneet's family was so far gone, what was one more casualty?

Suneet jumped in delight. I'd not seen him this happy even during our wedding.

The lotus grows in swamps because certain things only thrive in filth.

The next day, I went quivering to his brother's house. Suneet was already there. He didn't want us entering together, to show that he wasn't on my side. As expected, Kamini was breathing fire. She shot me looks that could've killed me. The knot at the back of my neck began to throb again.

'Let's begin,' Suneet said, barely able to contain his joy at orchestrating the clash of the sisters-in-laws. I knew that every word exchanged would go back to his parents, who were probably waiting eagerly by the phone to be updated. I wished this man would get a job.

Kamini began yelling. She said that I was an awful person, a liar, out to get her and her marriage, and all the things I knew she would rightly say. She denied telling me anything and added that she was merely listening politely to me, while I was bitching.

'I gave her advice out of the goodness of my heart,' she told Samit.

I didn't rebut her. I wished she'd been smart or courageous enough to tell the boys that she stood by her opinion, rightly so, and to go to hell if they didn't like it. But smart, courageous women wouldn't stay married to such boys. What did that say about me?

'God will punish you for this,' she said.

I deserved everything she was saying.

Suneet was glaring at me. I was not playing the part he had called me here for.

'I'm sorry, Kamini,' I said. 'I owe you an apology.'

'Of course you do,' she said.

'I agree. But perhaps this is also a good opportunity for us to air how we actually feel about Maa and Dad? We've been holding it in for so long, out of fear, but these boys need to hear our side of the story. Instead of bottling up our feelings and growing resentful, as we have been, it may help us as a family to get things off our chest.'

I was trying to turn the discussion around. Make it productive. Give it a positive spin. That did not work, of course. She began crying.

'Why would I be resentful? I love his parents more than my own,' she said. What would make her say that? Had Samit threatened her? Had he told her he'd leave her if she'd actually said those things? The poor thing. 'I would never say anything bad about them.'

She couldn't acknowledge even part of our conversation, because then she'd have to acknowledge all of it.

Samit asked me what exactly Kamini had said to me.

I couldn't repeat the things she'd actually said. That would be destructive.

'It's not about what she said, but what she feels, Bhaiya' I said carefully. 'She has the same issues that I'm having, honestly. She feels criticized all the time, like I do. She feels like you're all ganging up against her, as do I. She's told the same things that are said of me: selfish, immature, irresponsible, spoilt and a liar, though she's none of these things. I have told Suneet some of this. All I'm saying is, if we address the problems that Kamini and I are having in this family, it would help everyone. We would be stronger and happier if you guys listened to us.'

'What nonsense, Maneka,' Suneet said. 'Your situation is different from her situation. My parents have shown both of you so much love. They've sacrificed so much for both of you. Can you imagine how they feel when they hear you both talk like this? Maa has not eaten in three days. Her legs are cramping—'

These boys were too brainwashed to listen to their wives. Kamini knew this. She had learnt a bitter lesson through ten years. A lesson I should've learnt in one year. I was a fool.

Kamini was shaking with anger. She refused to meet my eyes. I felt terrible.

'I'm sorry, guys,' I said. 'None of this should have happened. I feel very bad that I said anything about Maa and Dad.'

'What's your intention here?' Samit asked me. 'What are you trying to achieve by doing this?'

I was stumped. What intention could I have? I had simply made a bad move while trying to get close to my husband. Frankly, it made no difference to me whether Samit was with Kamini or not. Suneet was the only one obsessed with their marriage.

'Bhaiya, these women were just being petty,' Suneet said. Fat chance of him defending me. He was doing this to make Kamini and me the villains while making his parents—once again—look like victims. Kamini had warned me that they'd never let us be friends but turn us against each other. I was a sucker for walking right into their trap.

'And what is your intention?' Samit asked Suneet.

Maybe Samit wasn't such a fool, after all.

Suneet looked aghast. I butted in, 'I'm the one who caused all this, and I am sorry, again.' I turned to her. 'I'm sorry, Kamini. I really didn't mean for all this to happen.'

She was too angry to even look at me.

'Samit,' she said. 'She told me that she can't stand you because you're a weakling who never helps her.'

'Kamini. I know it doesn't look like it but I'm trying to defend you. Please don't go down this path. You know I never said that.'

She was saying this to get Samit on her side. Pretending I bitched about him, when I didn't, was her way of doing it. I felt sorry for her.

'And Suneet, she said she's thinking of leaving you because you have nothing.'

I laughed. I actually laughed. Such a thought wouldn't cross my mind, as I'd proven over the last few months. 'I think you've misunderstood me, Kamini,' I said. This was a nice line that didn't make her look bad. 'Don't do this. Let's end this. Again, I'm sorry for having caused this.' I looked at Samit. 'If Kamini feels she said nothing wrong, then it must have been a misunderstanding on my end. You guys have just gotten back together, so let's put this behind us. I wish you both the best.'

'Yes, let's have dinner,' Suneet said.

'I'm not hungry. I'm going to go home,' I said. How could I sit down for a meal after all this? I wanted to get out of there.

'Stay,' his brother said. He turned to Kamini, 'Lay the table.'

Kamini got up fuming and began to bang dishes in the kitchen. I was too scared to ask if she needed help. I excused myself and said I needed to check my work email. I went up to their loft. A minute later, I saw Suneet crawling on all fours towards me. I was about to say something, but he put his finger to his lips. I kept quiet.

'You were amazing, jaanu,' he whispered. 'You came across as dignified and gracious. You made her look like a monster. I've never loved you more.'

I had never loved myself less. What had I become? How was this a victory?

'Why are you crawling?' I asked him.

Shhh, he said urgently. 'She'll be watching your reflection in the glass.' I turned to my right. Next to the desk was a glass railing overlooking the kitchen. She was there, but busy setting up dinner. He was imagining that she was watching me. A more troubling thought entered my mind: how did he know about this reflection in the glass? I had practically lived in this house and never noticed it. Is this what his family and he did to keep tabs on us? Ugh!

I watched him clamber back on his fours. He was pathetic. This was pathetic.

We ate in silence. I took two bites of my food. I couldn't even swallow. I felt horrid. This was not me. This was not who I wanted to become.

After we left, Suneet kissed me in the lift. 'You were astounding! You really showed her! I'm so proud of you, babe. This went off so much better than I could have imagined.'

What was wrong with him? Why was he playing games with his own brother's marriage?

As we were about to step out of the building, he told me to wait in the lobby.

'They will be watching us from their house. I want them to think that we fought in the lift. They should assume that I am angry with you. They shouldn't think I'm on your side.'

Because a husband taking his wife's side was wrong in this family.

I looked up. 'There's no one there, Suneet.'

'Trust me. Kamini is evil. She will be hiding behind the curtains.' *What?* 'Let me go first, so it looks like I stomped off in rage. Follow me in a minute.'

I stood staring dumbfounded at my husband's back as he went out into the snow. I followed numbly a few seconds later. I could no longer see him or his footsteps. I didn't want to. For the first time in our marriage, I realized that my husband wasn't at war with me, or with the world. He was a man at war with himself.

CHAPTER SEVENTEEN

WE HAD a great time in San Francisco, eating chocolate at Ghirardelli Square, driving down Lombard Street, drinking wine in Napa Valley, visiting Alcatraz Island, and having a romantic lunch at Pier 39. He came to drop me off at the airport as I had to get back to work and said he'd miss me. During the six-hour flight back to New York, I resolved to forget the horrible year that 2008 had been and make sure that 2009 was different in every way.

I called him on landing, but he didn't answer. I messaged him that I'd reached home, but there was no response. I didn't panic. He never called to check where I was, even if I was out late, as if I ceased to exist if I was not in front of him. This out-of-sight, out-of-mind attitude was meant to make me feel insignificant, of course, but he had promised that he'd work on showing that he cared. So, I let him be. Then a day passed, and another. I began to get worried. What if something had happened to him? What if he had had an accident, or had done something to himself? I called him and he didn't answer. I called Samit but, as usual, he never bothered calling me back. I called Bharti. She sounded awkward on the phone, said that he was

183

fine and she would tell him to call me. Still nothing. Two weeks passed.

One day I went to the ATM. Our joint account showed zero balance. I'd just transferred my salary into it. How was that possible? I walked into the attached bank branch. The teller told me: Suneet had withdrawn all the money from our account. That's when I freaked out. I had $20 in my wallet. How was I going to survive? I called him. He didn't answer.

Maybe he was in trouble?

I messaged him. I told him I had no money. There was no reply.

I could ask my parents for dough. Or my friends. But I would starve before asking someone for money. I had to find another way.

I remembered a bank that promised $100 for opening a zero-balance account with them. I had been seeing ads for it all over town. I went to the bank's branch that afternoon. I opened one account in Suneet's name and one in mine. They gave me $200 in cash. That would get me groceries for the week and pay for my train fare to work. What next? I requested two editors to expedite the payment for my articles published in their magazines. My desperation laced the emails, but I had no choice. One of them agreed. The other never used my byline again.

I began to pick up pennies from the road. Quarters on the days I was lucky. I didn't care who saw me. I was grateful that people in this city thought nothing of throwing their change on the road. I walked for hours to save $2 on the subway. On the days that I was too tired to walk, I'd jump over the turnstile to avoid paying the fare or enter through the exit door, ignoring people's glares. While shopping for groceries, I would hide a tomato or two, sometimes a chocolate bar, under my long winter coat. I'd put toilet paper at the bottom of the shopping cart, hoping the cashier wouldn't notice. I began to cook khichdi—it was the thriftiest meal option—and ate it in the office bathroom, hiding it from my colleagues who would buy salmon sushi and avocado salad for lunch. The only vegetables I ate were potatoes because they were cheap. I didn't eat fruit that month—it was expensive—though it was the one thing I couldn't live without earlier. I took two apples from the reception of a bank, where I had gone to ask if they gave credit for opening an account, and rationed those over four days. I didn't feel pathetic or guilty at that time. I just felt the need to survive.

A month passed.

Then one day, I came home from work and there he was, lying on the sofa.

'Where were you, babe?' I asked. 'I was sick with worry.'

He didn't reply but kept staring at his laptop.

What had I done now?

I went up to him and tried to hug him. 'Are you okay?' I asked.

He pushed me away and said, 'Look, don't take it personally, but I want to be alone.'

His words were like acid thrown on the optimism I had gathered for the last leg of our marriage. How could I not take it personally? What huge blunder was he punishing me for? At a time when we needed to be planning our future and sorting out our problems, he was shutting down completely. I had no idea why he was behaving this way. What was he trying to achieve? He was clearly not thinking properly. I held back my tears. I had to be supportive. I had to be the mature and responsible one for the both of us. So, I respected his space even though it was killing me. I tried to make him as comfortable as possible. I called up everyone I knew he loved—Bharti, Samit, even his parents—hoping they could reach him. I left food in the fridge, hoping he would eat properly. I was worried about him, about me. It was not normal to live day in and day out without talking to your spouse, but what choice did I have?

Suneet didn't talk to me for two months without telling me why. He did nothing in that time. I watched him grow a beard, smoke the snake, develop red eyes, leave empty packets of chips and chocolate all over the house, leave his clothes all over the floor. The dishes piled up. His laundry grew. I continued to cook and clean for him. I never cried in front of him. He still looked irritated by my presence. I refused to get provoked. I stayed out of his way.

Then, he started walking out of the house without telling me where he was going. If I asked him, he would not reply. Once he said 'friends' without telling me which friends. Then he began vanishing from the house for the entire day and night.

Was he at Tammy's?

It was too much.

When he stumbled back home with red eyes one morning, I asked him where he had been. He went into the bathroom.

I'd been patient for two long months. I'd managed the house and him in silence for sixty long days. I deserved an answer.

'If you don't tell me, I will leave. Enough is enough, Suneet,' I told him.

It was time to snap him out of his stupor.

'I was out of the house because you've been coming home late from work,' he said.

It was the first full sentence he had said to me in two months.

'I'm coming home late because you don't want me around, Suneet. Remember? You asked me to leave you alone? You can't start the fire and then cry when you get burnt!'

'Fuck off, bitch.'

We have to stop teaching women that putting up with pain is a sign of strength.

'Talk to me properly, Suneet. I have done nothing to deserve this. I am sick of the way you're mistreating me. If you want me out, just say so. I'll leave.'

As I said these words, I realized that it *would* be okay. It would be better for me not to live with this man. The last few months had taught me this. I could survive on my own.

I was clear-headed for the first time in our marriage.

'I'll tell you what,' I said. 'There is no need to act out like this. Just chill. I will stay over at Sherna's place tomorrow. Take this time to think about what it is that you're trying to achieve by stonewalling me.' He looked at me in surprise. He knew he didn't deserve this kindness after what he had put me through. 'And whatever it is that you want, we will do. Okay?'

It was like speaking to a toddler.

He nodded. I gave him a half-smile and called Sherna.

'Come stay with me forever,' she said.

I was glad for my friendships. At least there I got the love I gave.

The next day, I went to stay at Sherna's. She forced me to go out.

'When was the last time you did something fun, Manu?' she asked me.

Her attempts to make me smile made me realize how low I had fallen.

'Look,' she said, ordering apple martinis for us at a New York bar, a rare moment this year when I felt like a twenty-eight-year-old and not a ninety-year-old. 'He's a difficult man, but you made the choice to marry him and stay married, when any other girl would have run away in a month.'

'It's so complex, babe. I don't know what to do. I don't know what to think.'

'Okay. Let's break it down. What's your biggest issue with him?'

Everything, I wanted to say. Where would I begin? I had not once said a bad thing about Suneet to anyone. I knew that if I told anyone he hit me, nothing he did after that would make him redeemable. It would be a disloyalty to him, to my marriage. But I didn't feel guilty wanting to talk about it now. I was finally ready to offload my marriage. I told Sherna everything. It made me feel unburdened, unpacked, light.

But Sherna looked alarmed.

'What? Manu, seriously? He's hitting you?' she asked.

'I—I think so. Maybe not. We get a little physical once in a while.'

'Are you waiting for a calamity to prove him wrong?'

I shook my head. 'It's not that bad. It happened only twice. He hasn't hit me in a while.'

'Oh my god, Manu, can you even hear yourself? What are you letting this guy do to you? You're an amazing person. You're beautiful and smart. You deserve much better than this.'

'But isn't this normal in a marriage? A little bit of hitting. A lot of fighting.'

'What? No!'

'Come on. You're married. You're my best friend. Tell me, honestly.'

Sherna looked at me with such pity that I wanted to weep.

'This is not who you are, my love. Why didn't you speak to me sooner?' she asked.

I looked down at my drink. *What had I become?*

I told her about the knife. I still kept it under my pillow.

'Babe, if you're feeling this unsafe, get out.'

'Where will I go?'

She said I could stay with her, but I was asking a larger question. My entire life would change if I left him. Was I ready for such a big overhaul? Did I have that kind of strength?

'I'm just so . . . so exhausted,' I said. 'I'm too exhausted to change my life, Sherna.'

I teared up. She hugged me.

'You were the happiest person I knew. I can't see you like this, Manu.'

'I've been frozen for the last one year. I don't have the strength to act on anything right now, except to survive each day as it comes.'

'That's ok. Anyone would be. Do what comes to you. Get divorced later.'

'Divorced? I can't get divorced. That's for old people! I'm only twenty-eight!'

'Well, Manu, you have always been the trailblazer in our group.'

I smiled at her and said, 'Everyone will be so scandalized.'

'No, they won't. It's okay to be divorced.'

'No, it's not,' I said, 'Let's be honest. When we were growing up, couples never got divorced.'

'Yup. They just got bitter.'

We laughed.

'You're right, Manu. The only divorced person we knew was Mrs Coutinho. You remember her? The Anglo-Indian lady whose son was in our Eco class in college. The one who picked him up wearing shorts, chain-smoking . . .'

'. . . and who kept children's tears locked in jars. Do you remember what we used to say about her? I feel terrible about how small-minded and judgemental we were.'

'It was a different era. It's not so bad now. It's 2009. More Indians are getting divorced and it's not such a taboo.'

'But it is *still* a taboo. Let's be honest, Sherna. If I get divorced, no one will marry me, except a toothless man with erectile dysfunction and kids my age. My life will be over.'

'You're overthinking this, Manu.'

'No, like anyone else, I don't want to die alone and lonely.'

'Isn't alone and lonely better than together and miserable?' It was. But back then, I associated being alone with being lonely. I would learn that those were not the same things. Because the loneliest I had been in my life was when I was married.

'And you'll never be alone,' Sherna added. 'We are all there for you. We'll support you no matter what you decide.'

'I can't decide anything right now. Frankly, I'm surprised I'm even able to talk about this. What does that say about me?'

'It says that you did the right thing. Silence is not the answer to violence.'

I grunt.

'Listen, you are in the last stage of the five stages of grief: shock, denial, anger, depression and acceptance. You've accepted the truth. That's huge! Congratulations!'

'What congratulations? That would make my whole marriage a funeral,' I said wistfully.

'Stop it! You're still young and alive! There's so much you still have to do with your life.'

'How will I do anything with my life when I can't even take the first step towards changing it?'

'The first step is the hardest,' Sherna said. 'You'll be fine once you're out of that toxic environment. You are stronger than you know.'

'I am not strong.'

'Stop it, Manu. You're the strongest woman I know. Take your time. If you want to give your marriage a last shot and see if it works, do that. Otherwise let it go. Till then, cheers! I cannot party with this sad Maneka. Bring my old friend back!'

I laughed and said 'Cheers!'

We drank some more and went home. Sherna didn't let me leave till after lunch the next day. I messaged Suneet that I'd be home by 3 p.m. When I got home, he was there, smoking away.

'Sorry, I got a little late,' I said. 'Sherna made sali boti and didn't let me leave till I ate it. She's packed some for you. It's delicious.'

He got up. I saw that he had a duffel bag next to him. He walked out of the house. I stared after him. I had no clue where he was going, or when he was returning.

A man obsessed with punishing his wife can never let her love him.

Two days later, I spoke to Farah. It was her birthday. She'd had a party I didn't go for because I wasn't ready to show my friends who I'd become. She said she was sad not to see me. She hesitated.

'What, babe?' I asked.

'Look, I don't know whether I should tell you. Suneet came to my party. He was acting odd. When someone asked him where you were, he said, "How the fuck should I know". I'm sorry babe.'

'It's okay,' I said.

'Everyone is worried now. Is everything okay with you guys?' she asked.

'Everything's fine,' I said, furious that Suneet had made our private problems public.

When he reappeared at 2 a.m. on Tuesday morning, I couldn't go back to sleep. I went to the living room and saw him stir on the futon.

'Suneet, why did you go for Farah's party without me and then let everyone know we're having problems?'

'What? I didn't say anything to anyone. Your friends are all liars,' he said.

What was I expecting from my husband? Honesty?

'I see that you're deliberately pushing me away, Suneet,' I spoke to him calmly. 'I've never crossed the lines that you've once again crossed with me. I have been as kind as I could over the past months. I didn't leave your side in your time of need, and I hope you appreciate that. But I've also understood that you no longer want or need me here. I will begin packing my things and leave. Since you don't want to talk to me, you can drop me an email. I'll reply. I would appreciate it if those emails aren't forwarded to everyone in your family.'

'I think you should leave,' he said. He got up.

'That's what I just said,' I said plainly.

'But not for the reasons you think. If you're not going to give me money and are going to behave irresponsibly about money, then you get out of the house.'

I stared at him. What?

'Where is this coming from? I just had $3000 deposited in our joint account last week, from my salary and articles.'

'You've never given me anything.'

Well, if he wanted to keep score—'Should I remind you of the money I got from my savings in India, Suneet, which covered our rent for ten months? Or the fact that you haven't earned a penny since we got married, and we're still living here because of me?'

'You're wasting all that money going out with your friends and eating out.'

'I haven't gone out with a single friend, except Sherna three days ago. She insisted on paying. And I haven't eaten out in months! The only outside food I've been able to afford is a freaking $3 falafel from a cart.'

'Please. What do you eat in office? You don't look like you're starving yourself. Obviously you're hiding money to spend on buying lunch for yourself.'

God, he was petty.

'I've been packing lunch from home every day, so we can tide over. If you were awake in the morning or not out all the time, you would notice this.'

'What about your clothes and shoes?'

I looked at my $10 sweater and my $20 snow boots. Both had been bought in January last year when I'd just moved here. They were fraying because of their cheap quality.

'Seriously?' I said and held up my sweater that had a tear in it. 'I've not shopped since the day you told me about KMAT. You can't accuse me of making frivolous purchases when you're spending our money on weed!'

'I don't pay for that,' he said dismissively.

'Then who does?' I asked.

He blinked nervously. Fuck, it was Tammy. Why did I ask?

He quickly said: 'You withdrew a big amount of money without telling me.'

'How can I tell you anything when you refuse to talk to me? I bought a laptop for work. They're paying me for it in India. I'm getting that money transferred here, don't worry.'

'I don't need your charity.'

'Look, Suneet. Instead of always assuming that I'm doing something wrong, let's take a moment to look at what you've been doing. You withdrew all the money from our bank account without telling me. I don't know where it's gone. Was that responsible?'

'It was my parents' money. I had to pay them back.'

'Pay them back for what?'

'My tuition.'

'But Samit paid for that.'

He didn't reply. He was lying.

'At this time, when we have little money, what's the urgency to give them everything we have?' I didn't add that his parents had pointedly told us after he was thrown out of university that they wouldn't give us any money. 'Suneet, I have told you to do some consulting work so you can make a little money, but you're not doing that. You haven't been looking for a job here or in Dubai or in India. You haven't used any of the referrals I've recommended.'

'Why the fuck should I find a job when my wife is earning?'

I stared at him blankly.

'Because of your carelessness,' he continued, 'I had to borrow money from Bharti. A full $2000. Do you know how humiliating that was?'

I looked at him. I could tell that he was lying again.

'Excuse me,' I said. I went outside the house and dialled Bharti's number. It was before midnight in San Fran and she didn't sleep till 3 a.m. anyway. After a minute of chit-chat, I asked her, point-blank, whether Suneet had borrowed money from her. She sounded confused and said no. Sorry about this, I said. If I hadn't called her immediately he would've told her to lie. I walked back into the house.

'Bharti says she hasn't given you anything. Why do you keep lying, Suneet?'

I looked at him. He must have withdrawn the money and kept it for himself and—as usual—suspected me of doing something he himself was doing wrong. What a strange, complicated man! He assumed that the worst in him was also the worst in others.

I wasn't surprised. His parents were the same.

He stormed out of the living room and into the bathroom. I went to the kitchen and made chai for both of us. My head was hurting. But I was determined to reach a conclusion that day.

He came back after ten minutes and said, 'Look, I'm sorry about everything, Manu, especially my unreasonable behaviour.'

'Sit down, Suneet. Have some chai. We need to talk properly.'

He sipped from his cup like a helpless kitten. How did his demeanour change so quickly?

'You know it's too late for apologies, Suneet. You've broken my heart. You've left me wanting to tear the skin from my bones to stop the pain I've been feeling. I'm always crying. I'm miserable. And somehow you've become so insensitive that you only see what I do, not what you do to provoke that reaction. I think I've tolerated enough. It's time for me to go.'

'No, no,' he said, getting up. He made me sit on the sofa. 'I know it's been tough. You are an amazing person. You have been so strong and supportive. You deserve everything good in the world. I can never repay you for what you've done for me. And I promise I'll be a good husband from now on. Don't go anywhere.'

He began crying.

'I want to ask you something, Suneet,' I said. 'And please tell me honestly. Are you suffering from depression?'

No, he said, as if the thought had not even occurred to him.

I was surprised. One of the reasons I'd been hanging on was because I thought he was depressed. I couldn't leave a person alone if they were depressed. It was not human.

'Is it possible for you to talk to a psychiatrist? I think it will help you, Suneet.'

I wanted him to hear from a professional that what he was doing was wrong.

'You're the one who needs a psychiatrist, Maneka.'

I took a deep breath. I needed to stay focused and calm. I could not get provoked.

'Look, if you think you're fine, then it's time I left. There is no reason for me to stay.'

Losing him would be like losing a heart. The blood would have no place to go. But, it was time.

He fell at my feet. 'No! I love you, baby. Isn't that a good enough reason to stay?'

I shook my head. I was frozen and bloodless with fear and anxiety. But I had to go.

'Suneet, I kept making excuses for your behaviour. You were young. You were going through a bad phase. You were depressed. You didn't know what you were doing. You needed time, you needed help. Then I realized that you hit me before you were thrown out of university. That you were not young, you were older than I was. That you continued doing what you were doing after your "bad" phase was over. I can't keep justifying the way you're acting anymore.'

I kept blaming the circumstances, when I should've seen that it's not the circumstances that define a man, but his behaviour during those circumstances.

'Don't say that, baby. The walls of this house are asking for you, they're singing your name. You can't leave us.' I wondered what version of this he would spin to his family. 'You can't leave me. Please. I'm begging you. I will change.'

'Okay,' I said wearily. 'Let's talk about this tomorrow. I'm exhausted.'

I picked him up from my feet. He hugged me. To show that he was going to be a good husband, he said he'd do the laundry the first thing tomorrow morning. It had been six months since he had done anything in the house.

'Cool,' I said.

I put my head down on my pillow. This man continued to exhaust me. I needed a break.

When I woke up the next morning, I found myself buried under a pile of soiled clothes.

'What the hell!' I shouted. I threw the clothes off me.

He came storming into the room. 'You're such a lazy cunt. You sleep all day. You've even left the housework to me. Fuck off! I don't need this.'

What was wrong with this man? How did his mood swing like a pendulum?

'You're the reason we are where we are!' he continued shouting. 'My mother was right. You're a *panvati* (bad luck) to my family and me.'

That was it. I grabbed a pair of scissors from the drawer, picked up a T-shirt lying closest to me and cut it into pieces.

'You bitch,' he came towards me with his hand raised.

'Do it. It will give me evidence for the police,' I said coldly.

He hesitated and pulled back his hand.

'Last night was clearly a mistake,' I said. 'You told me you wanted to work things out. That's why I stayed.'

'You are a mistake. I don't want to talk to you ever again.' He stormed out of the house.

Tragedy doesn't change us, it reveals us.

I didn't hate him. What I felt for him was the opposite of love, but it wasn't hate. That would come later. There was no word for this feeling. What he felt for me was also not hate. But it was also not love. What he felt for me, what feelings I aroused in him to treat me the way he did, was something he couldn't explain. More so to himself than anyone else. Because he was not bringing my story into our lives. He was bringing his. The untold part of it that he didn't recognize because he didn't know his own story. It was sad, but I knew it was time to write myself out of his story.

This time, I was not scared to lose anything.

When he came back home an hour later, I told him that this marriage was not working. It was best if we took time out and separated. It was time we both stopped circling the ring.

The words coming out of my mouth did not surprise me.

From the lack of shock on his face, they didn't surprise him either.

He asked me if I wanted a divorce. I told him not yet, we could both work on ourselves and decide the best course of action later.

It was not that I didn't know how to end a relationship. Breaking up was something I'd never been afraid of. I'd broken up with the first and deepest love of my life, Aarav, who had cheated on me. I'd broken up with the wonderful Swiss boy, Mark, whose only fault was that he loved me too much. But I hadn't reached the point of no return with Suneet. This wasn't because he was better than my ex-boyfriends. He was just luckier. Because—despite my age, despite my generation—I considered marriage sacred. I considered breaking it taboo. The institution made me want to stay, even if the man didn't.

'You can't leave me like this,' he said. He started crying again. 'I love you.'

'This crap is not going to work this time,' I said firmly.

'I can't live in this house without you,' he said.

I took a breath.

'So, don't. Move to Samit's house.'

'We can't break the rental lease. And I can't afford the rent.'

'Find a subtenant.'

He looked like he was going to faint.

You don't kick a bleeding dog.

'Look, here's what we'll do, Suneet. I'll stay for a bit to help wrap things up around the house. We'll find a subtenant. After that, I'll leave. Does that sound fair?'

'Yes,' he said.

'While I'm here, I request you to please behave. I don't want any tantrums and bad behaviour. I can't take it anymore.'

'I promise,' he said. He hugged me.

I spent the entire first weekend deep-cleaning so we could show the house to potential subtenants. Then, I sorted his boxes from Boston, which he still hadn't bothered to open, and packed them away in our little storage closet. I then organized things around the house into *hers* and *his*, things he could keep and things I could keep. I sat him down one Saturday and went through each item to ask what he wanted. He wanted the Bart Simpson beer glasses someone had gifted us. I kept the candle stand we'd bought in Hawaii. A good three or four weeks passed. I didn't once ask for, nor did he offer, his help. I didn't want to speak to him more than was absolutely necessary. I didn't want to engage in any arguments. I just wanted to get out of that house knowing I'd been fair. I spent the next three weeks packing up my things. I couldn't afford storage, so I began keeping my belongings in the American-sized lockers behind my desk at office. Every morning I'd get up at 5 a.m., pack, lug a suitcase in the subway, up and down escalators and ramps and pavements, pass it through the heavy security at the New York Stock Exchange and avoid the strange looks that the guards gave me. I'd reach office at 7.30 a.m., before anyone else got in, and quietly tuck things away. The first time my colleagues saw me with a suitcase, they joked that I was living at JFK airport. I smiled. The joke got sour when they saw me doing this almost every day. They were too polite to ask or joke about it again.

I worked up a draft for the tenant hunt. I still sent Suneet job resources. I was still making his food, grocery shopping, doing the laundry, making the bed and picking up his damn socks, among the hundred other things that he kept throwing on the floor.

The day I was leaving, I put the knife under my pillow back in the kitchen. I gazed, one last time, at the house I had built and been destroyed in. I sat on the chairs I had spent a day at IKEA to buy. I ran my hand over the walls where I had been choked. I lay down on the bed where I had written stories to escape from my reality. I smiled at the bathtub where I had spent days studying. I bought an Entenmann chocolate fudge cake and put it outside the front door of my neighbour, whose newspapers I had used for a year; my apology. I stared at the broken kirpan hanging above the TV. It no longer had a hold over me.

Suneet was dropping me to Sherna's house in Samit's car. On the way there, he stopped the car.

'I want to say two things,' he said.

'Okay,' I said, looking out at the pier. There was a whole world out there that I had missed. Seagulls were dipping in and out of the water. Boats were swaying like drunk lovers. Parents were taking their children for a walk, holding hands, love still in existence.

'You have not had a responsible attitude towards the end. I am very disappointed.'

I continued staring ahead of me.

He stayed silent for a few minutes. I saw him clutch the steering wheel till his hands turned white.

'I also want to tell you that I love you. No matter what mistakes you have made.'

I didn't react.

'I want you to remember that we're still married. Separation is not a license to cheat.' Is marriage a license then, I wanted to ask, thinking about Tammy. 'Promise me that you'll not cross any lines.'

I turned to him. 'I am not the one who has crossed the lines in this marriage. And trust me, this is not because of you but because I still believe in the sanctity of the institution.'

He got his reply. Pleased, as if he had won a trophy, he drove me to Sherna's place. He helped me take my stuff up to her house. And then he left.

At last there was peace.

CHAPTER EIGHTEEN

FOR TWO months, I neither dwelt on Suneet nor our marriage. I slept on Sherna's couch, then Farha's. I got my health back in order. I got back into shape. I started attending writing classes. I began writing a novel and a book of short stories. I went to Cape May and Cape Cod with my friends. My mood was lifting as the dense cold gripping the city also lifted. Spring was New York's most beautiful time. Staying in the city was wonderful. I walked all the time, exploring nooks and corners. There was an air of gloom—with businesses shutting down and shutters declaring bankruptcy almost everywhere—but despite that New York's spirit remained merry. I wanted to learn from that.

I had told my parents of my separation. They insisted on coming to visit me. I was excited to see my parents and brother after almost eighteen months! My only issue was finding them a place to stay. I still wasn't sure if I was going to live in New York or move, so I didn't want to commit to a lease. I wished they had come when I had a house, but Suneet had never once invited them, and I hadn't seen a window in the tumultuous time I'd lived with him. So, I sublet an apartment in Manhattan for the three weeks they were there. The day they arrived, I wore a blonde wig to the airport, just for fun! Their worry turned to laughter when they saw me. I smiled. I didn't want my family to associate me with the broken image that had been painted of me during the time they hadn't seen me. I wanted them to know that breaking was healing.

When we reached the building where I'd rented an apartment, we realized it was a walk-up; there was no lift. Despite the fact that they'd left their house in India almost two days ago and were barely able to keep their eyes open, they lugged their suitcases up cheerfully. They didn't complain that we had to share a room, that my aloo-matar was too watery and that my brother and I had to sleep on the floor in sleeping bags. I had become so accustomed to non-stop criticism that I'd forgotten what it was like to be loved despite your mistakes.

It was good to have them here with me.

They loved New York. I loved discovering New York with them. We took the boat to the Statue of Liberty. We took photos with the naked cowboy at Times Square. I made them try hot dogs on Fifth Avenue. We ate peanut butter ice cream with crushed M&Ms from my favourite Cold Stone Creamery. We popped our ears at the top of the Empire State Building. They rang the mock opening bell with me at the New York Stock Exchange.

We didn't talk about my marriage or Suneet.

But, one day, my father saw me withdrawing money from an ATM.

'Why is your balance just $30?' he asked.

I was too embarrassed to tell my parents that their almost twenty-nine-year-old daughter was almost broke.

'Don't worry, Papa,' I mumbled. 'This is just a timepass account. My main money is in another account with another bank.'

'And how much money is in this other account?'

I couldn't say $120.

'Don't worry,' I said. 'My salary will be credited in two days.'

'Is that why you're making us walk everywhere?' he asked.

Taxis were expensive and the subway, for the four of us, would've been $8.

'Is that why the waiter was so angry at that restaurant yesterday?'

After a lovely Ethiopian meal with honey wine, I had left a 10 per cent tip, instead of the 20 per cent that Manhattan restaurants expected. The waiter had actually run after me and asked what he had done wrong. I'd never been more embarrassed.

'You should not have insisted on paying, Manu beta. We've been telling you from the beginning,' he said. 'What is this formality with your own family?'

But how could I let my own family know how low I'd fallen?

They refused to let me pay for anything after that.

A week later, my parents told me that Suneet had emailed, saying he'd like to meet them.

'How does he know you're here?' I asked them.

'We called him before leaving and told him,' my father said.

'Why?'

'He's still our son-in-law, Manu. It would've been rude not to,' my mother said. 'It would've created more problems for you if we hadn't.'

My parents knew the ways of the world.

They told him to meet us at Central Park in two days. We were having a picnic. I hadn't seen my husband in months. He had shaved. His eyes were no longer red. He didn't look like the world had hurled him over. I was glad to see that. While we all sat on a mat making polite conversation, I offered to make him a sandwich. He declined. He refused to make eye contact with me. Finally, when my brother and I went to the nearby swings, he told my parents that he wanted to speak to them and that it would have to be indoors as the park was making him uncomfortable. He said he would come to the apartment we were staying at in three days. When he came, he again refused to look at me. I ignored him too. He said he would like my brother and I to leave. I was glad to. I took my brother to Staten Island and we had a blast catching up along the harbour. By the time we returned, three hours later, Suneet had left and my parents were each nursing a vodka-Coke.

'Was it as bad as you expected?' I joked.

They smiled sadly. I could see they were trying to hide their annoyance.

They told me that Suneet had spent the entire time saying nasty things about me and analysing how badly I had treated his family and him.

'So, he repeated the same stuff he'd written in his eek-mails to you,' I said.

I opened a beer and sat down. I still hadn't told my parents what exactly he had done, not only to protect him, but to protect them, and—in many ways—myself.

'Yes, but he also said he's not left the US because he's waiting for you to decide the way forward,' my mother said.

'You have to make a decision about your marriage, Manu,' my father said. 'You can't avoid it.'

I changed the topic. 'Why didn't you stop him from talking nonsense about me?'

'He didn't pause once in the conversation,' my father said. He rubbed his forehead.

'The monologue, you mean?' I asked. We smiled.

'You must also understand that as the girl's parents it's tough for us to argue with our son-in-law,' my mother said.

'It shouldn't be that way. We're in the twenty-first century. His parents have no qualms talking badly to me. You should not hesitate to tell him when he's being rude.'

'We don't want to make things worse,' my father said.

'Worse? His in-laws are visiting his town for the first time, and he's not once asked if he can show you around, take you out or help in any way. He deserves your worst.'

'Forget keeping score, Manu. You'll be happy to know that we interrupted him once, when he said: "Maneka lies". We told him he was taking it too far. We've never caught you lying.'

I was thankful they put him in his place at least once.

'He said that you want a husband who does whatever you say,' my mother smiled.

'Yes, because that's what he is: easy-going . . . . adjusting . . . accommodating!'

We laughed. It was good to be able to joke about how ridiculous Suneet could be.

'He also said that since you've "hurt his parents" they expect an email from you.'

I stopped laughing. 'How can they say that after the way they've ill-treated me?'

My parents didn't know what to say. They couldn't imagine treating anyone this way.

I could see that the conversation with Suneet had taken a toll on them. They were straightforward people who lived and let others live. It was difficult to explain to them the complexities involved with Suneet and his family. But I had to speak to them frankly about what was happening. I told them everything.

My mother told me to leave him, but my father was more realistic. 'Listen, do what's best for you, but leaving him will not make your life easier. No one in our family has ever been divorced. You will be ostracized by people. It's 2009, but people still gossip horribly about divorcees, especially women. Be aware of what your life will be after divorce. It's going to be more difficult, not less than it is now. Whatever you decide, do it with your eyes wide open.'

We didn't know divorce the way we didn't know death. No wonder it was scary.

I rubbed my forehead. I had put my marriage and Suneet out of my mind for the past few months. Talking about him was like diving back into the quicksand I'd crawled out of.

'Honestly, I don't know what to do. I want to leave him. But I also don't.'

'Look, Manu,' my mother said. 'No one can help you reach a decision about your own marriage. It is entirely up to you. But you have to decide fast. He is staying back here for you. He's put his career and life on hold for you. Think about that. Think of the way forward. What will make you happy?'

'I don't know,' I said. 'I can leave the marriage without guilt only after I know I've done everything to save it. The problem is that because of the issues his brother and he faced last year, I don't know if Suneet is acting out, or if this is who he is. If I don't know the man I've married, how can I decide the fate of the marriage? Maybe we didn't give it a proper shot. Maybe if the circumstances were different, we would be a different couple.'

'Look, whatever has happened, let it be water under the bridge,' my father said. 'Suneet has been through a lot and doesn't have the maturity to deal with it. He wants to reconcile.

That's why he's still here. You were okay letting him meet us. Maybe you also want to give this marriage another shot?'

'Let me figure it out,' I told my parents. 'Let's not spoil our trip for this.'

We didn't. We went kayaking in the Pocono Mountains. We watched Lion King on Broadway. We ate chocolate pizza at Chocolate by the Bald Man. We attended my cousin's wedding in Toronto. We danced under the Niagara Falls. We drank ice wine and Tim Hortons coffee. We met friends and relatives. We had a lovely time. When my family left I knew my happiness was leaving with them.

But I had to find a way to it again.

I moved back into Sherna's place.

*

'Do you really want to get back with him after all this?' she asked me. Sherna and I were at the Costco store, buying food in sizes I couldn't believe were real.

'I don't know. I don't want to get back with him. But I'm also not ready to get divorced. I'm twenty-nine. My biological clock is ticking. I want to have children. I don't want to be alone.'

'Don't hold back because you think you'll end up alone. You will meet other men, better men, who'll treat you right. Have kids with them.'

Is it better for a dog to drink from its own dish or to roam the streets dipping its tongue into every dirty puddle?

'Finding another man will take too long, Sherna. I may not be able to have kids by then. And, honestly, all men are eventually the same. They all have some issue or the other. At least my husband is a known devil.'

Sherna picked up a block of cheddar cheese and said, 'Manu, people will not treat you the way *they* think you deserve, but the way *you* think you deserve. Don't undermine yourself like this.'

'Deep,' I said. 'Can I bite into the cheddar? I'm quite hungry.'

'Be serious, babe. Are you a bougainvillea or an orchid?'

'What?'

'You can treat a bougainvillea appallingly, keep it without water and it will still grow. But an orchid demands everything of you. It needs bright sunlight but not too much, you water it but not too much, and only then will it reward you.'

'Sherna, I can't think so much right now. I'm sick of overthinking everything.'

'You know the answer even when you don't,' she said. 'Here.'

She handed me the block of cheese. I opened the plastic wrap and bit into it.

Sherna leaned over and kissed me on the forehead, like I was a little girl.

She was right. The sun does not ask the planets to revolve around it. They do so of their own accord. It's a compulsion. Why was I even thinking of getting back with Suneet? I knew the answer but it sounded so ridiculous, given my upbringing, that I couldn't say it out loud even to my best friend. I had always been so eager to be a perfect woman—an excellent student, a well-mannered girl, a good daughter, a good sister, a good friend. I couldn't even imagine the impact a failure as public as divorce would have on my image. Back in India, it was assumed that only crazy, barren or evil women got divorced. As a divorcee, I would be assumed to be either. I would never be perfect again. I would always be flawed. I wasn't ready for that.

I wasn't ready to be seen as a failure after being a success all my life. Especially when it was not my fault.

'Look, I can lie down in the shopping cart,' I said. 'It's so big!'

Sherna laughed. 'I miss this. I miss who you were: goofy and fun.'

I smiled. I missed it too. I knew I would never be happy the way I was before marriage, not in that carefree reckless way, anyway. But I also knew that happiness was not about wanting what didn't come to you, but accepting what did.

As we were walking back to the parking lot, lugging two heavy shopping carts, Sherna told me that if I wanted to get back with Suneet, I'd have to do it with a plan in mind. 'Don't be impulsive and straightforward like you normally are. You'll have to operate like they operate, but you will also have to be the bigger person, because he'll never be. Suneet basically wants you to act like everything was your fault. So, write an email owning up to the mistakes he thinks you made. Stroke his ego. And then gently address what he did without accusing him. Then list down some conditions you need for the marriage to work. Things that were making you unhappy.'

'Pushing this cart is easier than that,' I joked, as I panted.

The next day, I wrote him an email.

'Will you read it?' I asked Sherna.

'It's private.'

'I want to operate like they operate.'

She smiled and read it.

'Too angry,' Sherna said.

'Don't I have reason to be?'

'Not if you want to reconcile. Listen, are you sure about this?'

I nodded. I was sure that I didn't want to be divorced and alone.

'Okay, then let's do it properly,' Sherna said. 'For example, remove the part about him hitting you. It's a deal-breaker. Say you might have over-reacted or misunderstood his intent.'

'No, that won't be right.'

'Look, Manu. Being who you are is not working with him. So, if you want to remain married, then be *chalu*, like his mother.'

I wrote the email admitting the ways in which I could've 'acted better' while listing his mistakes, including hitting me. I had to mention that. He replied saying he was glad that 'I was looking at what I had done wrong' but circumvented his issues. He said he would like to meet me. I agreed. When I saw him at a restaurant in Newport, I was glad that I'd worn the red lace dress Sherna had insisted upon. I realized that this was the first date we had gone on since we got married. This made me happy. He told me he was studying for his KMAT and would take it in two months. He told me that he was settled nicely in Samit's house and that our subtenant was not giving any trouble. He insisted on ordering me a Long Island Iced Tea, though he knew I was a lightweight. I got tipsy. We kissed.

'It's like the love never went anywhere,' he whispered at the end of the night.

When I was a little girl, my father would tell me on moonless nights that the moon had to go away in order to shine. It wasn't very different with love.

Suneet said that one meeting would not resolve anything. We had to meet more often. The cement of my soul was still wet. I was still open to changing my heart. I moved out of Sherna's house and rented a place in Newport, close to Samit's house.

Suneet and I met. We talked for hours. We heard each other out. We listened to one other. If listening was loving then this was love. By the time summer ended, we were back together. And it was nice. I took him for a spectacular show of Cirque du Soleil. I bought two tickets for the US Open. We walked across the Brooklyn Bridge hand-in-hand. He threatened to kill someone who was rude to me on the subway. He read every short story I'd written and edited them. He helped me move into a tiny rent-controlled apartment in Manhattan that I would share with a friend's girlfriend. He was attentive and loving. When I was invited by the Prime Minister's Office to the White House during Diwali, he came as my plus one. On his thirtieth birthday, I took him for an expensive dinner to Central Park's Loeb Boathouse with the extra money I was now earning from writing articles. We took a buggy ride, which was considered a benchmark of romance in New York.

One day, he came home and showed me a printout. 'Surprise! I got a 760.'

It was his KMAT score. A sign that he was ready to move forward with his life. It had been fifteen months since that night we'd received KMAC's email. I hugged him so tight he said his ribs would crack.

'We must celebrate,' I told him. 'Let's go out for dinner. My treat.'

'Isn't it always?' he said and hugged me. 'I love being a kept man.'

Once we had ordered our food and a glass of wine each, he said, 'I am so happy, jaanu. I can't wait for us to move to Dubai now.'

I froze.

'Dubai? I thought you were leaning towards India?'

'No. Not at all. I haven't lived in that country since I was fifteen. I have nothing to do with it.'

I didn't want to react. After all the progress we had made, it was pointless to dredge up his old habit of leaving me out of his life-changing decisions.

'And when——'

'I've decided to move next month. My parents have lined up interviews for me. I'm sure with Dad's contacts, I'll get a job soon.'

I drank the whole glass of wine in one gulp.

'Suneet, are you sure Dubai is a good idea? Are you doing it for the right reasons? India is a better option for us.'

'India is shit for me. I know no one there.'

'I do. I've sent you loads of leads. You haven't followed up. India is not hit by the recession. We'll be much better off there.'

'I prefer Dubai. I grew up there. I have friends there. My parents are there.'

He prioritized his parents even when it came to his career.

'Babe, trust me. I've weighed the pros and cons,' he said, without telling me what these were. 'I know you're apprehensive about moving to Dubai, but keep an open mind. Right now we need stability and that's what Dubai will offer us.'

'Are you sure, Suneet?'

'I promise you I have a plan. I will go to Dubai and find a job. You join me two months later, once I'm settled in. I'll work for a year in Dubai. During that time I'll send out my applications for a one-year MBA programme. I'll finish my MBA by 2012. I'll get a nice job and you can finally be a kept woman.'

I ignored his joke.

I took a deep breath, 'And where will we live in Dubai?'

He knew what I was asking. 'With Maa and Dad, of course,' he said. He looked at the chicken mince pie he had ordered. 'But that's temporary. Once you come, we'll move out.'

I felt as if a knife had been plunged into my heart. I couldn't breathe.

'Babe, relax. I promise you I'll keep a lookout for an apartment for us. We'll hardly be at their place. Chill.'

He smiled at me. I tried to gather a smile on my face.

There was silence at the table for a minute.

'What about . . . starting a family, Suneet? Have you even thought about that?'

'Look, I know you want kids, but this is not the right time. We are not financially stable. You will have to wait.'

'For how long?' I asked. I would be thirty next year.

'By the time I'm done with my MBA in 2012, you'll be thirty-two. You'll probably still be able to have kids. I promise you we'll try immediately and we'll be fine.'

'But . . . Suneet. You should've discussed this with me. This impacts my life directly. You decided all this without even asking me what I thought.'

'Look, I know you weren't expecting to have to move countries again or be the sole breadwinner or have kids late . . . but you're a strong girl. I expect you to be past all that.'

Past all what, I wanted to ask. I had already moved to a foreign country for his sake. I had given up a good career, a cushy lifestyle, family and friends, to be with him in the US. Yet, he had left me to fend for myself here. I was living in a house I could cover in four steps, picking pennies from the road and working non-stop, like a dog, to survive a life into which he had thrown me. I had done all this while seeing him, day after day, sitting at home achieving nothing. I had done all this without complaint, without making his life difficult. Still, he felt no hesitation in asking me to move to a country I didn't care for to live with people I couldn't stand.

'You can't keep taking me for granted like this, Suneet,' I whispered. I held back my tears. I couldn't breathe at the thought of living with my in-laws again. I couldn't imagine moving to a country where I knew no one. I couldn't gather the strength to once again uproot my life to find a new job, build a new home, make new friends, just because he was asking me to.

'Babe, that's marriage. Husbands and wives take each other for granted because that's what love is.' He put his hand on mine and wiped a tear with the other. 'Look, I know you have it in you to be a good wife. I can see that now. And it makes me want to be a good husband. We will make this work. Let's just wade through the shit that's been thrown at us. We're almost at the finish line. Be patient. We're better than most couples, and we will show them that.'

Show *whom what*? My red flags rang. I told them to quiet down.

'It's this or divorce,' a voice said to me. 'It's this or childlessness.'

It was one of the hardest decisions of my life, and I made it in a minute.

'Fine,' I told him. 'Let's move to Dubai.'

If you reach the edge of a mountain and there's no bridge, how do you get to the other side? You learn to fly. I was learning to fly.

CHAPTER NINETEEN

'THERE'S LESS sugar in the tea,' he said, his voice like fingernails scratching a blackboard.

I went back to the kitchen. I'd tried to stay on in the US for as long as I could. When the time came, I quit my job reluctantly. I walked my favourite streets in Manhattan and bid them goodbye. I cried and laughed when seven of my closest girlfriends took me for a farewell weekend to the Hamptons. Where would I find such good friends again? I wasn't ready to go to Dubai. So, I visited my folks in Mumbai for one-two-three-four months, and let myself be. I needed time to catch my breath before the sprint of marriage began again. Suneet kept calling me on Magic Jack and Google chat, ending each conversation with, 'When are you coming here?' Part of him felt I wouldn't return to him. Part of me didn't want to. What was the temptation to live with a family I despised and who despised me? Why would I want to move to a place where I knew no one except the three of them? Then, a close friend had a baby. Another celebrated his fifth wedding anniversary. My friends were all living the life that I wanted. The life that I thought I deserved. If everyone around me could be happy, why couldn't I?

I poured sugar into a bowl till it was a quarter full, the way he liked it, put a spoon on the tray and put it down in front of him. My hands were trembling.

'What's wrong with you?' he snapped. 'Is this the correct spoon to stir tea with?'

I looked blankly at my father-in-law.

'Get a teaspoon, not a tablespoon. Haven't your parents taught you anything?'

My days in Dubai were awful. I'd wake up at 6.30 a.m. and go straight to the kitchen to make breakfast. After serving it to my father-in-law, who left for work at 7.30 a.m., I would pack Suneet's lunch, mainly leftovers from dinner, have breakfast with him and see him off at 8.30 a.m. and my mother-in-law at 9 a.m. That's when the part-time cleaner, who did the mopping, dusting and bathroom, would come. My mother-in-law had given me strict instructions to follow him from room to room to ensure that he was cleaning properly and not stealing. The act was so stalkerish that I didn't do it the first few times. Somehow she figured this out. She yelled at me in front of Suneet. I wanted to ask who had monitored the chap before, but the cleaner grumbled to me about how they had changed his work timings since I was home. They had done it to increase my workload. After the cleaner left, I cooked lunch and had a quick bath. My mother-in-law went to school to teach for only four hours and returned home by 1 p.m. I had to serve her lunch. My father-in-law worked six hours a day and was back home by 2.30 p.m. I had to serve his lunch as my mother-in-law napped. I would have to wait in the kitchen till they finished their meals to see if they wanted refills, and then clear their dirty dishes and wash them. I then got one hour free at 3 p.m. I would write during this time. At 4 p.m., I had to return to the kitchen, make tea and serve it to them. By 5 p.m., I had to begin making dinner. Suneet usually came home by 7 p.m. The serving of dinner, eating it and doing the dishes went on till 10 p.m. I was on my feet for more than fourteen hours a day, most of them spent in the kitchen. When my friends and family joked that I was a woman of leisure in Dubai—with no job and working in-laws—I didn't know what to say.

My mother-in-law nagged me throughout the day about everything and anything—from the shape and colour of the groceries I was buying—snap each bhindi at its end, tap the melon and see if it's hollow, check each palak leaf for holes—to the way I cut the vegetables—lauki must be cut in 1-cm strips, cauliflower in 3-cm strips—to the order in which I was putting spices in the tadka—first add jeera, then chilli powder, then garam masala, then haldi—to the way I was washing dishes—rinse each dish before putting it in the dishwasher, with the cups on the top right, the glasses on the top left—to the way I was cooking—soak the rice for twenty minutes before boiling it, throw out the excess water and let it simmer for ten minutes before serving. 'It's my house and things have to be done my way . . . I don't run my house as carelessly as you ran yours in New York' were some of her relentless taunts. Then she'd bitch about how badly I made chapattis and go back to watching TV in the guest room, where she also slept. I didn't dare ask any of them why she didn't sleep in the same room as her husband. The monster that Suneet had unleashed on me lurked just beneath the surface in his parents. In my dreams, the three of them would lock me in the kitchen and burn me to death. Now that I was at their mercy, I realized that this was not impossible. I was petrified of them.

I washed a teaspoon and gave it to my father-in-law. He complained that the tea had become cold. A week ago my father-in-law had come home a little earlier from work. I was taking a shower. He was apparently hungry. He served himself the food. By the time I came out of my room, he was in a terrible mood. He snapped at me about how irresponsible I was and told me to pick up his plate. Later that evening, Suneet also snapped at me, and both men didn't talk to me for two days. Like his son, this man could carry a grudge.

'I'll warm up the tea,' I said, trying hard not to lose my mind.

'Don't you have any sense?' he said. 'I don't drink reheated tea. Make me a fresh cup, quickly. You've made me wait long enough as it is.'

I had never wanted a job more desperately in my life. But there were no jobs available. The global recession had chipped the gold off Dubai's shine. People were leaving their Maseratis at the airport. My father-in-law told me point-blank that I would have to change careers as he knew no one in media but many in banking. He had never approved of my job, or rather the salary that came with being a journalist. I didn't care. He had told me that the media in Dubai was like the democracy in China: non-existent; glorified public relations, where so-called journalists copy-pasted press releases and called it news. So, I dug into my knowledge of economics and finance from my MBA days, studying it mostly over the kitchen countertop, and went for job interviews. It was brutal. The interviews highlighted how mismatched I was with the world of banking, especially at a time when banks had applications from unemployed Wharton and Harvard graduates. I wasted six months on this.

I made a fresh cup of tea, certain that I'd set a new world record by spending an hour on making one cup of tea. Then, I went to my room and lay down. It was time for me to make dinner, but I didn't care. I was a metal they were forging into the shape they wanted. But I was out of sparks and reaching the point of breaking. I stared at the TV in front of me.

I had asked Suneet whether we could connect the TV in our room to the cable. 'How can you ask for such luxuries when you're not even making money?' he'd snapped. I asked him a few more times, but he refused. The only person allowed to watch TV in this house was my mother-in-law. She did that all day, usually till two in the morning. Even my father-in-law was allowed to watch news and sports only for an hour every night at 8.30 p.m. 'Watch TV in the guest room, like we all do, with the family, or not at all,' Suneet said.

I didn't say anything after that. Avoiding unhappiness was my only road to happiness. That forlorn, unused TV in my room became a reminder of how many things, like forgotten love, don't live up to their potential.

I got up to go to the kitchen. I was no better than a servant in this house. I had no rights. I had no voice. I had no joy. All I was expected to do was to wait on all three of them hand and foot.

A month after moving to Dubai I had asked Suneet if we could hire a cook, 'Please babe. It's exhausting making four meals a day, day after day.'

'I'm not asking my parents to pay for a cook,' he snapped.

'We'll pay for it.'

'We? I am not wasting my hard-earned money to indulge your stupid whims.'

I took a deep breath. It's amazing how I'd started thinking this was a normal way to talk.

'Fine. I'll pay for it,' I said.

'With what? Your parents' money? Stop throwing that around. We all know your parents are richer than mine, okay?'

They weren't richer. They were just not stingy.

'Suneet, please! Can't you listen to me for once?'

'Stop behaving like the spoilt princess that you are, Maneka. Thank your stars we're just making you cook and not clean bathrooms or wash windows!' he said.

We. Not us. Never us.

When I brought it up again two days later, he said, 'My father only eats food cooked by the women of the house. You'll have to cook. This is the least you can do for my family after everything they've done for you.'

What have they done for me, I wanted to ask. But that was the end of that discussion.

But last night, I had finally convinced him to do something for me, 'Please, Suneet. I need to get out of the house. It's been two months. We only ever go to your parents' friends' homes.' He, of course, had no friends, even in the city he grew up in. 'Can we go out tomorrow night for dinner? Just the two of us?'

'Okay,' he'd said. Suneet was a little better-behaved than he'd been in Newport. He didn't dare smoke up in his parents' house. He didn't dare vanish without informing anyone.

This was a small victory. Finally, one meal I didn't have to cook. That was till his mother came up to me and told me that I'd still have to make dinner for her husband and her. I was distraught. Now, instead of getting ready to go out without them for the first time in weeks, I had to cook for them. But I made dal without following the tadka sequence. I didn't soak the rice before cooking it. I didn't cut the lauki into 1-cm pieces. They would be pissed. I wanted to send a message.

The melodrama of the last two years did not happen this year. My in-laws' hatred for me was more subtle now, perhaps because they didn't want any outbursts to ruin their carefully cultivated image in glossy Dubai. While I was grateful that they'd all stopped ganging up on me or sending those eek-mails, I wished the toxicity and nagging would also stop. I was doing everything they wanted. Why couldn't they be happy and cut me some slack?

My father-in-law, in particular, continued to be prickly. One day he'd talk to me, and the next day he would stop talking to me for no reason at all. I didn't let it bother me anymore. I touched his feet when I saw him. I served him his meals and tea. I stayed out of his way.

He had also not returned the cash or jewellery I had given him in New York when he was visiting. I asked Suneet about it one Saturday evening.

'Look, I didn't say anything when Dad kept the $200 *shagun* that Kamini sent us when she had a baby.'

'As Maa said: why does Maneka need Kamini's shagun?'

'But Dad does?' I asked, my eyebrows raised. He didn't reply. 'Anyway, remember I'd given Dad three of my gold sets, a diamond set and Rs 25,000 of my cash for safekeeping? In Samit's house? The night before I left for India? I assumed he would return it to me when I moved here, but he hasn't. I can't ask him. You're the only one who can.'

He told me he couldn't ask his father for it either. 'We have to pay back my parents.'

'For what?'

'We owe them $50,000 for New York.'

This lie again. 'But Suneet, they didn't pay for anything there,' I said, again.

'Bhaiya paying or them paying is the same thing. We have to give them everything we're making, especially since we're living off of them.'

'But this house is rent-free. The electricity and water are free,' I said. These were all subsidized by the Dubai Police Department, where my father-in-law worked. 'And we're paying for the running expenses, like groceries, petrol and the cleaner. I'm doing the cooking and housework. So, how are *we* living off of *them*?'

'Enough! Don't speak like that about my parents,' he said angrily.

'What have I said?'

'It's not what you said. It's your tone.'

I understood. We were paying my in-laws to live with them, an amount much higher than what we would have spent living by ourselves. Or he was siphoning the money for himself.

'Tell me, Suneet, what exactly is your problem? You have a job. You're settled. I moved here for you. I do everything you ask me to. I don't talk back to your parents, even under provocation. Then why are you always angry with me? Why are your parents always pissed off with me? I live each second in this house walking on eggshells. What is—'

He slapped me. I took in a sharp breath. I picked up my glasses from the floor.

You cannot change someone. People will always remain who they are.

I told him I'd tell his parents. They were home.

'Go ahead. I'll tell them that *you* slapped *me*. Who are they going to believe?'

What a *chutiya*. 'Would you prefer that I go to the police?' I asked.

He had begun slapping me quite regularly since I'd moved here.

'Please. My father is a doctor for the police. They love him.'

That was the end of that discussion and many others that ended the same way.

I stopped raising my voice or protesting. I let him slap me once in a while.

I didn't tell him that silent crime also has a price to pay.

'Have you laid out the plates?' I heard my mother-in-law say. She claimed that she'd started taking orphenadrine injections for her muscle spasms. This was her excuse to make me do all the housework. One day, since I was the one clearing the trash, I found the orphenadrine dumped unopened in the garbage bag, next to open packets of glucose. She had been pretending. I was so unsurprised that I didn't mention this to anyone. I began to avoid even accidentally peeking into the trash. I couldn't bear any more hate.

But my mother-in-law could. She would enter the kitchen fifteen minutes before Suneet got home from work. She knew his timings because they called each other all day. 'You really don't know how to cook,' she'd say every time. She'd add masalas, bark instructions and make a great show of how hard she was working, in time for Suneet to witness. It was smart. I admired it because that's how little I'd begun to care about her obsession with diminishing me in front of my husband. Then the two of them would sit down together, watching *saas*-bahu serials, while I served them dinner.

I took the plates to the guest room where she ate. When she was not faking an illness, she watched TV, usually while knitting. The irony of knitting in Dubai didn't bother her. Suneet and she were watching a serial where the mother-in-law was forcing a red chilli down her teary-eyed daughter-in-law's mouth. This was probably from where she got her ideas about women and subjugation. She turned to me and said, 'At least we don't do that to you.' She looked at Suneet and laughed.

'I'm so lucky,' I said. I left the room.

When I'd first moved here, my in-laws had taken me to their friend's house for dinner. My mother-in-law had introduced me to a slightly cross-eyed girl called Neha. The minute Neha's back was turned, she said, 'This is the girl we wanted Suneet to marry. She makes perfect round chapattis. But what can we do if he likes burnt ones?' She didn't care that I sat alone for the rest of the evening, nursing another of her insults.

*

Finally, we got ready and left. It was our first outing alone in Dubai.

When I was ordering, Suneet said I could get only one main dish. We had to leave early.

'Why?' I asked. I was so glad to be out of the house.

He didn't say anything. When we got home I followed him straight to the TV room. My father-in-law made a face at me. I asked him what was wrong. He leaned over and whispered something in my mother-in-law's ear. They both looked at me and laughed.

The next day, my mother-in-law told me that Dad didn't like the way I made tea, so she would make it from now on. I was relieved. This would save me an hour and a half each day. But then she began to make tea for herself and her husband, leaving me out.

If I had been smart, I would have stopped trying to please them or to make food as per their exacting standards. But I had chosen to live with them, knowing full well who they were. I had no right to complain.

Like the tomato night in Newport, the teaspoon day in Dubai became another turning point in my existence. Suneet barely spoke to me. He stopped having breakfast with me. He'd come back from office and watch saas-bahu serials with his mother. On weekends, he would lock himself in the TV room or accompany his mother whenever she went, like a ten-year-old. He'd leave Post-it notes on the mirror in our bathroom. Through the steam, I would read:

> *You left a dirty glass in the dishwasher last night.*
> *You did not clean the dining table properly this afternoon.*
> *There was less jeera in the dal today.*
> *You forgot to buy apples yesterday.*
> *There are cockroaches in the kitchen because you are not cleaning*
> *it properly.*

I tore up each and every one of them and eventually stopped reading them, grateful that at least he didn't eek-mail these to my parents.

In September, I asked him, 'Suneet, you'd told me that you'd work for a year in Dubai while applying for your MBA. Admissions have opened. Should we begin applying?'

'No.'

'What? Why?'

'I'm not going to apply anywhere.'

'What? Why not?'

'Mind your own business.'

'This is my business.'

He stormed out of the room.

A month later, when this incident reminded me that there was little hope left, I asked him, 'Since you're not doing your MBA, should we plan kids? You'd told me in New York that we would start a family as soon as was feasible. Isn't this a good time?'

'Who told you I want to have children with you?' he said, his voice steady and calm.

Goosebumps rode up my body. Being a mother was all I had wanted for the last two or three years. I used to stop to gurgle at babies in strollers. I would sing 'Mary Had a Little Lamb' to my friends' toddlers and play with children in parks. I'd told him a million times how much I wanted a child.

'Suneet,' I said, trying to keep my voice even. 'You got me here on the promise that it was only a matter of one year. That you would apply for your MBA. And then we would have kids. How much longer do you want me to wait?'

'You can wait forever. I am not going to have kids with you.'

Everything around me went blank. Every promise he had made to me was a lie.

'Why not?'

'You will not make a good mother.'

This was worse than his beatings, more spiteful than his insults. It was the meanest thing that anyone had ever said to me. I held back the sob building up like a tsunami inside me, and said, 'That's a nasty thing to say to a woman, Suneet. How can you say that to me, your own wife? How can you be so cruel?'

'Am I wrong? What good are you for anyway?'

'Seriously? After everything I've done for you?'

'Look, you're a terrible wife and a terrible daughter-in-law. You're not a nice person. What makes you think you'll make a good mother?'

I began to cry.

Was it true? Was I a bad person? Would I make a terrible mother?

He didn't console me. He didn't say he was sorry for saying something so awful.

Things got worse as my brother's wedding approached in February. Suneet didn't bother to call up my family and ask if they needed help. He refused to participate in the dance I was organizing for the sangeet. He didn't even call up to congratulate my brother. I didn't say anything. But when I bought a wedding gift for my sister-in-law, Suneet took my debit card out of my wallet behind my back, and cancelled it.

'How can you cancel my card without my permission?' I asked.

'How can you spend this obscene kind of money?' It was 200 dirhams. 'That too on some random chick?'

'Random? She's my sister-in-law! Do you want me to go empty-handed to my own brother's wedding?'

'I don't care. Spend money when you earn money. Till then I'm giving you none.'

'But I need clothes for the wedding! What will I wear?'

'I don't care!' he shouted.

I could not buy gifts for my parents or brother. I asked my mother to bring her old saris and blouses for me. 'Don't you want to wear something new?' she asked.

I couldn't tell her I had no money to buy clothes for my own brother's wedding.

'I have no time to shop, Mom,' I said.

'I'll get your clothes stitched here,' she said.

'No, you have enough on your plate.' She really did. She was organizing a wedding.

'How will you fit into my blouses?' my mother asked.

I didn't tell her that I'd been eating my way out of a depression, again.

My brother's wedding was at Jim Corbett Park. Even though I was wearing my mother's saris and loose blouses, I had a great time. Anything was better than staying with my in-laws. Everyone asked me where my husband and in-laws were. I didn't know what to say. My in-laws had made an excuse that they couldn't get leave from work, while planning a trip to Shimla a month later. I was relieved. They were the last people I wanted to see during a family celebration. And Suneet? Even though he had left Dubai three days prior, he didn't show up. He messaged me to say that he was spending time with Bharti, who had moved to Delhi. He came on the day of the pheras, the last guest to arrive. He stayed for the wedding reception the next day. He didn't help out. He didn't mingle with anyone. The only time I saw him take an interest was during the *joota chupai* ritual.

'You stand back,' he told me. 'I'll take care of the girls' side. Who do they think they are, asking for so much money?'

What was supposed to be a light-hearted exchange began to turn sour as he argued with my sister-in-law's cousins.

'Please give them what they're asking for,' I told him, taking him aside.

'If you give them more than Rs 3000, I will never talk to you. Be firm.'

I didn't know what to do. My parents had budgeted at least Rs 15,000 for the ritual, but I couldn't defy my husband. I had to go back to live with him. I walked away shamefacedly.

Suneet said he was taking the earliest available taxi back, at 5 a.m. the next day, to spend a few more days in Delhi with Bharti. I didn't stop him. He hadn't stayed even two days for my brother's wedding, which was less time than any other guest. Everyone had noticed.

Before leaving he gave me Rs 20,000, a gift for my brother from his parents. I looked at the notes and laughed in shock. I had marked the bundle of Rs 25,000 I had given to my father-in-law in New York with a 25k at the top. There it was again: 25k in my handwriting. My father-in-law had returned my money to me, with Rs 5000 missing, and acted like it was a gift for my brother. I shook my head in disbelief.

My parents and brother noticed everything but didn't say anything. What could they say?

They had raised their son well, knowing that women were not rehabilitation centres for badly raised men. I wished someone had told the Sodis that.

CHAPTER TWENTY

I BEGAN to speak to Suneet about moving out. On my return to Dubai, I got a job at a leading media company as the editor of a new business magazine that I had to launch. It was so exciting! And it paid better than Suneet's job. It had been two years since we'd lived alone together. He kept talking about our lack of money, but with two incomes, his argument was thin. I told him we'd set aside a budget of 15 per cent of our income for rent. We would continue living frugally, I promised. He couldn't argue with that. We found a fully furnished apartment, close to Suneet's office and far from my in-laws place. It was perfect.

When we began prepping to move, he refused to pack. I did all of it. Even while loading the car, he refused to help. He was in a terrible mood. I ignored him. I'd been looking forward to this day for a long time. I could barely contain my excitement. When we reached our new apartment building, he told me to get the trolley to load the bags. 'Why don't you get it?' I asked him. I was not going to be his servant anymore. He told me to fuck off. There was no point arguing. I got out of the car. I was taking a few bags out from the trunk when he suddenly drove off.

The bag in my hand fell to the ground. I let it lie there. I couldn't move. He had left me all alone in an unknown place with nothing! Even my purse and phone were in the car. People were passing by, staring at me. The building concierge told me not to block the entrance. I moved the bags to a side and my eyes teared up. I felt so helpless. Why had I agreed to get back together with this man? Why had I thought he would change? Why was I being so unnecessarily optimistic? How could this be a new beginning?

He came back in thirty minutes. 'I hope you've learnt your lesson,' he said to me politely. What lesson was he trying to teach me now? 'How could you,' was all I said. I didn't want to make a scene in front of our new neighbours. Once we were all loaded up in our new apartment, he told me to sit down. The house we were renting was fully furnished. I sat down on the couch, dark clouds hanging above me. Come here, he said. He patted his lap. I didn't move. He got up and dragged me on to his lap. He gave me a tight hug.

'No matter what problems we have, I'm so happy that you're here with me today. This house would not be complete without you.'

He was trying to make up. A sorry would've been better.

'Suneet, why do you begin the new life we're building by trying to humiliate me? I—'

I stopped. I realized that no one could take my dignity from me, except me. Suneet could not destroy me if I took away the power he had over me. I would. Slowly and steadily I would.

'Suneet, this is the first time since our marriage that we have the chance to be a normal couple, okay? We're both working. We have our own place. We have our space. This is as stable as it's going to get. So things are going to be different from now on. Okay?'

'Of course,' he said cheerfully. He was in a good mood. This man was a see-saw.

'To begin with, in this house, I want our TV to have cable,' I said. 'Is that clear?'

'Whatever my princess wants,' he said. 'Why don't you unpack, while I sort out the internet and cable for the house?'

I told him to fuck off. It was Saturday night. Internet and cable companies were shut.

He laughed. 'Fine, you caught me! But it's been sixteen months since I smoked up. I need the snake.'

He opened the sheath of his kirpan and pulled out a joint.

'Where did you get that?' I said in alarm. 'It's illegal here! We'll get arrested.'

'Chill, babe.'

'Whatever. Smoke it later. You're not a ladla beta anymore. Come and help me.'

He listened. He quietly got up and helped me. We set up our new house together.

Time passed. I began to make friends. We called a few people over to our house and went to theirs. We made a trip to Kenya. It was the best time we'd had together since Hawaii three years ago. I didn't complain when he took our only car (his mother's) to work and made me take the metro, though my office was farther away than his, or when money was transferred from our joint account to his father's account. I was happy to be out of the hellhole that was my in-laws' house.

Despite our improved circumstances and his nicer mood, Suneet did not change.

It was my father's sixtieth birthday that July. I wanted to buy him something nice.

'We are not spending money,' he said.

'We did when your dad turned sixty, and we barely had money that time. We're both earning now, so what's the problem?'

He refused. I ignored him. I decided to surprise my father by flying to Mumbai for his birthday. It would only be for a day, but I knew he would love it. Meanwhile, by sheer coincidence, I got a swanky new Samsung phone at a press conference.

'I'll gift him this,' I told Suneet. 'His phone is ancient. It barely works. He'll love it.'

'You cannot waste so much money on a gift,' Suneet said.

'It's free.'

'It's expensive. I'll make 2000 dirhams if I sell it.'

'Suneet, I got this for free at work. I can do what I want with it.'

'There's no you and me in this marriage. What's yours is mine. I'm taking it.'

He snatched the phone from me. I couldn't take it back unless I got into a physical fight with him. I thought I'd get it later, but he hid the phone. I couldn't find it despite my best efforts. He must have taken it to his parents' house.

On the way to Mumbai, at the airport, I was empty-handed. No, I told myself. The last time I'd met my parents, during my brother's wedding, I had not taken them any gifts thanks to Suneet. So, I bought my father a 4000-dirham bottle of Blue Label. It came with its own suitcase. I used the credit card from the salary account my company had set up for me. I prayed Suneet wouldn't find out.

When I returned from Mumbai the next day, Suneet was all heart again. He showed up at the airport to pick me up with a bouquet of flowers.

'I missed you, my jaan,' he said as we drove home.

'Really?' I asked.

'Of course! I love you, my sexy Chikni.'

'If you love me then show it, Suneet. It's not that difficult.'

'How? Tell me. I'll do anything.'

'It doesn't have to be a grand gesture. Love is in the small things.'

'Like these flowers?' he asked. 'Like me picking you up?'

'Yes. But I need more.'

'Tell me what you need. I'll do anything for love.'

What had he been smoking? And who was I to question it? Nobody in the world rejects money, beauty, fame or love. My birthday was coming up in three weeks. Suneet had not once celebrated my birthday in all these years.

'Fine, start by at least asking me what I want as a gift for my birthday.'

'Whatever my baby wants.'

'Really? Well, it would be nice for you to get me a gift, something expensive, like a branded purse or a belt.'

'I don't know. I like my *sasta* and *tikau biwi*.'

'You've got to loosen the purse strings, Suneet. We've been so frugal this entire marriage. We never go out. We never go shopping. We're only saving money all the time!'

It was time to stop penalizing myself. It was time to show him I was more than a sasta and tikau biwi he could take for granted.

'I tell you what, Suneet. Since you're going to sell that free purse I got, buy me another purse of the same value from a brand I want.'

I had won a $2000 purse at a media event in April that year. Suneet had told me that the purse was too rich for our lifestyle and hadn't allowed me to use it. He'd told me he was going to sell it, but it was still lying in his mother's cupboard.

'Okay, my love, buy whatever you want, but up to 1500 dirhams. There's no one who deserves it more.'

So, on my birthday, I went to a Louis Vuitton store and bought a wallet. It had been years since I'd bought myself something nice. After all those awful moments of picking pennies, eating potatoes to save money, passing stores but never entering them, it felt good to finally reward myself.

Suneet met me at the store. He admired the wallet. He took me out for dinner.

But the next day, he came home furious from work. He barged into our room where I was still taking birthday calls and pulled out my wallet. He took out the cards for our joint account—both debit and credit—and cut them.

'What are you doing? Have you gone mad, Suneet?' I said, putting my phone down.

'You bitch! How dare you spend so much money? You think it's a joke?'

'What?'

'Your birthday extravaganza!'

'You told me I could buy anything up to 1500 dirhams. I did. What's the problem?'

The problem was that his parents had heard of the wallet and filled his ears.

'You have no self-control.'

'I'm not the one always losing control, Suneet.'

He glared at me and stormed off. He stopped talking to me for a week.

You can't stop a ticking bomb from exploding.

But it wasn't just my life he was blowing up, it was his own as well. Suneet began to have fights with his boss—with whom his father had been friends for decades—and colleagues. I sympathized with Suneet when he complained—better them than me—but knew there was nothing to be done. This was who he was. He couldn't go anywhere without colouring it with negativity. I gathered that the only person he got along with in office was a young Indian girl named Pooja. Her name would come up as his lunch and coffee buddy, as the Pooja whose engagement had recently been called off. In the duration of our marriage, Suneet had made only two friends. One was Tammy, the other was Pooja. Like Tammy, he never called Pooja home. I met her only once when I happened to be dropping him to office. I noticed that when I met his boss at parties, the man gave me a sad, knowing look. I wondered why this was. Was it because Pooja was another Tammy? There was no way to find out. Suneet wasn't conscientious enough to be honest. He wasn't naïve enough to get caught. And I wasn't in love enough to care.

So, we continued trying to live like a normal married couple: broken but together.

Then—ten months later, the magazine I'd launched went belly up. Dubai had still not recovered from the global recession. There were no funds, no investors, no readers. I lost my job. 'We can't afford to live alone anymore,' was Suneet's immediate response. The truth was that we could. We were saving my entire salary by then, as he had fortunately stopped paying his parents. We had more than enough to live alone, even if I didn't work for a year. But he wouldn't listen. He needed any excuse to go back to his parents. What was his obsession with them?

'You know how miserable that will make me, Suneet,' I told him frankly. 'Do you really want to put our marriage at risk again? We are on such thin ice anyway. Is it worth it?'

'Stop being a drama queen,' was all he said. 'We need money to settle down.'

He didn't care about the marriage.

'We are settled down. This is settling down. We have enough.'

'No, this is not enough.'

I looked at him and said plainly, 'To save a few thousand dirhams, which we can easily afford at this time, you are willing to throw your wife under the bus and jeopardize your marriage. Then be prepared for what will happen. Remember, it will be your fault.'

He laughed, 'I'll take that chance.'

So be it.

We moved back to my in-laws' house in April 2012. The same drama started again. I put on 3 kilos in a month.

But there was one silver lining in my life.

'Look, my debut novel is out,' I screamed in delight. My publisher had sent me three copies from India. 'And it's on the bestseller list in some bookstores! I can finally say I'm an author!' Writing had kept me sane through the past few tumultuous years. And now, it was rewarding me. I hugged my book. 'Do you want to read it?'

'No thanks,' Suneet said. He refused to even hold the book. 'Lay the table. It's lunchtime.'

If my spouse had published a book, I would've opened a bottle of champagne. Even if that spouse was Suneet. Knowing him, he was unhappy that I was happy.

Since I didn't have a job, I went to India for a month. My publisher had organized a book launch and some readings. It gave me a good excuse to get out of my in-laws' house. Suneet didn't wish me luck for my launch. He didn't congratulate me when it was successful. He didn't comment when I posted the photos on Facebook.

When I came back, because I got another job, better than the first, he told me, 'Don't get high and mighty now that you have some book out. Maa's not well. You'll have to cook.'

By this point, I could no longer deny that I would never be happy with this man. It was time to stop resisting the truth. Like religion, a marriage is not good unless someone is dedicated to its cause. I was no longer dedicated to the cause of my marriage. Fortunately, in my short time in India, my world had opened up. I'd heard of many divorces—marriages falling apart in a week, two months, many less than a year, on flimsy pretexts. Things had changed drastically in my country. People were more progressive. There was less judgement, especially of divorced women. There was no need to torture myself anymore. I no longer had to be scared of the stigma, of having my name attached to failure. For there were greater evils in the world than being imperfect.

I began preparing to leave Suneet. I didn't know how, of course. I wish women were prepared for divorce, the way they were prepared for marriage. For leaving a marriage—unlike getting married—is not an event, it's a process. I needed some more time to take that last step of leaving him. Till then, I would have to be chalu—like Sherna had advised me to be three years ago—or this family would keep treating me like some undeserving servant. I began by distancing myself from Suneet's family and him. I began to come home late from work, so my mother-in-law would have to cook and serve dinner. I told them I had to work weekends so I could go write in a café, instead of cooking and cleaning for them. I began to load the dishwasher without rinsing the dishes. If they told me to cook, I'd cut the lauki into 3-cm pieces and the cauliflower into 1-cm pieces. If they told me to clean, I'd purposely leave things unclean. My in-laws stopped asking me to do so much. With some free time finally in hand, I began taking stock of my belongings and finances, knowing I'd need money to survive alone. I didn't transfer money from my salary account, created by my new company, into our joint account, like I used to. I put most of my jewellery in a bank locker. I made a will in case they did something to me. I met the Consulate General of India to request his protection, if it came down to it. I met the cops who told me it was 'a private issue' and they could do nothing. I met a lawyer, who refused to take legal fees because she was shaken after hearing my case. I was ready for anything to happen.

And, soon enough, it did. One of my best friends, Masaba, who lived in Singapore, was visiting Dubai for two days with her husband. I hadn't seen her since my wedding. Since I couldn't call her home because of my in-laws, or take her out because Suneet would bitch about the bill, I told her we'd meet her that Saturday evening at a park.

That day, before we were to leave the house, Suneet asked me if I had washed the teacups my in-laws had just used for their evening chai. I told him no. He became angry.

'You think we haven't noticed how you're neglecting your responsibilities? Are you a maharani or what?'

'I'll wash the dishes when we're back,' I said to assuage him. I wanted to meet my friend.

In response, he pulled me out of our bedroom by dragging me by my long hair. I was so shocked that I couldn't even fight back. I saw his parents' faces as we passed them. They were in the TV room. They didn't say a word.

He took me to the kitchen and told me to start loading the dishwasher.

'Pick up that cup from the sink!' he screamed.

'I'll do it when we get back!' I shouted. 'What's the rush?'

'It's time you learnt that household responsibilities come before your stupid friends.'

'It's time you learnt that your wife comes before your stupid ideas of responsibility.'

He slapped me. I tried to run out of the kitchen. He pulled me back by my hair, towards the sink. He locked the door of the kitchen.

'Now. Clean. The. Dishes,' he shouted. 'All. Of. Them.'

'Why can't you do it?' I asked him. 'Do *you* have no sense of responsibility?'

He slapped me again. My cheek felt like it was on fire.

'It's the woman's job to look after the house, not mine. Fucking irresponsible bitch!'

I began to sob. I went to the sink and began to clean every dish before loading it in the dishwasher. He inspected each and every one of them, holding them up against the light.

'This cup still has chai *patti* on it. Are you blind?' he said.

He made me rinse it again. I continued sobbing.

He smiled. He was enjoying this.

The dishwasher was loaded. The kitchen had no air. I was suffocating.

'Now,' he said menacingly. 'Should I make you wait here till the dishes are done, so you can put them back in their place?'

'Please, no,' I begged him. 'Masaba is waiting for us. I haven't even been able to message her that we're late.'

'Fine. Since I'm such a good husband, I'll let you go now.'

I ran to the kitchen door and unlocked it. I went outside. His parents were now sitting in the dining room, listening to everything, pleased as punch.

They were all such fucking psychos.

I went to the bathroom, splashed my face with water and grabbed my purse. I messaged Masaba that we were late. I stood at the front door, waiting for Suneet. He was taking his own sweet time to get ready. I grew impatient. But I didn't dare leave without him.

*

'I think he's bipolar, Manu,' Masaba told me gently, later that evening, when we were alone for fifteen minutes. I couldn't hold back my tears. She had known me for twenty years, since school, and never seen me cry like this.

'I don't even properly know what that is,' I said.

'Look it up,' Masaba said. She was a doctor. 'Our husbands are walking towards us, so let me tell you quickly, leave this guy! It's breaking my heart to see you like this. This is not the Maneka I know and love.'

I wiped my tears.

Women are strong. But suffering is finite, not infinite. A woman can bear pain when it's temporary, not permanent. I had been married since December 2007. It was now June 2012. I had given everything I had to this marriage and nothing had changed. I'd done everything I could but nothing made him happy. I'd tried everything to save us but nothing was working. Enough was enough.

We all know the moment we fall in love. The moment we pour our whole selves into another person. But we never fall out of love in a moment. It's impossible to take our whole selves out in a flash. No, falling out of love asks for bits and pieces of us to crumble and disengage, till we have nothing of our selves left to give the other person. I had nothing more of myself left to give my husband. I was, finally, no longer in love with Suneet.

*

The next day, when his parents were out, I walked up to him and said, 'What you did yesterday. Not cool.'

'What did I do?' he asked, genuinely surprised. 'I thought we had a great evening with your friend.'

By then I had googled the term 'bipolar'. What I learnt had cleared up so many things that I hadn't earlier been able to put a finger on. I looked at him, my bipolar husband, and said, 'You don't remember what you did to me? The things you said to me before we met Masaba?'

'Look, all I want is for you to become a better person. Why don't you get that?'

'Suneet, in your eyes, I will never be a good person. I could be Mother Teresa, but I would still not be good enough for you. And this is after I've moved across continents for you twice, fucked up my career, fucked up my body, my social life, and done everything for you that I possibly could. It's taken me a long time to understand that the problem is not with me, but with you. You're the one who's fucked up this marriage, not me. Don't you see that?'

'That's not true. I have done so much for you.'

'Really? What have you done for me? Even when my brother came here for work last month, you told him to stay in a hotel. You didn't have the decency to invite him home for a meal. You know what you would've done to me if I'd treated *your* brother like that?'

'What the fuck are you trying to say?'

'I'm saying what I've been telling you for four years now, Suneet. I am miserable. I can't do this anymore. I've had enough. I don't think we should stay married.'

Till today I don't understand why he looked so surprised. Everything his family and he had done was leading up to this moment. Yet, he looked like I'd shot him.

'You think it's so easy to get divorced, Maneka?' he said. 'Let's see if you even have the guts to do it.'

He stomped out of the room. I let him go.

I stopped speaking to Suneet. For a few days, and then more. This was the first time in our marriage that I had done this. He didn't care. He began to spend even more time with his mother, if that was possible for a thirty-three-year-old married man. I completely cut off from my in-laws as well. The humiliation and disrespect they had shown me, thinking I was alone, helpless in the face of their ganging-up, gave me the strength to show them the power of a woman alone but not weak.

The next week, Suneet came to me, out of the blue, smiling, and tried to make up. 'I love you, jaanu. Why do you keep pushing me away?' His parents must have said something to him.

'Suneet, I don't have time for these mind games. What do you want?'

'Fine. My *dadiji* and *tayaji* are coming to stay with us next week. They'll be here for a month. Maa doesn't want you sulking in front of them. So tell me, what can I do to make you happy?'

They had to present a good face in front of other people. There couldn't be a single chink in their armour.

'Actually, we don't have to do this song and dance again, Suneet. You can tell your parents that there will be no problems from my end. I'll even pretend to be happy around your relatives, okay? I'm inundated with my job and my debut novel's promotions, so anyway I haven't been able to pack up my things and find an apartment. I need time, and a month is perfect.'

That one month turned into two. But, I was okay. Having an audience meant that all three of them were on their best behaviour. They were suddenly very charming around me. My mother-in-law began to cook all the meals. She'd make a big show in front of them and tell me to rest after work, instead of coming to the kitchen as I always had. My father-in-law began to smile at me and offer me wine to drink. Suneet helped me with my book promotions by taking photos of me that I needed to send to the press. They introduced me to a family friend who was a journalist, and who carried a big piece about me in the local paper. I'd never seen such two-faced people in my life.

Hypocrisy is a boil and lancing a boil is painful. But I'd finally drawn the blade and used their turning on a whim to my advantage.

It helped that Suneet's grandmom and uncle were sweet to me. It helped that I was super busy juggling two careers—that of a journalist and an author. For the first time since I'd been married, time passed quickly.

Of course, my mother-in-law couldn't pretend for long. During a large family lunch one day, Suneet's cousin, a darling really, asked who had made the dahi vada. My mother-in-law said with a trill, 'Obviously, me! Does my bahu look like she can cook? She doesn't even know how to make chapattis.'

Her and her bloody chapattis.

But if she couldn't fake it any more, I didn't need to either. Because I was no longer afraid. Because I knew I wouldn't fall like a ceramic ball and break. I knew I wouldn't fall like an iron ball and break everything around me either. I would fall like a rubber ball, rising higher, the harder I fell. They could no longer break me.

So I gave my mother-in-law the dirtiest look I had ever given anyone. Because bullies only respond to being bullied back. No one missed it. There was stunned silence in the room. After that, I went into my room and didn't come out till Suneet came to tell me the guests were leaving.

The fact that I'd done that sent a strong message to Suneet.

'What's wrong, baby?' he asked me that night.

I didn't reply. I was exhausted. We had moved to the TV room to accommodate Suneet's dadiji and tayaji, but my mother-in-law had continued watching TV on full volume till two or three in the morning, as I tossed and turned on the thin mattress laid on the floor. I was living on three to four hours of sleep. Only tonight, finally, she had left us alone.

'Tell me,' he said. 'Let me help you.'

'This is hell for me. Can we just end this? Please!' I said.

He blinked.

'I love you, baby,' he said. 'Give me a little time. Wait till dadiji leaves next week.'

'You've been saying that for two months now!' I snapped.

'What can I do for you till then?' he asked. 'I want to make it easier for you.'

Suddenly, there was consideration.

'Suneet, I don't need anything. But you, you must get help. You have to go to a psychiatrist.'

'I will. I promise.' He hugged me. Why was he making this so easy? 'But please be patient with me, jaanu. Give us a last shot. Without you, my life has no meaning. I know I don't show it, but I love you. You should know that.'

I pushed his hands away. As far as I knew, this marriage was over.

'I love you. I want everything to work,' Suneet said.

He was not one to know his own truth. I had to tell him gently that we were done.

'Look,' I told him, 'we've been together for seven years. We've been through a lot, more than most people do in a lifetime. For the sake of that, let's end things in a dignified manner.'

'I agree. But we will not end things. I love you.'

'Saying you love someone but never showing it is not how a relationship works, Suneet. What's the point of talking about love when every action of yours says "I hate you"?'

'Don't say that. We will make this work. You are all I have left.'

'Suneet, it's too late,' I said softly.

'Don't say that. I will change.'

'It's not that simple, Suneet. You are unhinged. You are bipolar. If you want to change, you'll have to go to a counsellor.'

'You're bipolar,' he snapped. 'You need a counsellor.'

I was the river that let him flow, but couldn't steer his direction.

'Fine, Suneet. Do what you like. I really don't care.'

'Wait! Wait! I tell you what, don't give up on us. Let's compromise. Let's keep talking. Let's go to a marriage counsellor,' he said slowly.

I sighed. Where would I even begin if we went to a counsellor?

'I love you, my jaanu,' he said, but I didn't respond.

Love is something that we're all born with. We spend our entire life finding the right person to pour this love into. But sometimes, we make a mistake. We waste our love on the wrong person. Knowing that we've made a mistake with love takes strength. That's why love is meant for the strong and not the weak. And so, I was being strong. For that was love. That was hope. And that was something he'd never know.

'Good night,' I said to Suneet, softly, gently, for I knew I'd never say 'I love you' to him ever again.

CHAPTER TWENTY-ONE

ON 8 SEPTEMBER 2012, he came up to me. His relatives had left three days ago. It was a holiday at work. I finally had time and was packing a few of my things into a suitcase. My process to leave him had begun.

'All this feels very sudden,' he said, looking at my suitcase.

I smiled sadly at him.

'Listen, let's not separate in front of my parents. It's making them very uncomfortable. Maa has been crying in her room since morning. She hasn't eaten . . . '

'Suneet, I'd told you this would happen.'

'I . . . I know. I've informed my parents.'

I figured. I'd heard the frequent fights Suneet had been having with his father, including a big one the previous night.

'You told me we will end things with dignity. For that we need to talk about our marriage in peace, jaanu,' he said.

'There's nothing to talk about, Suneet,' I said.

'I meant d . . . divorce. We can talk about it in peace. Maa and Dad are going to the US on the twelfth. Let's move to a hotel till then. Once they leave, we'll have the house to ourselves and can sort things out.'

'What? No! I have a lot going on. My book is launching on the twelfth in Dubai. I have to get things done for it. I need to be focused.'

'Look, it's just four more days. Okay? Please, for my parents' sake. Let's not involve them with our private life.'

I scoffed.

'Please, Maneka. For old times' sake,' he added. 'Think of it as a staycation. I know you need one. No cooking, no cleaning, no in-laws. You'll be able to focus better on your launch.'

'Suneet . . .'

'Please!' he said. 'It's the last time I'll ask you for anything. I swear!'

'Okay, fine,' I said. I knew it was a ruse. He was not trying to help me with my book launch or divorce. He was trying to get away from his father. I didn't care. I was happy to get out of that awful house and away from his horrible parents. I was also infinitely exhausted. My professional and personal life had been a roller-coaster the past few weeks, and I hadn't had a single moment to breathe in peace. I packed a handful of clothes, and we left with a small duffel bag. He drove me to some cheap hotel, five minutes away.

Once we were in the hotel room, he jumped up and down on the bed, something he did on every vacation. He looked delirious with joy. He said it was a relief to get out of the house. 'You're right, babe. That house is so stifling. We're meant to be adults. Stay alone together. We're a married couple, aren't we?'

I didn't know whom he was trying to convince. I didn't care for his bizarre thoughts anymore. I lay down on the bed and zoned out in front of the TV. It had been months since I'd watched a movie or show. I forced my body and mind to be still.

I needed it. Over the next few days, as I went back to working non-stop, he kept telling me how much he'd changed and how happy he was to be alone with me.

'See, we don't need a counsellor. We don't need family. We can sort out our own mess,' he kept saying. I didn't respond.

We continued to stay in the hotel. He made me pay for it every day, as though I would run away, leaving him with the bill. I didn't care. I was focused on my book launch.

On 12 September, before leaving for work, I asked him what time he wanted to check out of our room.

'Why do you want to check out?'

'Err . . . it's the twelfth. We have to go back to your parents' house.'

'We're not going back to my parents' house.'

'What?'

'We are not going back,' he said.

'What do you mean? You told me we were staying here only for four days.'

'We can't go back because you are not welcome back,' he said.

What fresh hell was this? What mind game was he playing now?

'Can we not do this now, Suneet? I don't have the bandwidth for it. I need my clothes. I need access to my things.'

'So, go live there by yourself then.'

'Okay, fine,' I said. I picked up my duffel bag to go. That's when I realized that I didn't have the house keys any more. Last week, his mother had come up to me, all sweetness, and asked me for my set of the house keys, since she'd lost hers. This whole thing had been a set-up!

I saw him smirk.

'Well played, Suneet. You've won. Congrats! But why are you still here?'

'Because I love you.'

This guy's head and heart lived in two different bodies.

'Suneet!'

'Did you think I was going to make it so easy for you to leave me? Did you think I didn't notice how you didn't transfer your salary to our joint account the last two–three months? That you stopped looking after my parents and my needs? That you were irresponsible and—'

'Suneet, look, I need my things from that house. Please. That's all I'm asking for.'

'Fine,' he said. 'You can take some clothes, if you want, but that's it.'

He drove me to his parents' house. He followed me to our room as I took some clothes from my cupboard. I went to work carrying a duffel bag.

The launch went off beautifully. The bookstore was packed. I was signing books for an hour. I was giving press interviews. Suneet showed up for it and stood at the back, watching me. No one there could've guessed the pain I was in, or the fact that I didn't even have a house to live in.

Once the launch was over, we went back to the hotel. He asked me where I planned to live now. That's when it fully sank in that my husband, along with his parents, had thrown me out of the house for good. Instead of waiting for me to find an apartment, they'd forced me into a cheap, trashy hotel! I wished they'd shown basic decency and humanity, but you can't ask a fish to fly.

I gathered some strength and told Suneet that since I wouldn't get an apartment to lease so quickly, I'd find another hotel to stay in.

I went to the bathroom to cry—I was exhausted—and noticed that my period had started. Perfect timing! It was the middle of the night. The chemist stores were shut.

I came out of the bathroom and told him, 'I'm bleeding. I need my sanitary pads urgently. Nothing is open right now. Can I pick them up from your parents' house, along with some of my other stuff?'

'No!'

'Suneet, please! This is not a game. I'm bleeding.'

'Fine. I'll give you five minutes,' he said.

Five minutes? I thought he was joking. But when we reached his parents' house, he followed me from one room to the other. He kept counting down—four minutes left, three minutes left, two minutes left, a minute left. I was in the house alone with a psycho on the loose. I ran to the bathroom first. No pads. They had moved my things. So, I ran to our room. I opened my cupboard but my pads were not there either. I ran to his parents' bedroom but the door was locked. Fuck! According to him, only thirty seconds were left. So I ran back to our room and grabbed some of my clothes and undergarments from the cupboard.

'I don't have a bag,' I shouted in panic.

'That's your problem,' he said.

I looked around for a small bag.

'Your time's up,' I heard him say behind me.

I held the clothes against my chest.

'Please, just let me find my pads, Suneet. I'm bleeding.'

He grabbed my arm and pulled me away. Some of my stuff fell on the floor.

'Five minutes mean five minutes,' he said. 'I shouldn't even be letting you into the house.'

There was only hate in this man.

While we waited at the lift lobby, I felt like I was reliving the horror of the first year of marriage. The lift door opened. There was a man inside. He looked at the clothes I was carrying in my arms. One of my bras fell down. He looked at me. My eyes had teared up. He looked at Suneet. Suneet was smirking. The man bent down to pick up my bra, gave it to me and then moved to a corner, as far from us as the lift would allow, as if he didn't want to breathe the air we were breathing. He scuttled out quickly when the lift door opened.

On the car ride back, I began to howl. I could no longer hold back my sorrow. I'd been treated worse than a stray animal. Demeaned and humiliated more than I could've imagined. What had I done to deserve such hatred from someone who claimed to love me?

Once we were back in the hotel room, I stopped crying. I put the few clothes I had in my hand into the duffel bag. I put toilet paper in my undies for the blood. I left the room and went out for a walk. I didn't take my phone or wallet, just the hotel key. I didn't care how late it was. Or how dark. Or unsafe. I didn't know where I was walking to or who was around. I just kept walking.

After an hour passed or two, I went back to the hotel room. Suneet had turned off the lights. I said calmly in the dark, 'This is the last night I'll ever spend with you.'

He turned around but didn't reply.

I slept without another thought.

The next morning, I packed my duffel bag. He was waiting for me.

'Suneet,' I turned to him. 'I was trying to end five years of marriage with some shred of dignity, a little bit of kindness. But, once again, your parents and you have treated me worse than barbarians would. Thanks for proving my point. I should've left years ago. I didn't have the courage. I didn't have the wisdom. Today, I have both. So, this is the end. I wish you all the best in life.'

I turned to go. He fell at my feet. 'Don't say that. Don't say such things, jaanu. I love you. I've always loved you. Don't leave me. I'll die. I am begging you.'

I looked at him and smiled.

'All I ask is that for the sake of the love we once had, the seven years we were together, please cooperate for the divorce. Goodbye.'

I left the room.

'I will not let you divorce me,' he shouted. 'You hear me! I'll never give you a divorce!'

Despite my bravado, I was trembling after I checked into an affordable hotel close to my office that evening. A Middle Eastern country was not the safest place for women who were alone. Outside my thin door, I heard groups of men walk past, laughing, talking loudly. Did any of them know there was a girl behind that door? If they did, would they come in the middle of the night and do something to me? It was scary. I was all alone. No one knew where I was. It didn't help that my room was right next to the elevator. I heard it loud and clear every time it went by, every time its doors opened, as though I were living inside it. I didn't sleep the entire night. Still, I didn't cry. I had to be strong. I had faced worse demons and survived.

The next morning, I went to the ATM to withdraw money. It showed zero balance. Not again! I walked into the adjacent bank branch. The teller told me, rather sadly, that there was no money left in the account. Suneet had withdrawn all of it the previous week. Almost all the money I'd earned since coming to

Dubai was gone. Fortunately, I was prepared for this. I had my salary account. There wasn't much money in that, but it was enough to see me through for now.

The weekend came. My mood cheered. I knew I had made the right decision.

As I was cooking khichdi in the kitchenette in my hotel room, glad not to have to eat outside food again, my parents called.

'What's going on, beta? We heard you've left him?' my mother asked, really concerned.

'They threw me out of the house. It was a set-up,' I said plainly.

'That's not what they're saying. His father called me. He said that five days ago you told Suneet you're filing for divorce and then stormed out of the house!'

I laughed. What had I expected?

'Should I send them the hotel bills from the last ten–twelve days as proof?'

Their collective lies could not stifle my individual truth.

I told my mother about the crafty way in which his mother had taken the house key from me. And how Suneet had physically thrown me out of the house the night I got my period.

The line went completely silent. Then, I heard a sob. Then two.

'How can they do this to you?' my mother said. 'What kind of monsters are these people?'

'Do they have no sense?' my father said. 'They're doing this to a girl, leaving her alone in a foreign country? Do they have no sense of responsibility? No conscience?'

I didn't say anything.

'Where are you now? Why didn't you call us?' my mother asked.

I told them I needed to be alone.

'Come back to Mumbai. You are a girl. You cannot be living alone in Dubai at a time like this. It's not safe. It's not healthy.'

'Don't worry, Mom. It's because I'm a girl that I should be living alone in Dubai at a time like this.'

'Maneka—'

'I promise you that I'm fine. I'm feeling better than I have in years.'

I was. A burden had lifted off my shoulders. I felt light.

'Please, come back here.'

'I will,' I said. 'But not like this.' This was not the state I wanted my family to see me in. I wanted to be whole again. I wanted to prove to myself, and to them, that a woman could survive without a man, anywhere and anytime.

'Do you want us to come there?'

'No. I want to do this by myself. I owe it to myself.'

'Can we help?' they asked.

'Actually, you can. Since we got married in Delhi, I cannot get divorced in Dubai or Mumbai. I need you to initiate the divorce proceedings in Delhi as quickly as possible.'

A week later, I was handwashing my clothes and undergarments, as I did every day after work. If my colleagues thought I was strange for repeating the same four outfits, they didn't comment. In fashionable Dubai this was a faux pas, of course, but I no longer cared about being somebody else's idea of perfect. I was hanging my clothes to dry on the radiator when my friend Niloufer called. She had gone to school with Suneet, but was closer to me than to him. When she heard about what he had done, she insisted I stay with her. It was the kindest thing that anyone had done for me. Despite my bravery, I needed a friend. So, the next day, I went to stay with her. She lent me her clothes and a room. She forced me to go out, to talk, to laugh. This helped me feel better.

'Please help me get my things back from that house,' I told her. 'I've emailed and messaged Suneet several times, but he's not responding to me.'

She tried. I tried. But for more than a month there was nothing. When a man shows no tenderness in togetherness, how will he show it in separation?

At the end of October, with Niloufer's help, I found an apartment. I told my parents to call Suneet's parents and ask them to return my things. Finally, Suneet emailed me to come on 4 November at 6 p.m. to his parents' house. I requested Niloufer to accompany me. It was safer that way.

'I'd help you, but my back's not good,' I heard him tell Niloufer when we entered. Niloufer and I looked at each other. I felt only disgust for him. Did he ever speak the truth?

He waited in the living room while I went into what used to be our bedroom. I felt no nostalgia when I entered. I put my things into the two suitcases I'd left there. I didn't open the locked suitcase I'd brought from India during my last visit there in August. I went to his parents' room, where my other suitcases were lying, but the door was locked.

'They're still in the US,' he said.

'But surely you have the key? They wouldn't leave it locked for months!'

'No, I don't have it.'

I'd have to let go of half my belongings, including jewellery, the $2000 purse and the Samsung phone. So be it. I realized that the reason he was sitting in the living room so cavalierly and not following me around, as would be in his nature, was because he'd already planned exactly what I'd be able to take and not. Everything, except my cupboard, was under lock and key.

I couldn't give this sadist the pleasure of another win. I told him I was done.

Niloufer told me that she'd bring her car to the front gate. She left.

I went into the common bathroom to pee. When I came out, he handed me a form.

'What's this?' I asked.

'It's to move our joint account to a single account in my name,' he said.

I signed it without reading it and left. I didn't even think to ask for my share from the joint account, which he had emptied.

'You're so naïve,' Niloufer said later in the car. 'You should have refused to sign it.'

'I want that guy out of my life. I don't want to hear his voice, see him or read an eek-mail from him ever again,' I said. 'I want him to be history.'

But I should've heeded Niloufer's advice. When I got home and opened my one locked suitcase, I found that all the cash I'd brought with me from India (more than Rs 4 lakh of my savings) along with some jewellery and expensive gifts were gone. He had broken into my suitcase and then relocked it! This was a new low, even for him. I didn't know his expertise also included stealing.

It was almost midnight. Still, I called him.

He picked up on the first ring, something he'd never done before. He had been waiting for my call.

'What happened to the cash in my suitcase?' I asked.

'I've taken all of it,' he said bluntly. There was still so much evil left in this man.

'How can you be so blasé about it? That was my money. My things.'

'There are no "your" things and "my" things in marriage,' he said coldly. 'I have a right to everything you have.' I realized that he was deriving pleasure from seeing me suffer. He was still trying to destroy me. Nothing would ever change with this man. He wanted to make my life as tough as possible, even when I was no longer with him.

'Keep the money. Clearly you need it more than I do,' I said.

I hung up.

That day I learnt an important lesson. You don't crawl out from under a divorce. You carry it around like a brick in your pocket, a weight you can never lift. I would never forget.

CHAPTER TWENTY-TWO

'AND I hope you didn't have to see him ever again?' Anmol asks.

I saw him thrice after that, I tell him. But only for the divorce proceedings. I'd told my mother to handle my divorce as I wanted nothing to do with Suneet or his family. Suneet had initially refused to give me a divorce. He'd told our lawyer: 'I'll stay separated for the rest of my life, but I'll never let her move on.' I was ready to contest that. My lawyer advised against it: 'Contentious divorces take years in India. Try for mutual consent, where both parties agree to divorce. You'll be done in six months.' He then warned Suneet that if he didn't agree to a mutual consent divorce, we'd put him behind bars using the Domestic Violence Act since there was evidence of physical, financial and emotional abuse. Suneet apparently told him, 'Put me in jail. I'd rather rot there than give her a divorce.' He was the type who'd be happier in jail.

It was time for serious action.

We hired one of India's most famous lawyers, Neeta Guthra, who was based in Delhi. As she read my case file, I remember her telling me, without sentiment, that she'd never seen such savages. Her anger spilled on to the firmly worded email she sent them, clarifying that we were in a position to send Suneet and his parents to jail for abusive behaviour and they would be left with no reputation to salvage. That's when Suneet finally agreed to the divorce; to save his *bechari* Maa. But they had two conditions: they wanted both parties to hire a mutual lawyer of their choosing (not Guthra, obviously) and they didn't want to give alimony. I didn't care about the lawyer, but I wanted alimony. From that man, I deserved it. I made my lawyer send them an Excel sheet with a breakdown of the amount of money I'd spent on Suneet during the course of our marriage, as well as the amount he'd stolen from me in cash and from our US and Dubai bank accounts. But my parents counselled me otherwise: 'Knowing Suneet's stinginess, he'll give you nothing, but make you waste five-ten years fighting over it. You can make much more money in that time. Let it go.' My parents were right. Although I wanted my hard-earned and stolen money back, obviously, I let it go. Freedom was more important than money.

My in-laws found a cheap lawyer in Delhi to take the case. Exactly five years after our wedding in Delhi, we filed for divorce there. At our first hearing in February 2013, I saw Suneet as a complete stranger, someone I'd never known. I'd always thought that he was handsome. Now he looked like a wrung-out washcloth, a loser. I couldn't imagine why I'd fought so hard to be with such a man. The judge asked us if we'd been separated for more than a year, and whether we were sure about the divorce. We said yes. Our order was passed in one minute.

At our next hearing in May, Suneet forgot to get his proof of address. Our hearing was postponed to 5 December 2013. I was scared that Suneet had done this intentionally. Anything could happen in that time. He could go back on his word. He could become unreachable. He could change his mind. I was working in Dubai till July. He could have me killed, a genuine fear I had, given his father's contacts.

But Guthra's words still rang in their ears because it was I who almost didn't make it to the final hearing of my divorce. A few months prior, I had moved back to Mumbai. My second book had been published. I was getting invited to literature festivals all over the country. I was with family and friends. I had lost weight. I was happy again, at least happier than I'd been in years.

On the way to the family court in Delhi that day, my mother and I got stuck in traffic. We were pretty nonchalant about it. The last two times we'd had to wait for more than an hour in court. But our lawyer called to say that the judge was on time today and there were only two hearings before us. If I didn't make it on time, our case would be further postponed. We panicked. While we were not far from the court house, the car we were in was not moving.

Like in the movie *Dilwale Dulhania Le Jayenge*, where the father tells his daughter, '*Jaa* Simran, *ji le apni zindagi*', my mother turned to me and said, '*Jaa* Maneka, *karle apna* divorce. This is your chance. Run!'

I got out of the car and ran towards the court building. Despite the winter chill, I was sweating in three minutes. My shoes kept coming off. The lawyer kept calling me: 'Where are you? Hurry!' I realized I would take forever to reach the court. I couldn't miss the hearing, not after everything that had happened. So, I waved to the traffic passing by, hoping to get a lift. A man on a scooter stopped and asked what had happened.

'Bhaiya, it's a matter of life and death,' I told him in Hindi. 'Please give me a lift till the end of the road.'

That man, bless his soul, told me to hop on to the back seat of his scooter.

'Where exactly should I drop you?' he asked, as I told him to go faster and faster.

'Outside the divorce court,' I said.

The man actually stopped his scooter and turned to stare at me, like I was mad.

'Please, I beg you,' I said. 'It's a matter of life and—'

'—divorce,' he chuckled.

The man revved his scooter, and in twenty seconds flat, he dropped me right outside the courthouse. I shouted out a thanks and scrambled up to the first floor, to hear my name being called out.

'You arrived just in time,' my lawyer said. His shirt was drenched in sweat.

I looked at him and said. 'You have no idea how.'

I entered the courtroom and that was the last time I ever saw my ex-husband.

The day I got divorced was one of the best days of my life.

That's when I realized that divorce is a celebration. It's the start of a new beginning. And I decided to throw a divorce party.

*

'So, in all this, *when* did you decide to kill him?' he asks.

I smile at Anmol. We stare at each other for a minute. I look at the fifth cup of green tea I'm having and say, 'Who says I killed him?'

'I would if I were you,' says DCP Sahib.

I look outside his office window. I can see light after the darkness. I can hear birds chirp. I can feel the city come back to life. It's morning time. I open my mouth to say something when he adds, 'Stop. Don't say anything. Let me guess *how* you did it. You killed him in a way that you wouldn't get caught. So, it must be—'

I look at him, while he searches for answers.

'It's easy to kill someone with castor seed husk,' he says.

'Would I want to kill him in such an easy, obvious way?'

'No,' he says. 'Let me see. Cyclosarin is a popular option. It's odourless. You can put it in someone's coffee. It kills them in seconds.'

'Yes, but the victim bleeds. Did Suneet?' I say. The cop smiles.

'You could've used ricin poison and put the powder in his weed?'

'Long shot. Ricin is tough to get.'

Anmol takes a sip of his green tea. He's stumped.

'Well, since you want to let your imagination soar, maybe this is what I did, DCP Sahib. Maybe I planned Suneet's murder in advance. Maybe I waited patiently till I knew the marriage was over. And then, maybe, I laced his weed with fentanyl.'

'Fentanyl?'

'It's a pain reliever that becomes poisonous when mixed with cocaine, heroin or weed. An incorrect dose and it becomes a silent killer. It was just a matter of time till Suneet smoked up, right?'

The cop looks at me. 'So, the only gamble you took was not *how* but *when*?'

I nod. 'Maybe.'

'But you would not poison the stash while you were living with him, of course?' he asks.

'No, I imagine that would be too risky.'

'So, then—' He thinks for a minute. 'The only other time you were in that house was when you went with Niloufer to take your suitcases?'

'Smart. Maybe I knew he wouldn't help that day. Of course! So, maybe, while he was *not* helping, I opened the back of the TV in our room, that same unused TV he never let me watch, and I found the kirpan he used to hide there, the one with all his stash.'

'But how did you know he'd risk taking drugs after you left him? In his parents' house?'

'He took risks with drugs all the time, whether flying them from Goa to Mumbai, or New York to Jamaica. He loved the challenge of it all, the thrill of outsmarting others.'

'Why not do it while you were still in the house? When you could make sure he took it?'

'And become a widow?'

Anmol gives a little chuckle, 'Widows are blameless, divorcees are not, right?'

I grin, 'Sure, everyone in a bad marriage knows how convenient it is if a problematic spouse dies before divorce. And nothing would have given me more pleasure than watching Suneet die. But the best way to murder someone is to not get caught doing it, no?'

The cop nods. 'But something makes no sense. All this knowledge of pharmacology . . . all that access to fentanyl. You couldn't have done this alone.'

I smile, 'Who says I'd do something like this alone?'

'Who would've helped you?'

'Sometimes, DCP Sahib, we women stick together.'

'Sherna?'

I shake my head.

'Who do you know with pharma knowledge?' he asks.

I smile.

'Her?' He stares at me incredulously. 'But I thought you hated each other.'

'Maybe we didn't. Maybe, since we're making all this up, we decided: why stop at one?'

'All four of them?' he asks incredulously. 'But you were abused by Suneet. Why go after his family?'

'Was I abused by only Suneet, or was I abused by his entire family? Isn't emotional and financial abuse also abuse?'

'Even Samit?'

'Nah! She needs him alive. He's the father of her child.'

'Ok, then. Dare I ask—how would someone go about doing all this?'

'I'd imagine it to be effortless. For example, killing my father-in-law—easy. I'd imagine that we'd switch his hypertension medicine metoprolol with carvedilol. He's deathly allergic to it, so even one dose will kill him. The two medicines are the same shape, size and colour so—despite being a doctor—he'll not notice the rogue.'

Anmol looks horrified.

'Don't worry. It would be quick, DCP Sahib. We're not savages like them.'

'And when would you have possibly done something like this?'

'I'd imagine doing it the same day as I imagine I'd done for my *pati parmeshwar*. Remember, we know our abusers well. We know their worst habits and we can, if we want, use those against them. Suneet was a druggie. His father is stingy. He keeps almost two years' worth of medicines in the common bathroom's cabinet. It's free for him.'

'So, you'd go into the bathroom the day of the suitcases and—?'

'—and it wouldn't be to pee. Dr Sahib takes a metoprolol tablet every day at 9 p.m. sharp. I know because I was responsible for giving it to him. But he's so engrossed in his one hour of TV at that time, he takes the metoprolol tablet without even looking. The day I'd gone for my suitcases, there would be eight bottles in the cabinet. I imagine that I'd open one, using the guest towel, so it wouldn't have my fingerprints and put one—just one—carvedilol in it. He could take that tablet anytime. Maybe today, or maybe tomorrow, or maybe right before his son's funeral. That would be redemption. What say?'

The inspector smiles. 'You're unbelievable.' He takes a sip of his tea.

'And her?'

'Oh, I wish I could swing her by her plait and toss her into the sea. But, well, I imagine that her we would torture, like she tortured us, slowly. We would extend her suffering to after she loses both her husband and her precious ladla beta.'

'No!'

'Yes. She has it coming.'

'How?'

'Same strategy, I'd imagine. Use your abuser's weakness against them. Remember those imaginary health issues she'd keep making up? Remember those injections she was pretending to take to avoid doing housework?'

'The ones in Dubai?'

'Yes. Once she's in America, mourning the loss of her husband and son, her muscle spasms will become more frequent—obviously—so she doesn't have to lift a finger in Kamini's house, right? That's when Kamini will put the idea in Samit's head to help Anju by injecting the orphenadrine himself. Anju will not be able to refuse Samit.'

'And then?'

'Do you know, DCP Sahib, that diabetic insulin, if injected into someone, can cause a cardiac arrest? It goes undetected unless one is looking for injection points. In Anju's case, no one will get suspicious because of her orphenadrine needles. And—it gets better. Kamini will convince Samit that he created an air bubble in the injection which went into Anju's heart, causing her death. He will think that he caused his second mother's death as well.'

'That's horrible!'

'I imagine he deserves to be punished a little bit as well, right? He's not completely blameless in all this. But the best part—he'll think Kamini is covering his mistake and love her more. Everyone wins. Brilliant, no?'

'Remind me to never fuck with you.'

'I'll never give you the chance, DCP Sahib,' I say and smile.

He smiles back at me and says, 'But haven't you asked yourself, Maneka, whether they really deserve to die for what they did to you? I mean, it's not like they tried to burn you, or throw acid on you, or actually try to murder you.'

'This is the problem, DCP Sahib. Do you know why India's billionaires are the least charitable in the world? Because they've grown up seeing so much poverty that they're immune to it. It's the same with society. We've seen so much abuse of women that we've become desensitized to it. We don't react the way we should. Silent crimes go unpunished. Do we catch women who speak up? Do we break the male code? No! Since society and the state are not protecting us women, we must protect ourselves.'

Anmol looks at the photo of his wife and daughter. I see his eyes glaze. He understands.

He takes a sip of his tea: 'So tell me, where and when could Kamini and you have possibly come up with this plan, if it's real?'

'Not in those eek-mails, I'm afraid. Wouldn't make your job so easy,' I say and smile. 'Do you remember when Kamini broke that heating rod by "accident" in Egypt? Well, I'd imagine that she's ace at "accidentally" breaking other things as well. Including the—'

'—kirpan?'

'Yes, to protect me. Symbolic, no? That's when I would've known that I could trust her.'

I smile as I remember the way she'd winked at me after breaking the kirpan.

'See, DCP Sahib, I imagine that we would continue using their weaknesses against them. The first thing we'd do was to stage a fight. The family would assume that Kamini and I were enemies because we'd let them believe that. We'd use their obsession with controlling us against them. Once that premise was laid, it would be pretty easy.'

'Brilliant! But I have to ask: how do I know what's the truth? You've told so many lies in this story.'

'No, DCP Sahib, I've told only *one* lie in this story. But it's the lie that *you've* believed.'

'Because not telling the complete truth is also a lie, right?' He pauses. 'So, what was the one lie?'

'I've told you this story from two perspectives: the victim's and the survivor's. Only one version is the truth. Whether you believe the *abla nari* or the *krantikari* depends on the lie that *you* want to believe. This is what I told you at the start.'

He shakes his head in disbelief and stares at me. I stare back.

'Aren't you scared of saying all this on record?' he asks me, nodding at the camera.

I smile at him, 'No.'

'How do you know I won't use it against you?'

'Because I know what version you've believed. It's better to believe a lie than to doubt the truth, isn't it?'

He shrugs his shoulders.

'Besides, it could never be us who killed them,' I say. 'It could only be their karma.'

'How?'

'Because, I imagine, we'd leave their deaths to destiny. Think about it. What would be the chance that Suneet would ever get to the doobie? What would be the likelihood of the fentanyl working after months or years?'

The cop nods.

'Each of them will die only when their time comes,' I continue. 'What's the chance that Manjrekar will take that tablet without looking? What's the chance that Samit will give the injection to Anju? We would increase the probability of them getting killed, but eventually it's their karma that'll kill them.'

The cop shuts his eyes and takes a deep breath. Then he breathes out. He does this five times. I pick up my phone from his desk and check my messages. I see him open his eyes. I hear him chuckle as he takes a sip of his tea.

'You knew I was not going to take you to court from the start, didn't you?'

'Yes.'

'How?' he asks.

'You arrested me at night, without a lady cop. You let me keep my phone and purse during interrogation. You have no respect for the law of the land.'

He chuckles. 'You're using my weakness against me?'

'No, only your strength.'

We smile at each other. He takes another sip of his tea.

I get up and take the tape out of the camera.

'What are you doing?' he asks.

'The best way to murder someone is to not get caught doing it.'

'Wha—' He tries to get up but slumps back on his desk. He's sweating profusely.

'What have you done?' he asks, his voice shaky.

'Nothing. I imagine that if I wanted to do something, I would take out the oleander flower from my hair. I'd cut it in half. I'd stir your green tea with it while you were meditating. Because what I forgot to tell you is that the oleander carry a poison that protects them, but can kill everyone else.'

'What? But I'm on your side.'

'I know. And I'm on your side as well. So, don't worry, I imagine it will not kill you. Not if you close the case of Suneet's murder. Not if I give you the antidote, which you only get in the US.'

'What?'

'Do it. Close the case. You have two minutes, after which I can't do anything to save you.'

He finally sees me for who I am. He sees the truth in my eyes.

The abused has become the abuser.

Anmol calls someone on the phone and says something in Marathi. He stamps 'Case Closed' in a red stamp on Suneet's file. Constable Wanave enters his cabin. He murmurs something and takes the file. He salutes me on his way out and says. 'You are free to go. Have nice day, Madam.'

'I will,' I say. I get up. I take out a tablet from my purse, shaped like a broken handcuff, and put it in front of Anmol. 'Take this. Go home and rest. Spend time with your daughter.'

Anmol nods.

'I better go home to my friends,' I say. 'I've told them that I've been set free.'

The truth is, I haven't. I just want to get back home to my oleander. For that's the beauty of a flower that never forgives even what it's forgotten.

ACKNOWLEDGEMENTS

What began as a story of abuse in 2007 has become a story of redemption fifteen years later. It's a story that not only took me more than eight years to write, but also asked for all my courage, strength and grit. It shape-shifted from a heart-wrenching tale of marital violence into a crime thriller with an urgently relevant text on mental health, patriarchal systems and women's issues.

For that I'd like to thank super-agent and friend Kanishka Gupta, who picked up the book with the vigour and vitality of the powerhouse that he is. The wonderful team at Penguin Random House India, who helped *Boys Don't Cry* come together beautifully. Vaishali Mathur, my prodigious editor and advocator, who poured heart and soul into the book. Saloni Mital, Shreya Dhawan and Pallavi Narayan for the astute edits. Marketing gurus Vidushi Khera and Prateek Agarwal for taking the book to more readers. And, the superbly talented Akangksha Sarmah for her brilliant cover, as always.

Success is talent that is recognized. And for that a big thanks to the marvellous Shobhaa De, Aditi Mittal and Anees Salim, who enthusiastically and generously graced this book with their early praise.

My amazing mother Sujata Pant—the smartest and bravest woman I know—who caught me when life seemed ragged and rancorous. My unwavering friends Shahnaz Shroff (especially you), Vahbiz Engineer, Benaifer Hussain, Priya Shah, Bhavya Kalsi and Tina Talwar for being my greatest consolations in my darkest hours. Sahil Kanuga, you are god making up to me, the magical thoroughfare that carried me out of the wasted oblivion of my heart into an overflowing abundance of love. Thanks for keeping your panic at bay when you saw me google 'how to kill your husband without getting caught'.

My readers. Thanks for the love that you've shown me with every new book. You give me wings.

Ultimately, this book is dedicated to victims and survivors of domestic violence. If you're one of the 200 million abused women in our country, or know someone who is one, please don't stay silent. Silence is the biggest violence. Maneka's uplifting story shows that physical, emotional and financial abuse does not have to fit snugly into our private world of awfulness or turn into an aimless monochrome of regret and shame. As a survivor I can tell you that once the veil around your eyes lifts, you'll open up little sifts of light under those clouds of darkness. Like me, you'll be able to see again, breathe and even smell those little flowers in the sidewalk. Your smile will come back to you, on some days wider than usual. That rupture point will become your most defining moment that takes you from strength to strength. So—let's break the taboo, shatter the sites of violence, and teach our boys that a slap is not an act of intimidation but a war cry for society to leave a safer world for our daughters.

Speak up. Fight back. Be strong. Keep the courage. We're in this together.